TORN TO BITS

KINGDOM OF WOLVES

KATIE MAY

EXPRESSO PUBLISHING, LLC

To my grandma who tells all of her friends I write "literature porn." No, I will not allow you to read my books in your book club. I refuse to traumatize you and your friends like that. Love you.

CONTENTS

FOREWORD

This is a shifter mafia/MC reverse harem romance and is not suitable for anyone under the age of 18. It contains strong language, sexual situations, and psychotic males.

This is a part of the Kingdom of Wolves shared world. However, you do not need to read the other books in the series to enjoy this one. Each author has put her own twist on the wolves and world, so please keep that in mind while reading. There will be differences from one book to the next.

Torn to Bits will conclude in Ripped to Shreds.

Enjoy!

BLAIR

I lower to my stomach and grip the ledge with my fingertips. Slowly, being extra mindful not to make any noise, I begin to pull myself to the very edge, so only my eyes are visible if anyone decides to look up.

The noisy air conditioning unit does very little to combat the stifling heat in the corrugated iron warehouse. My shirt sticks to my skin with a fine layer of sweat, and I'm pretty sure I'm going to get a rash on my thighs from chub rub.

Still, I remain silent, barely even breathing, as I stare at the wiry man directly below me.

He's completely oblivious to my presence as he unpacks a large crate from the back of a semi truck. I count three grunt workers with him. Maybe fellow bittens? It's impossible for me to tell. They seem fearful of the man, despite the fact that they're three times the size of him and appear to be chiseled from solid stone.

Either way, they'll be easy targets for me to take out if the need arises.

But fuck, I hope it doesn't come to that.

The warehouse itself is one large open room with a garage door at the back and twin swinging doors near the front. There are a few empty shelves scattered throughout the spacious room, and even more shelves full of haphazardly wrapped boxes farther back. Fluorescent lights are positioned intermittently across the ceiling, their reddish-golden glow hidden by black beams that crisscross the entire length. There's a small ledge that I'm currently perched on, roughly five or so stories above, with no discernable way to get on or off. It's why none of the fuckers thought to look up here before they began unloading. I just barely have enough room to lie on my stomach, my legs squished at an unnatural angle behind me.

One of the workers makes a crude joke involving his dick and a hole in one of the crates, and the other two roar with laughter. The smallest man, and the obvious leader, levels him with a ferocious glare, one that even makes *me* shiver, though I'm not the recipient.

"Shut the fuck up, bitten piece of shit," he snaps as he grabs a cigarette out of his pocket and places it between his lips. From this angle, I can see that there's nothing significant about this man whatsoever. He almost reminds me of a child playing dress up, pretending to be a big, bad, scary mobster. He's practically *swimming* in the white suit he wears, and there's a noticeable stain on his shoulder, though I can't tell if it's blood or something else. His brown hair is slicked away from his broad forehead, emphasizing the numerous scars marring his skin. Combined with his too large eyes and crooked nose, he's the type of man you would glance at once on the street before immediately turning away from.

Forgettable.

Maybe that's what makes him the best dealer in the entire state.

Everything from drugs to weapons to skins. Revulsion ripples through my body at the latter thought, and the only thing stopping me from putting a bullet in that fucker's head is the fact that the boxes they're currently stacking are too small to hold any human, even children.

Pezzo di merda.

Piece of shit.

If my sources are correct, which they always are,

then the shipment today is weapons. Everything from handguns to automatic rifles to machine guns.

After all, you can't have a war without the tools to fight it.

I lick my lower lip as my back pocket vibrates with an incoming text message. Probably Papa Gray, wondering when I'm returning.

Keeping my eyes on my target, I reach behind me blindly and pull out my phone, using my hand to shield the light from any wayward eyes. As expected, Papa Gray's name blinks up at me, along with a message asking when I'm going to be home. Well, maybe *asking* is the wrong term. More like *demanding*.

Soon, I respond before flipping the phone off and placing it back into my pocket.

The weapon's dealer, who my contacts named as Leopold Hayman, glances down at his own phone, irritation etched onto every haggard line of his face.

"Where the fuck are they?"

"Where the fuck are who?" a cold, calculating voice inquires, and I instinctively blanch, scooting farther away from the edge so as to not be seen. Less than a second later, two figures appear almost directly below me, stalking towards Leopold with the stealth and gracefulness of twin panthers on the hunt. And maybe that's what they are. Fuck only knows how many prey the Davenport twins have devoured.

Shit, why are they here? Why didn't they send some low-level lackey to complete this job? Why did it have to be them?

My eyes flicker to the girl first, looking completely out of place in a tight black skirt that stops just above her knee and a modest blazer. Her dark brown locks are immaculately brushed away from a face that would make angels weep. Her eyes appear almost amber in the glow of the blood-red fluorescent lights, though even that warm color does nothing to dispel the iciness radiating from her in palpable waves. With her ruby-red lips, she looks as if she's seconds away from stabbing everyone here... and then bathing in their blood with a sinister grin plastered on her face.

Her movements decidedly lazy and indolent, she takes her phone out of her clutch and begins to text away, almost as if this meeting is beneath her. Fucking rich, murderous, *sadistic* pricks.

And also...fuck her for having such pretty nail polish, dammit.

The man, her twin, places a hand on the small of her back to steady her as he keeps his eyes on Leopold.

From this angle, I'm able to see every inch of his

painfully beautiful face, and I swear I stop breathing, my heart thundering beneath my rib cage. That reaction lasts only a second before I remind myself that he's a psychopathic murderer and doesn't deserve an ounce of my attraction.

He's not necessarily muscular, though his shoulders are broad and lead down towards a tapered waist. He looks as meticulously groomed as his sister, bedecked in a form-fitting black suit that makes his wavy brown hair appear even darker. And his eyes...

Unlike his sister's honey-colored ones, his are twin abysses. I wonder if it's merely a trick of the lighting or if he truly does have black eyes.

Soulless.

This man looks absolutely soulless, as if what little love and joy he's ever had has been snuffed out of him years ago, leaving behind a bitter, empty shell.

Vincent and Valentina Davenport.

"Do you have it?" I nearly jump out of my skin at the rumbly voice coming from the cold, impassive man's lips. Vincent. It reminds me of thunder on a normally tranquil day, when the sky turns gray with heavy storm clouds and you're forced to run to avoid the sudden downpour. My nipples harden where they're pressed against the platform, and I can't even blame it on the chill.

Leopold looks as if he's sweating, but he nods once and gestures towards one of the many crates situated behind him.

Vincent removes his hand from his sister's back as he stalks forward, pulling open one crate partway and then immediately shutting it. He nods curtly in Valentina's direction, though her eyes remain glued to her phone, her manicured fingers tapping faster across the screen than my racing heart beating in my chest.

"Is it to your satisfaction, my lord?" Leopold's lower lip trembles, and I just barely hold in my snort. My lord? Really?

But I suppose being a Davenport comes with some perks...mainly having other shifters treat you with the utmost respect and admiration. Leopold's eyes flicker hungrily back and forth between the siblings, as if he would quite literally get on his knees for either one of them the second they asked him to. And not just to bow. No, he looks as if he wants to fuck both of them with his tongue. Or cock. Or any body part, really.

Ew.

"Val?" Vincent quirks a brow at his sister, and she

finally lifts her head from her phone, a slow, cunning smirk pulling up her luscious lips.

"Kill them all," she says simply, her grin widening.

Oh fu—

I don't have time to finish that expletive before Vincent has a gun placed to Leopold's head, the silencer on. He shoots once, and I watch as the slimy man falls to the ground in a pool of his own blood.

The shifters Leopold came with begin to scream and run in every direction, but Vincent treats it like a game you would play at a carnival—shoot as many assholes as you can before the timer runs out.

Click.

One down.

Click.

Two down.

Click. Click.

Three down.

When the last body falls to the cement floor, I realize only five seconds have passed.

In that time, Vincent Davenport managed to kill four shifters, all on behalf of his sadistic twin sister.

His sadistic twin sister…who is currently glaring at him, her golden eyes spewing vitriol. She places one hand on her hip and cocks it to the side.

"You got blood on my new shoes," she snaps,

raising a perfectly manicured hand to brush at a loose curl that has fallen in front of her ear.

Vincent scoffs, using the tip of his polished loafer to turn Leopold's body over, giving me a glimpse of his vacant eyes and bloody forehead. At least the skull didn't completely shatter, leaving brain goo on the floor.

I've seen that before. Never again.

"I'm sorry that I didn't kill them far enough away to not get their guts on you, little sister." Vincent's voice is heavy with his sarcasm, and she scoffs.

"Whatever. It's done. Now are we going to grab the product or just sit here twirling our thumbs like we're a fucking idiotic member of BS?" she jests, flipping her shiny hair over her shoulder and very carefully stepping towards one of the crates.

BS. Bloody Skulls. The name of the local motorcycle club that rivals even the Davenports in power and stature.

"Calm yourself." Vincent shoots her a glance over his shoulder, and it's somehow...warm. I didn't think that expression was possible on a man molded entirely from ice. Fuck, he reminds me of one of those snowmen I used to make when I was a kid, complete with a top hat and button nose.

Though, now that I'm thinking about it, I'm

pretty sure a snowman would be more expressive than this bastard.

Without another word, Vincent opens up the crate once more and moves to the side so Valentina, and consequently I, can see the contents.

Fuck.

There are more weapons than I initially expected. And that's just one fucking crate!

My pulse skitters with a strange mixture of trepidation and anticipation. I always get this way during a job, and today is no different.

Almost instinctively, my hand twitches around the trigger that will detonate the bombs I planted a few hours earlier, before Leopold and his crew arrived.

But if I set it off now...

There's no doubt in my mind that Valentina and Vincent wouldn't survive the blast, even with their lycan genetics, and though I don't mind killing them —quite the contrary, actually—we can't afford to have a full-blown war on our hands, especially if they figure out it was me. They're already slaughtering my people like we're vermin. No, like we're *less* than vermin. Like we're creatures so horrific and disgusting that we're not even worthy of being eradicated with the minimum amount of human decency.

We're butchered.

Slaughtered.

Mutilated.

I bite down on my lip hard enough to taste blood as Valentina stealthily steps over one of the corpses and leans against the wall. Her phone is out once more as she types away, her amber eyes narrowed on nothing in particular.

"Hurry up. I want to get home as soon as possible," she snaps, and Vincent rolls his eyes, already moving to load the crates back into the truck Leopold removed them from.

Fuck! I can't allow the weapons to leave this room. Not when they're going to be used against my people.

But I also can't detonate the bombs while the fucking Davenport siblings are present. If it were anyone else, I wouldn't hesitate. One less lycan in the world is a good fucking thing. Instead, I'm faced with the two people whose deaths could quite literally lead to my species' complete annihilation. The Davenport family would wage a war against my people, one we couldn't possibly win, if word ever got back to them of our involvement.

Fuck. Fuck. Fuck.

I need to get them out of here.

Now.

My mind sifting through all of the possibilities, I quietly move to my knees, keeping my hands wrapped around the edge, before climbing to my feet. There's no railing, so if I lose my balance and plummet, I'll have nothing to stop me from a five-story drop. I might survive it.

But there's a very good chance that I won't.

The window, however, leads to a fire escape that travels down the side of the industrial-sized warehouse. It's why I picked this location to begin with—a good escape route when the building goes boom.

I move on silent feet to the already opened window, reveling in the cool breeze that caresses my skin and blows back my hair, before launching myself over the railing. I land gracefully in a crouched position on the metal fire escape, one story down, before continuing the rest of the way.

The staircase ends a few feet from the ground, but I don't bother using the rickety metal ladder to climb down the rest of the way. Instead, I propel myself off the ledge and land on the pebbled ground, directly adjacent to the entrance of the warehouse.

I can hear Valentina bitching about something, followed by Vincent's low laugh. For some undefinable reason, his laugh sends goosebumps rippling up and down my arms. I ignore my body's visceral reaction towards the sound and mentally chastise my vagina for being a shameless hussy.

You'll have some dick in you soon, girl. Don't worry. You don't want that mobster's cock, anyway.

Bending down, I grab the small handgun which I hid in the bushes directly below the fire escape. The weapon is already loaded with silver bullets.

You got this, Blair.

With that admittedly pathetic pep talk, I creep towards the nearest opened window—and considering the fact that this warehouse has been abandoned for years and is now sporting a fine layer of graffiti and dirt, that isn't too hard to find—and peek inside.

Vincent is pushing another crate onto the truck, while Valentina perches on the very edge of the truck bed, her feet dangling. She's chatting incessantly, more animated than she was mere moments ago when they were with Leopold. There's an actual, honest-to-God smile on her face that somehow makes her look almost ethereal.

You just need them to abandon the truck and move out of the warehouse.

Without getting killed.

And without killing them.

No pressure.

As my mother once told me…

Che vita di merda.

What a shit life.

With a shrewd eye, I aim the gun to hit the truck just over Valentina's shoulder. And then I fire.

Their reaction is instant. Valentina, the renowned ice princess and badass mafia member, squeals at the top of her lungs, pathetically raising her arms to cover her head.

Vincent drops the crate he's been carrying—his jacket now off and his white dress shirt rolled up to his biceps, revealing muscular, bronze forearms—and pulls out his own gun. The same gun he just used to kill Leopold, a loyal member of the Davenport family, without remorse.

The same gun that's currently pointed at the window where I'm standing.

I move to the side of the warehouse just in time, barely missing a bullet to my shoulder.

I hiss out a breath and wait until the firing stops before aiming my gun back into the building and shooting wildly. This time, I'm unable to see who the fuck I'm shooting at, so I can only pray that they're smart enough to move the fuck out of the way.

I can distantly hear Vincent hollering at Valentina to leave out the back before his gunshots start up again.

Fuck. Fuck. Fuck.

How much longer is it going to be until the human authorities become aware of gunfire? We're in an abandoned stretch of the warehouse district, sure, but I'm positive that someone, somewhere has heard something and reported it. And the last thing I want to deal with is the fucking police, especially when the majority of them are on the Davenport's payroll.

I cautiously move around the side of the warehouse just as Vincent exits from the front, his eyes wild with fury. He's an angel personified. An avenging angel, yes, but an angel all the same. I half expect dark wings to explode from his back as he stalks forward, his body trembling with barely contained rage.

His eyes lock on mine briefly before I move farther away, disappearing around the corner of the warehouse, and I pray he didn't have enough time to get a good look at me.

"I smell you, runt," Vincent growls out, his voice causing goosebumps to form on my arms.

Ignoring him—which is really fucking stupid, considering he's a psychopath—I peer through the window, ensuring that Valentina has left as well.

Empty.

Besides the truck and the half loaded crates, the warehouse is empty.

I'm sure my grin is positively savage as I grab my necklace once more and finger the pendant.

The pendant that also happens to be the trigger to the bombs I planted.

Vincent appears around the corner, his lips curled away from his teeth and his fingers already elongated into keen claws, but I don't wait. I don't hesitate.

His steps falter when he catches a glimpse of my deranged smile, and he tilts his head curiously to the side.

But before he can stop me—hell, before he can even think one coherent thought—I press down on the pendant.

And the entire warehouse explodes in a kaleido-scope of bright, cheerful colors.

2

BLAIR

In the chaos that follows, I'm easily able to slip away while Vincent runs to find his sister.

But I don't leave.

I tell myself I'm staying behind to make sure they're still alive so I don't inadvertently start a war, but I'm only able to breathe easier when a soot-covered Vincent rounds the corner a few minutes later carrying a coughing Valentina, her brown hair disheveled and ash covering every bare inch of skin.

I quietly creep through the back alleys, stopping only when I reach my forgettable gray Chevy, approximately five miles away from the warehouse. I slip into the driver's seat, pausing only briefly to ensure that I haven't been followed, before slowly inching out of my parking space on the side of the street and onto the road.

In the distance, I can hear the raucous blare of sirens, and red and blue lights fill the air, flashing intermittently. I can also see a sleek, black limo a few streets over, and I have no doubt the Davenport siblings will be safely nestled inside, planning their sweet, sweet revenge on the strange little wolf girl who blew up their weapons shipment.

Fortunately for me, I'm forgettable. A ghost. They can look for me—and I know they damn well will—but they won't find anything.

My anonymity has kept me alive for many, many years. There's no way it's going to fail me now.

...

I arrive back home a few hours later, having taken numerous random turns and side streets on the off chance someone is following me. You can never be too paranoid about safety.

The trailer park is nestled deep in the woods, tall maples interspersed with thick oaks. Starlight weaves its way through the thick branches, creating an aperture of light towards the community of campers and tents all scattered around a large log building. The building itself serves as a community recreation center of sorts and has a few rooms with board games, a swimming pool that's seen better days, a basketball court with hoops hanging precariously from the wall, community showers and bathrooms, and an area that serves as a school for the pups.

There are approximately thirty trailers in the immediate vicinity and ten more on the outskirts, where the guards watch over the community. A few tents are scattered throughout, heavy tarps draped over the weatherworn fabric.

A campfire has been started, and I spot over twenty people laughing and jostling around it. The distinct smell of chicken fills the air as I put my car into park and climb out.

Immediately, a pack of tiny wolves weave around my legs, trying to get me to play. I pet each of their cute, fuzzy faces as their flustered parents attempt to corral them back to the fire.

"Jacob Hanson Wheeler! You get your ass back here!" A large, robust woman hurries through the throng of parents, one hand on her hip as she cocks it to the side. Her brown hair hangs around her face in soft, delicate curls, streaks of gray scattered throughout. Her blue eyes are narrowed as she glares at her son, currently curling around my ankles.

The tiny wolf whimpers at his mother, but I simply laugh.

"Martha," I say, greeting the woman as I bend down to pick up Jacob. The wolf pup immediately begins to lick my face, his tail shaking like crazy with his excitement.

Martha's face softens when she sees me, and she accepts her son from me gratefully.

"I'm glad to see you're in one piece, girly." Her voice is strident, firm, and she tries to appear unaffected, but I can see the relief in her eyes as she gives me a once-over. The woman can try to pretend she hates me all she wants, but I know she has a soft spot for little ole me.

"Is Papa around?" I inquire as a few pack members around the fire finally take notice of me. Howls fill the night air, immediately followed by even more farther away. Soon, the entire camp is alive and vibrant with the jovial noise.

Martha clicks her tongue as she holds her squirming kid. "If he didn't already know, he sure as hell knows now. You should go see him, girly, before he sends the guards after you."

I smirk at her with a devilish wink. "I can take them."

"I bet you fucking can. But I'll have to be your backup, and I'm too old to be in a fight." She sniffs daintily as Jacob begins to wiggle, demanding to be put down so he can rejoin his friends. Martha is one of the very few parents in the camp who actually has her biological kid with her. Most of the stories are much more tragic.

"You're not old," I insist with an eye roll, giving her forty-year-old body a slow, lazy glance. I allow my lips to twist into a predatory leer, knowing it'll annoy the shit out of her. "You're just...like a human thrift store—old and gross and broken."

Martha glares good-naturedly. "Your hoo-ha is a thrift store," she retorts without pause. "Old and used up, and nobody knows what that black stain is but it ain't coming out."

"Well you're as dumb as those shapeless, ugly mom jeans that kids these days think are cool."

I cackle with glee as she lunges at me, and a few of the younger wolves wrestling behind us stop to join the fray. It becomes a playful fight of snapping teeth, half-hearted growls, and tummy rubs. I swear, shifters are more like dogs than you could ever fucking imagine.

"All right. All right." I hold my hands up in a placating manner as I begin to walk backwards, in the direction of my own tiny trailer. "I'll be back in a second. I need to change before my meeting with Papa."

A few of the wolves whine, but Martha snaps at

them to give me space because, in her words, I'm "a deranged, antisocial psychopath."

Fuck, I love that woman.

With a wide grin—both because of what I accomplished today and the innate sense of family and security being with my pack evokes within me—I bounce up the steps and slip inside my trailer.

It's one of the tiniest in the forest, the wooden flooring deteriorating with age. Black spots cover the wood, though I don't know if it's mold or water stains. Either way, it's squishy beneath my feet as I walk.

A couch rests against the right wall, though I gave all of the pillows and blankets away years ago. On the other side is a simple table, so tiny that I can barely fit one plate on it. My bed rests against the far back wall on a raised platform. Only a threadbare blanket, scratchy, stained sheets, and a yellowing pillow rest on top of it. The bathroom on the other side of the trailer is just as sparse, with a toilet, sink, and shower, all three of which are covered in a fine layer of rust.

And where there was once a set of bunk beds…

There's only one place in my entire trailer I worry about. One place I clean religiously and treasure above all else, even my bed.

My weapons stash.

When I bought this trailer, many, many years ago, I removed the mattresses on the bunk beds and gave them away so some of the younger pups could have them. And on the wooden bed frame, I created a kickass collection of weapons I acquired over the years.

Gleaming knives, katana swords, a few grenades, and even some handguns I was able to steal off of unsuspecting Bloody Skulls.

My fucking pride and joy.

Part of me wants to give each of my weapons a kiss like some sort of crazy psycho, but I settle for caressing the hilt of my favorite longsword. Simple, elegant, and so fucking deadly, I can slice through any man or woman like butter.

Sighing heavily, I reluctantly peel my eyes away from the beautiful, orgasm-inducing weapon and slide into a clean pair of shorts and a bright pink T-shirt that has a picture of test tubes with the saying, "Are you staring at my rack?" on it. Classic.

I pull my long, wavy brown hair into a messy bun, a few flyaway strands framing my face, before I slip on a pair of Docs and head back outside.

Martha and Jacob have moved to sit around the fire once more, the kid now back in his human form, and the rest of the young pups are wrestling on the ground while their adopted parents look on with tiny smiles.

I ignore them all and head towards a trailer even smaller than mine, with row after row of dirty windows. I told the old man he needed to take better care of his shit, but he simply smirked at me, the wrinkles around his eyes turning even more pronounced with his smile. Once, when I got super drunk and apparently had a death wish, I spray-painted the side of Papa's trailer with the hope that he'll finally get off his lazy ass and clean it. Of course, the blood-red cock is still there to this day, the ballsack having faded with time and the squirted cum beginning to drip down the sides.

My other fucking pride and joy.

I knock on the door twice but slip inside before he can actually respond.

The rich, tangy smell of smoke permeates the air, and I make a face instinctively, kicking the door shut behind me with the toe of my shoe.

"Did you miss me?" I singsong, skipping inside, pausing, and then striking a pose in the middle of the hallway.

Papa Gray snorts, rolling his eyes at my antics, before nodding towards the torn couch across from him.

"Take a seat, kid." He coughs, holding his cigar

away from his mouth before reluctantly placing it on the table beside us. He knows how I feel about smoking, even if it is a simple cigar. He steeples his hands together and spears me with a long look. "How'd it go?"

My joking mood vanishes, replaced by the persona I wear when I'm the eyes and ears of the bitten faction of wolves. When I'm the thief. The killer.

The assassin.

"Their supplies are gone," I answer simply, and his shrewd eyes narrow further. He's an older man, though no one knows for sure what his exact age is. Could be sixty, could be over one hundred. I imagine he was once handsome, but time and responsibility have chipped away at his looks. Wrinkles mar his face, and even his smile can't demote him from intimidating to approachable. The sweater he wears now is riddled with holes and cuts, and his jeans are covered in stains. Poverty has not treated him well.

"And did anyone see you?" Papa inquires, his hand twitching for his cigar.

I debate lying to him, but I can't do it. Our entire relationship is based on trust in a world that wishes to destroy us all. Every single one of us in this community has had our human lives brutally ripped away. We didn't have a choice or a say. One second, our lives were normal. Peaceful, even. And the next...

And the next, we're beasts.

Monsters.

Sometimes when I close my eyes, I can still hear my parents' bloodcurdling scream, my older brother's enraged shout, and my little brother's gasping sob.

Forcing those memories in a barricaded steel box where they belong, I admit, "Vincent and Valentina Davenport arrived to oversee the shipment."

Papa Grey curses viciously, finally giving in to his impulses and puffing on the cigar. The long, wrinkled fingers of his other hand tap against the armrest of his chair.

"Did you kill them?" he questions at last.

I have to give my pseudo-dad credit. He doesn't freak the fuck out that I might've inadvertently started a war with the Davenport family, one of the largest crime families in the entire United States and *the* largest crime family of shifters. Lycans, to be exact. Werewolves that are more powerful than any other type and are forced to shift during the moon cycle.

"No." I clear my throat and shift uneasily, wondering how pissed he's going to be. But I can't lie to him. I won't. Not after everything he did for me and continues to do. "I lured them out of the warehouse before I destroyed the weapons." I keep my voice curt and formal, not allowing any of my own emotions to bleed into my debrief.

"And did they see you?" Papa reiterates, cocking a bushy white eyebrow. He doesn't seem mad. More... resigned. Tired. Weary. He scrubs a huge hand down his face, his fingers catching on his scruffy beard.

"Vincent Davenport saw me a second before I pressed the detonator," I confess, my fingers automatically reaching upwards to finger the pedant around my neck. It's a device I made myself, and something I'm immensely proud of.

"Vincent Davenport," Papa Gray repeats, disbelief evident in his tone. He reaches towards his minifridge, close enough that he doesn't even need to get out of his chair, and grabs a beer. He doesn't bother to offer me one. He knows what my answer will be.

Drowning half of the bottle in one swoop, he wipes his lips with the back of his hand.

"I don't think he got a good look at my face," I continue, my voice devoid of any inflection. I sound as robotic as the man we're speaking of, the stone-cold killer. "He was more worried about his sister."

Papa rubs his chin in contemplation, and just when I think I might die of uncomfortable silence,

Papa nods his head. Just the tiniest dip of his chin, but it's enough for me to know that he's not mad. That whatever happens, we'll figure it out.

As a family.

"But the weapons have been destroyed?" he asks for clarification, finishing his beer and placing the empty bottle on the table beside his still burning cigar. I'm surprised he doesn't start a fucking fire in this place. Heaven knows it's a complete and utter fire hazard. Does he even own an extinguisher?

I try for a smile. "Everything went boom."

Before he can respond, the door to his trailer is pushed open and a man I recognize as one of the nighttime guards hurries in, appearing frazzled. "There's been an attack. Jerri's dead." He takes a shuddering breath, but before he can continue, Papa and I are already on our feet and pushing past him. I reach into the pocket of my shorts and grab out my small pocket knife. It's not going to do much for protection, but it's better than nothing.

Outside of the trailer, chaos reigns.

My pack scatters around like chickens with their heads cut off. A few of the male wolves attempt to herd the children into the recreation center, while Martha herself stands on a plastic chair and begins shouting orders. Those who are capable run towards where the battle wages, nothing but distant cries and screams for help.

"Blair, wait—" Papa Gray begins, but I don't hesitate, shredding my clothes and my favorite T-shirt of all time as I allow my wolf to take over. In my wolf form, I'm approximately the size of a small horse, my fur a luscious brown highlighted with gold, just like my natural hair. Despite my unnaturally large size, I'm the fastest wolf in our entire pack. And the strongest.

I could easily fight Papa Gray for the position of pack alpha, but I don't want that responsibility. I'm many things, but a leader isn't one of them.

My paws beat against the ground as I race in the direction of the enraged growls and pained whines. I can only pray that my packmates are winning.

When I arrive at a clearing, just at the outskirts of our camp, it's to find one of our younger guards, Darren, being held up by the scruff of his neck by an older man with thick black hair and tan skin. One sniff confirms he's a totemic wolf.

A member of the cleverly named Totemic Tribe, just to the north of us.

Fuck!

I don't hesitate.

Opening my jaws as far as they will go, I throw myself at the pathetic man and clamp down on his neck. Hard. His dark eyes widen in his face as blood squirts from the opened wound, darkening my fur. I pull until I hear the satisfying snap of tendons and his head rolls to the side, illuminated in the pasty, starlit night.

"That's enough!" The voice is cold, strident, and unflinching.

I immediately bare my teeth, a growl reverberating through my body, as a figure stalks through the trees. I recognize him as another totemic wolf instantly, though something about his smell seems off. Almost…sweet. Addictive.

I shake my head rapidly from side to side as he steps into the clearing, giving the fallen wolves a dismissive once-over. His eyes flicker to the dead totemic I'm standing over, and something hardens in his gaze for just a brief second.

"We just came here to talk," the man continues in his honey toned voice.

"By killing my wolves?" Papa Gray demands as he staggers into the clearing, leaning heavily on his wooden cane. His shrewd eyes are anguished as they land on Jerri, the only other causality of this attack.

"It was an…unfortunate accident," the newcomer responds curtly.

The shift fizzles over my skin before I can stop it.

One second, there's a seventy-pound wolf standing beneath the low-hanging tree branches, and the next, I'm me again. I level the asshole with a glare capable of making a lesser man shit himself. But this wolf...

He's not a lesser man.

He's *all* alpha.

I don't bother shying away from my nudity as I swagger forward, my hips swaying and my breasts on full display. I watch as his eyes instinctively dip to my pert nipples before he forces his gaze back to my face, a scowl marring his features.

I can't help but notice that he's ridiculously handsome, just like Vincent. And also like Vincent, this man screams danger, though his type of danger doesn't feel nearly as cold as the mobster I shot at. A black, form-fitting shirt conforms to his muscular chest and shows off every chiseled line of his eight-pack. Tattoos line the bronze skin of his arms before curling up his neck. I imagine he has tattoos on every inch of skin available, and that shouldn't appeal to me as much as it fucking does. His hair is dark, appearing almost blue in the starlight, and is cut short on the sides with a longer, wavy strip directly on top. He's sex on a stick, my wet fucking dream...

And my enemy.

I continue moving until I stop a few feet in front of him.

One of the wolves he came with, a man only a few years older than myself, releases a low whistle. A *wolf whistle*—get it? Snort.

Immediately, Sexy releases a savage growl, whirling around to face his fellow pack member with a murderous expression on his face.

"Shut the fuck up, Paiter," Sexy—because now that I started with the nickname, I can't stop—hisses. His friend pantomimes zipping his lips shut and throwing away the key.

"Who the fuck are you?" I demand, crossing my arms over my chest and forcing all eyes to fall back on my breasts. Only Papa Gray doesn't ogle me, as he purposely stares over my shoulder at the newcomer.

"Put a damn shirt on!" the man hisses as his packmates continue to leer. When I don't immediately respond, continuing to glare at him with blood dripping down my naked body, the man rips off his own shirt and hands it to me with a glare.

I'm right.

He's covered in tattoos.

Hot damn.

I eye the shirt like it's laced with poison, and

when I don't immediately make a move for it, he attempts to forcibly shove it over my head.

"I will peel your dick like a banana and then feed it to you," I warn, backing away and allowing the shirt to fall into a mud puddle between us.

He snarls savagely, glaring at every male in the clearing, before he takes a deep breath and forces himself to relax.

"I'm here to remind Grayson Turner about the summit meeting occurring in two days' time," Sexy says, turning to face Papa.

I barely, just barely, hold in my snort.

The summit.

Where all of the leaders of the werewolf territories come together to discuss territory disputes and issues that may have arisen with the humans. Oh, and to find the best ways to kill us bitten wolves for sport, despite the fact that *they're* the ones who turned us in the goddamn first place.

"We'll be there," I answer immediately, ignoring the glare I can feel on my back from Papa. Sometimes, I'm content to allow him to take the reins and lead our pack. Other times, like today, I can't control myself. My alpha dominance comes out to play, and trying to reel my wolf in is virtually impossible.

Something flickers in Sexy's eyes, but I can't read what it is. As quickly as it arrives, he shuts that shit down and lowers his gaze once more to the wolf behind me. The wolf I killed.

The wolf he *saw* me kill.

The treaty between our territories states that he's allowed to sentence me to death for that. Or even kill me himself.

But I'll be damned if I don't fight tooth and nail until my very last breath.

Instead of saying anything, instead of attacking me or demanding my compliance, Sexy simply glares at me, eyes spewing acid, before whistling sharply beneath his breath. Immediately, the forest comes alive as all of his wolves begin to stalk back towards him. I count at least thirteen, if not more. We would've been fucking slaughtered if they'd chosen to attack.

Paiter—the man who whistled at me—gives Sexy a curious look, his eyes dropping to the body of the wolf I killed before he cups his mouth and releases an ear-piercing howl.

Sexy pauses near the edge of the forest, his tattooed hands clenching, but doesn't bother to look over his shoulder.

"Two days, little wolf. Two days."

3

TAI

My wolf howls and whines inside of my head, pacing relentlessly. He lifts his head and spears me with an eloquent look, one that demands an explanation.

Why?

Why did you leave her?

Claim.

Possess.

Devour.

I clench my jaw to contain the growl that boils up my throat like scalding water. My hands grip the steering wheel until I can see the blue of my veins.

Paiter, in the passenger seat, drums his fingers against his knee, the only obvious sign of his discomfort. Like me, Paiter has bronze skin that appears almost copper in certain lights. His black hair is cut short, nothing more than dark fuzz on the top of his head, and accentuates the roundness of his face. Dark brown eyes, currently shrouded with annoyance and a tiny bit of amusement, stare back at me.

"Sarai isn't going to like this," he points out, and though he tries to smile, it falters on his face, turning the expression into more of a pained grimace.

"Don't care." The words are only a step below a growl, distorted around my mouthful of rapidly sharpening teeth.

"But, Tai—"

"Don't care," I repeat, and he sighs heavily. Out of my peripheral, I watch him pinch the bridge of his nose in exasperation.

"Crim's dead, Tai. That bitten wolf killed him," Paiter points out, probably trying to appeal to me.

But I don't want to hear it. Not for a second.

I know all about Crim's death—I watched him get cut down myself. Imagine my surprise when the wolf who'd slain him transformed before my very eyes, coarse fur being replaced by smooth, dewy skin and a sexy as fuck body that will provide fuel for my spank bank for years to come.

Little wolf.

My little wolf.

The possessiveness of my thoughts startles even

me, but nothing can compare to the way my wolf howls his approval. He throws his head back, his black fur glinting like ink, and releases a noise that has goosebumps jumping to attention on my arms.

"So you're not going to tell Sarai that the little she-wolf killed Crim?" Paiter asks for clarification, but something about his tone has me whipping my head in his direction, momentarily forgetting that I'm supposed to be driving. He holds his hands up in a calming manner, his eyes flickering towards the road with noticeable wariness. "Woah. Calm yourself, man. And eyes on the road."

With a growl, I turn my head to once more stare out the windshield, though I track Paiter like a predator out of the corner of my eye.

His too-acute eyes narrow on me as his mouth compresses into a grim line.

This mission was supposed to be fucking easy.

Travel to the bitten encampment. Remind Grayson of the upcoming summit. Maybe scare him a little bit. And then leave.

But when I heard that some of my father's men were going, I demanded to take the lead, knowing that we couldn't trust the others not to take things too far. Dear old dad, or Sarai, as the rest of the tribe refers to him, allowed me to handle this task, a wry smirk playing on his lips when he did so.

I prayed to the moon goddess that this wouldn't end in bloodshed. And my wish would've come to pass if it hadn't been for Crim.

Crim, one of my father's trusted advisors, was a wicked man with a murderous streak a mile long. The second we arrived at the camp, Crim began taunting one of the bitten wolves patrolling the border. One thing led to another...

And the innocent bitten wolf had his throat ripped out.

Now, Crim's dead, at the hands—or jaws, as the case may be—of an unnamed female that is quickly consuming every single one of my thoughts. When I close my eyes, I can envision her powerful wolf racing through the forest, pouncing on Crim. The way her eyes flashed amber in the glow of the moon. The way she pulled her mouth away from his neck, her teeth stained with blood. And then the way she transformed from wolf to girl, though I have no doubt that both are just as dangerous and fearsome. That they're both formidable predators.

If I were to close my eyes, her image would be etched onto my eyelids. Those perfect features high-lighted by the moon, displaying pouty lips I want to see wrapped around my cock, bright blue eyes, and a tiny nose. Brown hair cascading around her, streaks of gold woven throughout. And then her body...

The image of her body coated in blood will forever be seared into my mind.

Mine, a possessive voice growls in my head as phantom tendrils of jealousy wrap around my heart, squeezing the organ until blood wells. I didn't like the way the other wolves had stared at her. The way *Paiter* had stared at her.

Mine.

Ours, my wolf corrects in irritation.

Ours.

"So what's your plan, Tai?" Paiter continues, oblivious to my internal turmoil. He continues to tap his fingers against his knee, one after the other. "Take the blame for Crim's death?"

"Yes." Short and concise. There's no need to give a better explanation than that.

I'll tell my father, our alpha, that Crim disobeyed me and I had to put him down like one would a rabid dog. That will keep all eyes off of the little wolf until I can figure out what the fuck to do. I'll be punished, of course, but it'll be nothing I haven't experienced ten times already.

Claim.

Possess.

Devour.

I shush my wolf's internal monologue. Some-times, it's irritating having an entirely separate and primitive soul inside of you. None of the other shifter species have to deal with it, though I can't imagine being so disassociated with your wolf. The prowling beast stalking my mind is a part of me, an intricate piece of my very soul that I'll never want to get rid of.

And both parts of us currently want one thing and one thing only—the little wolf with the fire in her eyes.

"I won't tell Sarai the truth, you know," Paiter continues, still drumming his fingers against his jeans. He keeps glancing out the window, as if the dancing trees will answer all of the world's problems. "And I can see why you want to protect her. I mean, did you see her tits—"

I slam on the brakes so suddenly, his head bangs against the dashboard. He releases a startled yelp, rubbing at his skin as his eyes narrow into thin, unforgiving slits.

A translucent veil bathed in blood darkens my vision. A virulent storm wages a fierce battle inside of me.

"Don't," I warn around bared teeth before driving forward once more.

Don't push me while my wolf is so close to the surface.

Don't talk about her fucking tits.

Don't.

Don't.

Don't.

For a moment, his eyes flash amber before he wrestles control back from his own wolf.

"Asshole," Paiter grumbles, but he mercifully drops the subject.

For all of two seconds.

"But there's a flaw in your plan," he presses. "That bitch—" A growl escapes me before I can contain it, and Paiter wisely chooses to correct himself. "That *woman* was seen killing Crim by Calian. And you know Calian will go straight to Sarai with the news."

The familiar haze of red once more clouds my vision as I tighten my hands on the steering wheel. I drag my eyes up towards the rearview mirror where, in the distance, I can see six other cars' headlights. All of them belong to my pack.

And one of them contains Calian.

Threat. My wolf perks his large head up, growling sharply.

For the second time tonight, I slam on the brakes.

"Motherfucker!" Paiter screams as his head once again collides with the dashboard. He throws me a scathing glare. "Really?"

"Shut up," I hiss out as, behind me, the other cars stop as well.

As I watch, the members of my pack begin to get

out of their vehicles one after another, all with visible confusion etched onto their faces.

In the car directly behind me, Calian sits. Alone.

Thank fuck there weren't any other occupants in the car with him. I might've had to kill them all on the off chance that he talked to them during the drive.

Threat.

Protect.

A growl rumbles up my throat as I stalk out of the car like death personified, ignoring Paiter's muffled curse behind me.

I stalk directly to Calian's car, rip open the door, and drag the wolf out.

"What the fuck do you think you're doing?" Calian screams in rage, flinging a clawed hand at my face. I stealthily duck out of the way, still maintaining my hold on him.

Making sure to keep my voice loud and strident, and containing the growl that threatens to escape through clenched teeth, I say, "Calian, for crimes against the Totemic Tribe, you have been sentenced to death."

His mouth drops open in shock, his eyes widening.

"What the fuck did I—"

"For the murder of Crim, you have been

sentenced to death," I continue, and the whispers spread like wildfire. I catch tidbits here and there, but the gist is simple—people are shocked. Scared. Confused. Calian has been a model citizen since my father took control of the pack many, many years ago. But the term "model citizen" connotes unspeakable and depraved acts implemented by my father and his men. A model citizen he may be, but a loved community member he is not.

No one stands up for the man.

Not after all of the horrible things he has done to the community. To the *women and children* of the community. His life may have been spared time and time again by my cruel and malevolent father, but I'm *nothing* like the man whose DNA I carry.

Nothing.

And while he forgives those who least deserve it, I remain wrathful.

So tonight, I'll kill him, protect the nameless she-wolf, and rid the world of one more monster.

Calian's eyes harden, his mouth opening to no doubt scream his truths to the world, when I slash my claws across his throat. Blood bubbles as pure terror reflects in his eyes.

"The demons of hell are here for you," I whisper in his ear, my voice superimposed with the growl of my wolf, "and they've come to collect your pathetic, miserable, broken soul."

Threat.

Kill.

Protect.

Her.

Her.

4

BLAIR

While the guards make another sweep of the perimeter, ensuring that our unwanted visitors have truly left instead of seeking retaliation for the fallen member of their pack, the rest of us convene in the makeshift conference room in the rec center.

It's furnished with nothing but a long table with twelve chairs planted around it. Each chair is filled with an important member of our pack.

To my immediate left, we have Johnson, the head of security, and to my right sits Papa Gray himself. Martha, Bri, and Letty are the only other females present, running the daycare, armory, and self-defense training, respectively. The rest of the table is filled with the wolves that deal with mundane things, such as hunting, agriculture, maintenance, job placement, and schooling.

"So, what the ever-loving fuck are we supposed to do now?" Martha snipes, never one for softening her words. That woman has the mouth of a fucking sailor, and I love her for it.

Papa Gray rubs at his forehead, where a heavy crease has developed between his bushy eyebrows. If it's even physically possible, he looks even older than he did a mere hour ago when I met him in his camper. The lines on his face are even more pronounced, zigzagging down his face and causing his lips to distort unevenly.

"Isn't it obvious?" Salmon, the wolf in charge of trading with the other packs, cuts in with a scathing look in her direction. When he turns towards me, his features soften instantly. "Blair's gonna have to go to the summit with Papa."

"You know that's not a possibility," Papa interjects with another heavy frown. He turns towards me, one eyebrow quirked, and I can see the entire monologue he's attempting to articulate without words.

If the Davenport twins are there, if they recognize you, then they'll declare war on us. We can't afford that. We already lost so many members of our pack this year alone when they started hunting us for sport. But if you don't go, that Totemic fuck from today will hunt you down. For some reason, he wants you to go, and that makes me wary.

Over the years, we've gotten immensely skilled at reading each other. He doesn't have to say a word for me to understand exactly what's going through that analytical head of his.

Speaking slowly, so as to not alarm the others about what transpired just a few hours prior in the warehouse, I say, "The Davenport siblings haven't attended a summit since they were in diapers. They think it's beneath them. And with the death of their father," my upper lip curls, "they'll be more paranoid than ever. They'll send a representative. I'm sure of it."

Johnson, the head of our security, eyes the two of us suspiciously. He's always been more perceptive than the other wolves in our pack. His bald head and chiseled features give him a severe look, but I know him to be a big softie. If you can look past the scowl always darkening his features. And the muscles causing his black T-shirt to strain. And the fierce glint in his eyes promising pain and suffering to those who dare hurt his family.

You know, just a great, big teddy bear.

"Did something happen with the...?" He trails off, casting a quick glance at the faces of the others present. No one, besides him and Papa, knows the truth about where I went only hours before. Has it really been only a few hours since I blew up the warehouse? Fuck, it feels like it was a lifetime ago.

"Nothing we can't handle," Papa states with a sniff. "So it's settled then." He pauses to level each of us with a cold, unwavering stare, his gaze lingering on me the longest. "Blair and Johnson will both accompany me to the summit in two days' time. I'll fight my damnedest to protect our people," he vows, his throat bobbing as he swallows. "But until then... we need to pray for a miracle."

THE FIRST VACATION I WENT ON WAS WITH MY FAMILY, only months before the...incident. My mother took us to her hometown in Italy to visit my grandma, who was on her deathbed. I remember that Percy kept squirming in my mother's arms, but he finally settled when I held him. My older brother, Brett, continuously poked me in the stomach until I squealed and smacked his arm. I don't know why that particular memory is etched in my mind, tattooed on my closed eyelids, but it is.

It's one of the very last good memories I have of my family.

That trip.

My parents.

My two brothers.

Most of my other memories are bathed with the blood of *that* horrific night…

Shaking my head, I focus on my suitcase once more.

The summit's location alternates year to year between the Bloody Skulls, the Davenport's mansion, and the Totemic Tribe's land.

Never in bitten territory.

This year, the Bloody Skulls MC—or BS, as we so eloquently nicknamed the motorcycle club of fenrir wolves—is hosting. They rented out a hotel directly in the center of their district. According to Papa, we'll stay two nights. On the first day, we'll have an introductory, completely optional session where everyone will introduce themselves and mingle. And on the second and third days, we'll discuss territories, politics, trading, and new legislation. Because even criminal organizations need some semblance of control and order, don't they? If they don't have that, they're left with nothing but anarchy.

And they can't rule a nation in anarchy.

Papa had taken to drinking as he discussed the days' events with me, just an hour earlier.

Because every damn year, Papa attends, hoping for more rights for bitten wolves. And every damn year, the leaders of the three ruling gangs laugh in his face. Half the time, he arrives back home sporting bruises and fresh scars. The other half, he's drunk off his ass and unable to function for days after.

As I pack the suitcase Martha loaned me, I allow my mind to wander.

I know almost everything there is to know about the three gangs that rule our city, unbeknownst to the humans.

Directly north of us is the Totemic Tribe, cleverly named after their wolves. According to legend, they perform a ritual on their members when they come of age, and that ritual allows their wolves to emerge. Unlike a lycan, they're not born with a wolf and they're able to shift on command. The leader of the tribe goes by the name of Sarai, though not much is known of the alpha, except for the fact he's a sadistic fuck who runs most of the drug trade in the city. Gambling, revels, drugs...that all falls under the Totemic's jurisdiction. The spy I have inside of their territory told me that the alpha's son, Tai, has recently shown signs of being an alpha himself, causing discourse within the community. It makes me cackle with glee. I don't honestly believe that such a diminutive fracture will lead to the entire organization crumbling, but a girl can never be too hopeful. Either way, I need to be prepared if Tai *is* able to take control from Sarai. Will he be a just and kind leader like his grandfather? Or a malevolent one like his father?

To the west of us, and our host for the summit, is the Bloody Skulls Motorcycle Club. They can always be recognized by the tattoo located somewhere on their person—a pale white skull weeping blood from its empty eye sockets and gaping mouth. They're the cruelest of all the gangs, simply because they don't give a fuck about anyone who isn't in their little club. They especially hate bitten wolves, like us, and humans. Rumor has it that they keep humans and bitten wolves as glorified slaves, forced to spend their days sucking their disgusting cocks and cleaning floors. It's despicable. They also serve as the cleanup crew for all three gangs. If you have a dead body that you need to get rid of, you call a BS member. I have no idea what process they use to get rid of the dead bodies—acid? Pigs?—but they're renowned for their skills. But unlike the Totemics, I haven't been able to get an inside guy to spy for me.

Well, I've tried, but they never come back to me alive.

And finally, we have the Davenport family. The richest fucking family in the entire city and made up entirely of lycan wolves—wolves who were cursed by a Gypsy a long time ago to transform into beasts during the moon cycle or something like that. Their dad died only a few months ago, leaving his impressive fortune to his wife, Annabelle, and her two children, the twins from hell. The Davenports are known for dealing in skin, as in humans, and are ruthless and vicious. Stone-cold killers who won't hesitate to shoot you between the eyes and then stare impassively at your decaying corpse.

I can't help but think of Vincent's apathetic expression when he killed Leopold and his crew. There was nothing remotely human about him in that moment. He was all wolf. All beast.

All monster.

The door to my trailer opens and closes just as I'm shoving my favorite longsword into my bag. I'll keep a few daggers underneath my clothes, but I'm not leaving here without my fucking baby. No chance in hell.

Besides, according to Papa, the assholes running the summit never bother to check us for weapons.

They don't think us "poor, pathetic bitten wolves" will be stupid enough to bring any.

But that's always been the world's problem when it comes to me.

I'm not one to be underestimated.

"You don't have to do this," Papa pleads from directly behind me, and I don't need to look to know that he'll be leaning against the sink, his cane extended as he leans heavily on it.

"You should've knocked," I deadpan as I attempt to fit my blade into my duffle bag. Fortunately, it's one of the biggest Martha could find for this exact reason, but it's like putting together a puzzle. After a few tries, I'm able to snuggly fit my sword amidst my clothing. Take that! I totally do a victory dance and punch the air a few times. "What if I was naked?"

"We're wolf shifters, girl," Papa says with a disgruntled snort. "I've seen more of you than I ever, *ever* want to. I still have nightmares to this day."

"Ha. Ha," I respond dryly, finally spinning around to face him. I cross my arms over my chest and lean against the wall that leads to the bathroom. "But you know why I have to go, right? I weighed the pros and cons. The Totemic fucker saw me kill one of his wolves. By law, he's allowed to punish me for the action. But he didn't, and we can't piss him off. I don't know about you, but I don't want to die just yet. There are too many people I want to stab beforehand. Too many *stronzi*." My Italian heritage always comes out with a vengeance when I'm feeling stabby.

"And the cons of going?" Papa inquires, ignoring my half-hearted joke.

The smile that was attempting to make an appearance on my face dissipates instantly. The mood turns somber. "The cons? If the Davenport siblings show up, we're fucked. If the Totemic asshole decides to air his grievances to every member of the summit, we're fucked. It doesn't matter that they were in our territory and killed one of ours first. To them, we're just bitten wolves. Scum. That's all they'll ever see us as." I stare angrily over his shoulder at a darkened water stain. "Even if we didn't ask for this."

Papa nods sagely, tapping his fingers against the counter while his other hand grips the head of his cane tighter.

"Did you make contact with Jerri's family?" I ask after a full minute of silence. His eyes whip down to my face, his features shadowed by sorrow.

"I did." He sighs. "We'll have his wake tomorrow night before we leave for the summit." Pure fire spews from his gaze when he speaks next. "I promised my people I'd fight for us, and I fucking meant it. We're not leaving the summit until we can get actual goddamn rights for the bitten wolves."

My answering grin is savage. Taunting, almost. I pull a knife out of the holster on my thigh and hold it lovingly against my chest, stroking the emblemed hilt.

"Fortunately for you, old man," I wink, "I'm ready to go to war."

5

BLAIR

I've never been inside the Bloody Skull's territory before, and I'm not prepared for it to be so...dilapidated. Rundown. I've heard rumors, of course, that while the members of the motorcycle club themselves were thriving, the rest of the area was virtually a wasteland, but seeing it with my own two eyes is something else entirely.

The houses appear to be no bigger than rundown shacks, each one ravaged by vandalism and graffiti. Most of the buildings' windows have been broken, tiny shards of glass splattered across the street we drive down. Even inside the car, the pungent smell of stale garbage and bodily fluids reaches me and permeates the air, causing me to wrinkle my nose in disgust.

Papa glances at me out of the corner of his eye as

he steers us expertly through the crowded street. Johnson is in the car behind us, and through the rearview mirror, I can see his own face wrinkled in disgust.

"Just you wait, kid," Papa says as we pull to a stop in front of a moderately nice hotel with sun-bleached wooden walls. Hell, compared to the rest of this dump, the hotel is a fucking paradise. "Things are about to get ten times worse."

With that ominous statement, Papa parks the car and waits for me to climb out, my neck canting backwards to stare up at the five-story building. The sun has bleached away some of the coloring, but it's apparent that unlike the rest of the town, this hotel has been well maintained.

Directly next door is a sleazy dive bar with numerous motorcycles parked out front. I've heard from my sources before they died that this is their clubhouse where the leader holds church every week.

I find it ironic that the BS members always talk shit about us bitten wolves living in poverty, and yet the majority of them live the exact same fucking way. Sure, we live in trailers in the woods, but at least our home doesn't look like we should be up-to-date on our tetanus shots. At least we do the best we can to set up safe living spaces. Theirs is a garbage can.

As if the universe itself is agreeing with me, a fast-food bag blows across the parking lot before getting caught on a tree. Actually, it's the only tree I've seen since we crossed into BS territory. The majority of the area is made up of industrial warehouses and rickety apartment complexes.

"You need to be careful about who you talk to and how you talk to them," Papa says in a rushed whisper as I grab my duffle bag out of the trunk and throw it over my shoulder. I grab his suitcase as well as he hobbles forward on his cane. "The leader is Grim, and he's a fucking brutal, savage asshole. He doesn't give a fuck about humans or bitten wolves... Hell, he doesn't give a fuck about anyone who isn't a member of his club. And women?" He scoffs, and I can hear the derision he holds for the man in that one sound. "He treats them as nothing but toys for him to use and discard. Steer clear of him."

Well, it's not like I was planning on having a nice conversation with that asshole. Unless it ended with my knife in his throat.

"His son is named Bullseye—"

"Bullseye?" I interrupt. I think I remember getting word about him from one of my sources... but then that source was brutally slaughtered, so I can't be certain how reliable his information was. "What type of name is that?"

"The name of someone who can shoot you in the forehead from miles away, pretty girl," a masculine voice that doesn't belong to Papa responds. My alpha freezes, his hand clenching around his cane, but I remain nonchalant as I spin around to face the newcomer, releasing the death grip I had on Papa's suitcase.

And my breath rushes out of me.

He's probably the most gorgeous man I've ever met. Not because he's sexy or rugged or handsome... but because he's too fucking pretty.

His golden blond hair is messily styled, the honey streaked strands having a natural wave that most girls would kill to run their hands through. It hangs just to his shoulders, framing a face models would sell their souls to obtain. Normally, I don't like long hair on a man, but fuck, he makes it work. His vibrant green eyes, the type of green that reminds me of nature with fresh buds and manicured grass and large leaves, sparkle with his mirth. He wears a leather jacket that conforms to his muscular shoulders and reveals the tight gray shirt underneath.

His luscious lips quirk upwards the longer I continue my appraisal, but fuck it. I don't plan on stopping when he's doing the exact same thing to me.

"And who are you?" I question coldly, my eyes flicking to the insignia on his cut. A Bloody Skull.

Papa clears his throat beside me, his face taking on an ashen quality, but I'm done being bossed around by these little bitches. We came to the summit to fight back, didn't we? To demand more rights?

Well, I'm gonna start now. Why should I cower in front of this man?

"What would you do for me to get that information?" he asks with another cocky ass grin.

My god. He really is too pretty for his own good. His features are so perfectly proportionate and angelic that I sorta hate him.

"If you're asking if I'd be willing to suck your cock, then I'd rather just call you Choir Boy," I say, crossing my arms over my chest. This gorgeous little fuck doesn't deserve a better nickname.

And I wonder...

Has he ever attacked my people? Two months ago, when Malcom didn't return home from work and was found murdered on the street, did he play a part in that? How about when Mandy and Elizabeth were attacked and killed, only six months prior? Or

Lucien? Mike? Tommy? Did this angelic man help slaughter my people?

Each thought only exacerbates my rage.

Both of the man's eyebrows raise until they touch his hairline. I can't help but note that they're a slightly paler color than his gorgeous blond locks. "Choir Boy, eh? I can't say that I've ever been called that before." He gives me a salacious perusal, one I can feel in the very depths of my soul. My nipples pebble beneath my shirt, and I can tell he sees them when his grin widens to disarming levels. "Can I at least have your name, pretty girl?"

"For one, don't call me that," I snap, my anger bubbling and frothing inside of me. His smile grows. "And for two," I take a step closer until I'm toe-to-toe with him, "you wouldn't know what to do with the name of a bitten wolf." I speak slowly, reminding him that I'm nothing but the scum of the earth in his eyes, but his gaze only turns even more molten.

Papa makes a strangled noise in the back of his throat, but he doesn't comment. He may be the alpha of the pack—hell, he may even be my alpha—but we both know he doesn't own or control me. No one does.

"Bitten wolf. Lycan. Fenrir. It doesn't matter to me." He smirks. "I never have a shortage of women sucking my cock."

My temper burns white-hot as I ball my hands into fists. "And how many of those women are willing?" I snark, knowing the reputation of each and every member of this godforsaken club.

The lust filled fire dies from Choir Boy's eyes, replaced by a fierce anger, one that takes my breath away.

"Wow." He scratches at the back of his neck, blowing air out through his flared nostrils. "Look at you acting so high and mighty when you're making assumptions about a complete stranger. You know what they say about assumptions, pretty girl?"

"That they make asses out of us all?" I cross my arms, refusing to be cowed.

He releases a dry and humorless laugh. "That they lead to consequences. An action always has a reaction. And a judgment? It can create a formidable enemy."

His words cause goosebumps to rise on my skin like angry fire ants. It feels as if razor blades are being dragged down my throat, and each time I swallow, they slice my skin raw.

"Is that a threat?" I cock an eyebrow.

"Nah. Consider it a warning. I'll let you have this one for free. Because as 'warning prostitutes' go— that's my new title, by the way, because I hand out warnings instead of blowjobs—I'm a pretty damn cheap one." He flashes a smile, one that quirks up only the right side of his lips. It doesn't meet his eyes, those verdant green orbs still swirling with anger and barely suppressed rage.

"You would know all about prostitutes, wouldn't you?" I take a step closer, keeping my voice low and deadly. "After all, the Bloody Skulls are known for their girls on every corner."

"Blair—" Papa hisses, but Choir Boy waves him away, not tearing his gaze from mine.

"No. It's fine." Another smile. Another spark of anger jumping in his eyes. "It's always interesting to hear strangers' opinions on things they know nothing about."

The condescension in his voice is plain to hear.

But instead of mollifying me or even making me regret my quick judgment, it only serves to piss me off.

"You say that, Choir Boy, but you don't know a damn thing." I bare my teeth. "You can shove your hypocritical judgment up your ass."

That anger I saw before returns, darkening the green to a mossy color. His lips peel back from his teeth, even as a cocky grin remains firmly in place.

"Right back at you, pretty girl. Though I'm not sure your judgment would fit with the stick already there."

With a forced wink, he steps away from me as if my mere proximity burns him and then storms towards the entrance of the hotel, leaving me and Papa behind. He doesn't look back once, his muscles bunching beneath his leather jacket.

I watch him go with my heart beating rapidly, almost erratically, inside of my chest as anger continues to liquify my veins and turn my brain into mush. Stupid, cocky, arrogant bikers with their too-pretty faces and delectable bodies.

"What did I say about stirring the fucking pot?" Papa bellows when he's sure Choir Boy is out of earshot. Irritation laces his tone.

"I can't help it," I grumble as I grab his suitcase once more and trudge towards the entrance of the hotel. "I'm a fucking spoon."

He snorts at my shitty analogy but follows me inside.

The summit hasn't even officially begun yet, and I already know it's going to be a whirlwind of a ride.

All I can pray is that Papa and I make it out relatively unscathed.

6

MASON

Who was that beautiful woman with eyes brighter than the Caribbean Sea and hair that would look fucking fantastic wrapped around my fist as I fucked her?

And why the fucking hell am I so enraptured with a dumb slut who dared to accuse me of something so…fucking disgusting?

I'm not my father. I worked my ass off for years not to be like that vile man and the other members of this club.

So how fucking dare she accuse me otherwise?

I don't need validation from some girl I don't even know the name of, but fuck, it's hard not to get upset by the vitriol spewing from her eyes when she looked at me like I was the scum of the earth. The sticky gum beneath her combat boots.

I'm still fuming when I enter my hotel room, throw off my jacket, and kick off my boots like I'm a fucking three-year-old having a tantrum.

I'm so lost in my own thoughts, I don't realize that there's a naked girl in a bed with my best friend.

"For fuck's sake!" I snarl.

Grunt gives me a very, *very* annoyed look as he sits up in bed, his scarred chest on full display while his lower half stays, mercifully, covered. The girl in bed with him releases a high-pitched giggle, almost as if she's feigning nervousness. The cover slides down to reveal her large breasts and perky pink nipples.

I don't bother acknowledging her, growling sharply at Grunt until he releases a sigh and gets out of bed. I avert my eyes as he pulls on a pair of pants and leans down to kiss his slut. And yes, I understand that word is demeaning, but it's not like this woman means anything to him. She's just a desperate gold digger who would spread her legs for any powerful man if he were to ask her. Including me.

As if to prove my point, she swaggers past me as naked as the day she was born, large breasts bouncing, and purposely runs a hand down my arm. One smell confirms she's a fenrir, like me, though not one I'm familiar with. Probably a new girl my dad chose.

I offer her a tight-lipped smile, allowing my eyes to travel over her curvy form the way my reputation in the club requires me to. And normally, I would be all for fucking her senseless. She's hot enough, with sandy-brown hair, abnormally large breasts with swollen nipples, and a pussy glistening with cum.

But fuck, even thinking about sticking a finger in her cunt or sucking one of her breasts fills me with unease.

Why?

Why the fuck shouldn't I bend her over a chair and fuck her senseless?

As if my mind is battling my body, I reach a hand up to stop her and give her a slow grin, watching her eyes turn half-mast with lust.

"Did my friend here show you a good time, baby?" I murmur as I move a hand up her side, stopping at the underside of her heavy breast. Bile rushes up my throat, but I have no idea why.

What's happening to me?

"Why? Do you think you can do better?" she asks in a sultry voice, gripping my wrist to place my hand over her breast, her nipple pushing against my palm. Grunt makes an amused noise behind me, but the sound abruptly cuts off when I jump away from the girl as if I'm on fire. And when I fucking growl at her like a feral beast?

Yeah, I'm just as confused as both of them.

The girl runs as if her ass is on fire.

I turn towards Grunt to see both of his eyebrows raised, but I simply spread my hands out on either side of me. Fuck, I don't understand my reaction either. Maybe I'm just not in the mood for pussy?

"Please tell me you didn't get cum on the floors?" I ask scathingly in an attempt to change the subject, moving to my own queen-sized bed on the other side of the room. For the summit, Grim commanded that all of his representatives stay at the hotel with the rest of the wolves. And since I'm here, of course I'm gonna bring Grunt. There's no chance in hell I'm leaving him behind at home, even if it's only a few minutes away.

Grunt's a bitten wolf, and as such, the men of the club treat him like a slave. He was their fucking whipping boy until we became friends, and now I protect him. At least as well as I can in the world we live in. His entire family was fucking slaughtered by the wolves that turned him, and it also caused his body to become mottled with hideous scars and his vocal cords to turn to shit, hence the name Grunt.

"Grim wants us down there to scope out the representatives. Ran into Gray. The fucker didn't come alone this year. Had a girl with him."

Why does my voice lower at the mention of the

unnamed female? And why does the thought of Grunt—in all his rugged charm—setting his eyes on her make me murderous with rage, almost blinded by it?

"So we need to get our cuts on and head down," I finish, determined to put any and all thoughts of the girl out of my head.

Grunt continues to give me a strange look, but he doesn't question me, sliding his cut on over his shirt and running his fingers through his messy black hair.

Fuck, I hate these summits. It's a cesspool of whining and crying and sobbing and stabbing. Yes, stabbing. There have been more than a few fights that have broken out during the meetings. Hell, even I got stabbed once, and all I did was try to get in between a Totemic wolf and a Davenport.

Shaking my head ruefully, I lead Grunt down the hall of the hotel, past the elevator—because like fuck am I going to be trapped in a tiny, enclosed box for even a second—and to the staircase. We descend in relative silence, me fuming over the blue-eyed female and Grunt lost in his own thoughts. Probably lamenting over the loss of his girl.

As we move to the lobby, I'll never admit to anyone the disappointment I feel when I don't spot

Grayson and his...daughter? Lover? Fuck, she better not be his lover. I would go apeshit.

Why am I so obsessed with this girl? I've never been obsessed with anyone or anything in my life... unless you count that Britney Spears phase in middle school, but we don't need to talk about that. Either way, I'm irritated as fuck that I can't get that nameless bitten wolf out of my head, try as I might to eradicate her image from my brain. I need to take fucking bleach to my mind and scrub all traces of her away. Then, and only then, will I be able to breathe easier.

I do, however, spot Tai himself leaning against the bar on the opposite side of the room. The bartender hands him a glass of bourbon, which he downs in one shot, wiping his mouth with the back of his sleeve.

As always, Tai is intimidating as fuck in his leather jacket, his tattoos peeking out from his sleeves and curling around his fingers. His black hair is tousled, a few wayward strands brushing against his cheek, and his scowl is firmly in place. I call it his murder scowl, mainly because it's an expression that promises extreme pain and suffering to everyone in the general vicinity.

Curse my father for wanting an alliance with these asshole wolves.

Plastering on a cocky smirk, I swagger towards the scary fucker, Grunt trailing behind me like a silent sentry.

Tai doesn't look up when we arrive, though I know he senses us. His scowl deepens, a feat I didn't think was possible, and the hand around his glass tightens, his knuckles turning a stark white color.

"Fenrir," he growls sharply, still keeping his eye on the glass. One of his bronze fingers moves to lazily trace the rim, and I try not to let my agitation bubble inside of me. But fuck, if there's one thing I hate most in the world, it's being ignored.

"Totemic," I seethe, moving to perch on the barstool next to him. Out of my peripheral, I spot Grunt moving farther down the bar, giving us space to talk while still keeping me in his direct line of vision. And also to watch my back, because I know for a fact that there are over a dozen wolves currently prowling through the lobby, all of whom wouldn't hesitate to put a blade through my skull. But the humans loitering about keep those primal urges adequately at bay.

The one rule all of us wolves have to follow—we can't risk discovery.

Tai nudges his empty glass in the direction of the bartender—a member of the club my father hired— and the wolf growls, baring fangs and flashing yellow eyes, but pours the damn drink. I glare at the wolf pointedly, nodding my head towards the oblivious humans, and he storms away, growling beneath his breath.

My dad considered closing the hotel this weekend for the summit, but we need the business. And this is the one hotel in the entire area that isn't a complete shit show. But we can remain cordial so as to not make humans aware of our presence, right? Right?

For three days only, we're all…friendly. Yes, that's the word I'm thinking of. Friendly. We have to be, or the consequence will be absolute bloodshed. It'll be an all-out war, and frankly, I'm betting on us winning. How can we not when this is our territory and the hotel is run by our wolves? Hell, I could slit all of their throats myself if the desire hit me and face very few repercussions due to my position as VP.

"Your father talked to my alpha," Tai continues in that cold, detached voice he always uses. I grin at him sharply but allow him to gather his thoughts. I find it funny that he refers to his own father as "alpha," when the entire wolf community knows he's more powerful than him. If he wanted to, Tai could take complete control of the Totemic pack and every wolf in it.

But for some reason, he resists.

"About the alliance," I add when it becomes obvious he's not going to say anything else.

Tai swirls the golden-brown drink around before chugging it back. "You think that's a smart move? An alliance between our two packs will be an unofficial declaration of war against the Davenports and the bitten wolves." He speaks the words casually, as if he doesn't give a damn either way, but his shoulders have gone rigid beneath his jacket, the tattoos on his neck rippling.

I recite the words my dad has drilled into my head. The speech I perfected. "The Davenports are weak. Their entire lives revolve around the moon. And the bitten... We all know they're weak too." Weak. Impoverished. Practically extinct. And while the community surrounding the MC is struggling immensely, we, as a pack, are flourishing.

I know not all cities and states and countries see bitten wolves as "less than." Some even cherish and protect them. I visited this one chick at Silver Falls University in Wisconsin, and the bitten wolves were revered there. Loved, cared for, and admired.

But unfortunately, our city does not regard bitten wolves that way.

At the same time, when bitten wolves try to leave, we attack them. Kill them. Hunt them down for sport. We don't want them gaining back any of the power we stole.

Besides, how can they possibly leave when poverty is even more crippling to them than any wolf attack could possibly be?

Nobody can say for sure what caused this intense hatred against the bitten wolves. Maybe one of the older wolves can tell you, but not even my father knows the truth. It's just the way it's always been in our city. The fenrirs, totemics, and lycans are revered and respected, if not feared, while the bitten wolves are discriminated against and hunted down. Hell, for all I know, the ruling packs were fighting over some bitten female wolf, and when she chose none of them, declared war on her people.

Bile swirls in my stomach as if someone stuck their hand down there and is sifting through the meager contents. Fuck, sometimes I hate the choices I have to make for my family and club. Sometimes, I hate the fact that we're considered the "bad guys." At the same time, I know I can't stop any of it—the threats, the deaths, the attacks…all of them on innocent, defenseless bitten wolves.

But what can one wolf do? What can *I* possibly begin to do without risking my life or Grunt's?

"Just think of the proposal," I grit out, hating

myself a little more for playing puppet for my deranged father. "Our resources—"

"What can a poor MC offer us?" Tai bites out, his tone loud enough to make Grunt's back stiffen. I eye the asshole totemic wolf coldly, but he continues, unperturbed by my ire. Or maybe just too drunk to fucking care. "We have a self-sustained community," Tai continues on, slapping the bar to get another refill. "Doctors, teachers, farmers… We don't need you."

"You might not have a choice," I say simply. Because if I know my father as well as I think I do, he'll stop at nothing to get what he wants. And what he currently wants is the Totemic Tribe on their knees for him, begging for whatever scraps he wishes to bestow upon them.

"Is that a threat, not-wolf?" Tai hisses, and I bristle at the common Fenrir insult. He knows that most of us are sensitive to the fact that we can't shift into anything even remotely resembling a wolf.

Smiling through gritted teeth, I respond, "No. It's just a warning." I remove my leather wallet from my pocket and slide a few twenties in the direction of the bartender. It's a grave fucking insult, implying that Tai won't be able to pay for his own drinks, but I'm too wound up to care. "Have a great day."

Because I can be civil as shit when I need to be.

I storm out of the lobby, ignoring the metaphorical daggers Tai hurls at my back, as Grunt steps up to my side.

He lifts one eyebrow and signs, "The gym?"

"No." A growl reverberates through my chest before I can contain it. "Outside. I need to beat the shit out of someone, and unfortunately for you, big guy, there's no one else around."

7

BLAIR

I sleep like the dead.

While Papa Gray knocked on my door the night before to tell me he was heading downstairs to mingle with Johnson as backup, I chose to stay in my room, buried beneath layers upon layers of blankets.

I can't remember the last time I slept that good.

When I wake up the next morning, I stretch lazily, feeling like an overgrown housecat, and push back the covers. I take a quick shower, throwing a brush through my tangled brown hair, and then dress in a purple leather tank top that clings to my breasts and a pair of jean shorts. I complete the outfit with a pair of thigh-high, lacy, black stockings and combat boots, my knife holster clasped firmly to my left thigh. Staring at my reflection in the mirror,

I decide I appear presentable enough and leave my room to find coffee.

Oh, and Papa Gray and Johnson.

But coffee's more important.

The two of them are in Papa's room when I waltz inside, my eyebrows lifting to my hairline when I see Johnson lounging in Papa's bed beneath the covers, naked from the waist up. He eyes me astutely, daring me to comment, when the bathroom door is pushed open and Papa Gray waddles out with a towel clasped firmly around his waist.

"Don't you ever knock, girly?" Papa growls out with an exasperated eye roll, his eyes flickering between me and his chief enforcer still in his bed. I bite my lip to contain my grin, but fuck, the two of them are too cute for words. Like I give a shit who they share their beds with. They're both consenting adults, and I know Papa's been lonely since his wife died many years ago.

As long as I don't have to see or hear anything, I don't give a damn.

"Wanted to know if you have..." I trail off when my eyes lock on the coffeemaker on top of the minifridge. Coffee. Without waiting for them to even acknowledge me, I make a beeline towards my beloved coffee and immediately make a pot.

Why does he get a coffee pot and I don't? Fucking BS. Literally.

"You making that for all of us?" Johnson asks, and I hear the sound of him getting out of bed and throwing his clothes back on.

"Fuck no." I wave my hand without turning around. "You guys will ruin it with all of your creams and sugars." I shudder delicately. "Get your own damn coffee."

"That *is* our coffee," Johnson grumbles good-naturedly, and I roll my eyes.

"Semantics."

Papa Gray snorts as he grabs his own clothes out of his suitcase and heads back into the bathroom to get dressed.

Silence descends as I pour myself a cup of liquid gold, and Johnson watches me with shrewd eyes. As I sip the drink, humming happily beneath my breath, he says, "You swear too much."

"You don't fucking swear enough," I retort immediately, and he ruffles my hair, ignoring the half-hearted swats I aim at his head. I may be the most esteemed spy and assassin of all of the bitten wolves, but sometimes…

Sometimes I feel like a little girl, desperate to get the attention of the men she sees as family and looks up to.

"You ready to go?" Papa Gray appears in the doorway, dressed in a cozy-looking gray sweater and blue jeans, and hobbles forward with his cane extended in front of him.

"Let's go liberate some fucking wolves," I say with forced cheer. Both men give me yet *another* eye roll, but the humor that had been prevalent mere seconds ago is nowhere to be found. The tension resembles an electrical current vibrating in the air, sparking in my bloodstream like errant fireworks.

Because what we're about to do…

It's never been done before.

And it may just get us all killed.

THE MEETING TAKES PLACE IN THE HOTEL'S ONE ballroom, located just off the lobby. Unlike the rest of the hotel which is rundown and archaic, the ballroom is gorgeous, almost as if modern architecture exists side by side with *Bridgerton*-style decor. It's the one room in the entire hotel that appears grander than what it truly is.

Immediately once I enter, I'm overwhelmed by the sheer amount of gold. Burnished red-gold walls, brown-gold carpeting… Even the table in the center of the room has a goldish sheen that screams wealth and opulence. Chandeliers are suspended from the ceiling, casting the room in soft hues of yellow and brown.

But even the grandeur of this ballroom can't mask the evil lurking within the people situated inside.

When we enter, Grayson on one side of me and Johnson on the other, almost every seat is already full.

My eyes drift over the men present—and make no mistake, all of them are males, minus the one female Davenport representative—and spot the man who must be Grim, the leader of the Bloody Skulls. He sits near the head of the table, a scowl marring features that might be considered handsome in any other circumstance, but now appear cold and unwelcoming. Light blond scruff covers his jawline, the color matching his white-blond hair. At his side, his arms folded over his chest, is a familiar man who must be his son.

Bullseye.

And also the man I insulted yesterday.

Oh, shit.

Yup.

I'm fucked. On a scale of one to anal probed, I'm having a finger shoved up my butthole so high, I see stars.

Fuckity fuck fuck. Why, oh why, do these things happen to me? Why?

His golden hair hangs loose around his chiseled face, and his sparkling green eyes glimmer with mirth. He wears a cut that signifies him as the VP of the Bloody Skulls. He hasn't noticed me yet, deep in conversation with a man who has his back turned towards me, so I take a moment to survey him uninterrupted.

He really is a gorgeous man. Beautiful, really. It's not fair that a man is capable of looking that attractive. Even his lashes are thicker and darker than mine, fluttering against his cheekbones like twigs of ebony.

The man he's talking to squeezes his shoulder, rises from his chair fluidly, and stalks out of the room, not once sparing me a glance, but Bullseye lifts his head up and meets my eyes with a smoldering gaze of his own.

A part of me wants to cower, wants to shy away from the sheer intensity of his penetrating green stare, but I keep my head held high as I maintain eye contact. At first, anger darkens his features as he no doubt recalls the conversation from yesterday. But then a mask slips into place, one that uses his sinfully good looks to his advantage, and his full lips begin to twitch as if he's fighting off a smile. I watch in rapt fascination as he bites down on his pillowy lower lip, the move far too sexy for my mental capabilities.

In a move that I know will piss him off, I turn away and focus on the rest of the table.

The Bloody Skulls have brought four representatives—five if you count the man who just left—but I only recognize Grim and his son. The other three must be some low-level grunts or hired muscle.

Fortunately, the Davenport siblings are nowhere to be seen. Like I expected, they sent representatives in their place. A man and a woman, both of them in their mid-thirties and looking out of place in their immaculately-pressed suits and with their carefully combed hair.

Finally, my eyes land on the representatives for the Totemic Tribe. Their alpha, a tall and arresting man with a strong jawline and high cheekbones, is dressed in a pitch-black shirt and ripped blue jeans that show off his strong, muscular legs. He has an easygoing smirk on his face, but that smile does little to hide the darkness swirling in his eyes. At his side, a scowl firmly in place, is the shifter who invaded my community and demanded I attend the summit. Sexy.

Paiter sits beside his friend, murmuring softly beneath his breath. Whatever he says has Sexy's scowl deepening to epic proportions. As if he can feel my eyes on him, Sexy's head snaps up and his gaze drills me in place. A fire dances in his brown depths, one that I don't think even my barbs or cruel words can put out. He stares at me with a ravenous hunger that makes my nipples uncomfortably aware of the scratchiness of my tank top, even as I bare my teeth at him and move towards one of the three empty chairs.

Johnson, ever the gentleman, holds my chair out for me, and I smile at him softly, placing a hand on his arm as I sit.

Two growls echo throughout the room before the sound is immediately cut off, almost as if they're clenching their teeth.

I don't need to look to know that the growls belong to Bullseye and Sexy. Somehow, I'm able to recognize their wolves' noises the same way I would their speaking voices.

Why the fuck are they growling? And why do I care so much that they are?

I swear it's like a bubble machine goes off inside my stomach, and now each individual bubble is growing bigger and bigger until it feels like I'm floating. But still, I can't deny how weird their reaction was. Or how weird my *own* reaction was. Has hell frozen over? Has the world gone mad? Have I fallen down the rabbit hole and ended up in Wonderland, where instead of Cheshire cat grins, there are a bunch of howling wolves with glowing yellow eyes?

Fortunately, the room is still alive with murmured conversations and hushed whispers, so no one notices their little…slip. Or whatever the hell they were doing.

When Papa finally sits down, resting his cane against the table, Grim stands and pierces us all with a searing look, one that sends prickles of unease racing down my arms and legs. It's easy to see how dangerous this man is from one look alone. How deadly. There's a reason he's named after the Grim Reaper. He practically radiates danger and a malevolence that steals the breath from my lungs.

This is a man who quite literally evokes death.

Cold eyes land on me for a brief moment before he flicks his gaze away, studying Papa Gray with unnerving intensity.

"I would like to call the annual summit to order." His voice is low and raspy. A smoker's voice. My unease only amplifies at the guttural noise.

A chorus of howls follows his declaration, and my eyes latch on the hollow of Bullseye's throat as he throws his head back. When he catches me watching him, he winks at me flirtatiously, his smirk growing. I glare at him in response.

He can be a shameless flirt all he wants, but I can still see the darkness swarming in his gaze. The beast is just waiting for a chance to be set free.

Bullseye…

He's dangerous. I'll have to keep an eye on him.

Sexy, one of the few wolves not howling, scowls at all of them, his body tilted away from mine as if he's doing everything in his power not to stare at me.

"We need to discuss Taylor Street," he snaps, his strident voice causing Grim to stop howling and arch an eyebrow. Sexy continues on with a fierce glare. "Your wolves have been encroaching on our territory."

"Really, Tai," Grim begins lazily, resting his forearms on the table. "Is it always straight to business with you?"

Tai. The sexy man's name is Tai, and if my sources are correct, he's the heir to the throne of the Totemic Tribe. The next alpha.

Sarai, the alpha of the Totemic Tribe, exchanges a droll, almost conspiratorial look with Grim, and apprehension ripples down my spine. It's almost a look of…familiarity. But that's impossible, right? The Totemic Tribe and the Bloody Skulls loathe each other, constantly at war and disputing territories.

So why the hell are they grinning at each other like long lost lovers?

"Down, boy." Sarai waves a hand at Tai, and the tattooed man stiffens. "We'll get to that."

"But before we begin, does anyone have anything they would like to add to the agenda?" Grim queries. This is nothing more than a formality. According to Papa Gray, we always talk about the same three fucking things—territory disputes, grievances between the packs, and bitten wolves' rights. Only two of those things ever get handled.

"I have one," a feminine voice announces stridently. All eyes turn towards the entrance to the ballroom, where Valentina Davenport stands ramrod straight in the doorframe. She looks as beautiful and elegant as ever with her brown hair curled in perfect ringlets, ending just above her waist, and a white blouse and skin-tight black skirt. She moves gracefully towards the table, her golden eyes, so unlike her brother's, never leaving mine.

Oh, fuck.

Fuck. Fuck. Fuck.

I'm nearly positive that she didn't see me at the warehouse, yet there's something akin to familiarity in her amber gaze. And when she smiles, I know without an ounce of hesitation that I'm well and truly fucked.

Johnson casts me an anxious look, but Papa Gray is better at schooling his features, adopting a bored, nonchalant expression as his eyes follow the striking bombshell while she moves towards the head of the table. She stops only once to address her delegates— offering them both simple nods which they return— before she pierces Grim with a stone-cold look, one that befits her nickname as Ice Princess.

"Valentina Davenport." Grim's brows are furrowed, just as surprised with her presence as the rest of us. I also detect a hint of unease, barely noticeable in his steely gaze. I doubt anyone else would've noticed if they haven't been trained to decipher every damn facial tic of all of the wolves in this room. "How nice of you to grace us with your presence."

She offers him a blood-red smile, but it's about as pleasant and sincere as his words were.

"Fergus," she says, breaching protocol by calling him by his real name. His hand tightens into a fist on the table as she continues to offer him that saccharine sweet grin. "How lovely of you to host the summit this year in such a...quaint hotel."

She smooths her brown hair and sits gracefully in a seat one of her delegates have pulled up for her.

Clasping her hands together on the desk, she levels us all with a cold look, her gaze lingering on mine.

"The Davenports would like to make an offer to the bitten wolves," she begins without preamble, turning her gaze towards Papa. I watch my mentor straighten almost imperceptibly in his seat, his eyes clouded with suspicion.

Murmurings begin to take over the table.

No one, in all of the years the summit has been around, has offered any deal or olive branch to the bitten wolves.

"And what would that be?" I'm proud when Papa's voice doesn't shake.

Valentina's smile broadens almost coquettishly, and this time, I swear it's genuine. Her honey-toned eyes sparkle in the artificial lighting of the ballroom.

"The Davenport pack will offer you full protection and support," Valentina says simply, and the hushed murmurings turn into outraged cries. Grim and Sarai exchange a narrowed-eyed glare, while Bullseye and Sexy both stare at Valentina with their mouths agape. For some reason, I feel irrationally irritated that their eyes are on her, despite the fact that their expressions are a mixture of distrust and anger.

Maybe because she's fucking gorgeous and they're two hot-blooded males.

I very wisely choose not to look too closely at my turbulent emotions.

"I feel like there's a catch." Papa's voice cuts through the mutterings like the crack of a whip. Even Grim and Sarai stop talking, their eyes fixing on him.

"No catch. At least, not really." Valentina straightens in her chair and tosses back a strand of silky hair. "More of an exchange."

"Exchange," Johnson parrots dryly, his fingers tapping against his jeans. It's the only indication that he's anything other than calm.

Valentina finally allows her eyes to drift to me, and I stiffen in surprise.

"Our protection...in exchange for the pretty bitten wolf. Blair, is it? Blair Windsor?" She doesn't wait for me to respond, pulling out her phone and shooting off a text, her red nails like lightning over the screen. When she's satisfied with whatever she just sent, she lowers her phone and turns to Papa. "We'll protect the bitten wolves as if they were our own, as if they were members of the Davenport family, in exchange for Blair. You have until the end of the summit to decide."

8

BLAIR

Papa Gray demands a recess after that bombshell, and surprisingly, no one argues with us. I think the other pack leaders are readjusting their entire strategy, now that they know how important I am to the Davenports.

Cold, icy dread skates down my spine as I recall the smirk Valentina gave me just before I was ushered out of the room by a glowering Johnson and stone-faced Papa.

Do the other packs understand that she's going to kill me? I have no idea what game she's playing, but I'm not dumb or oblivious to the rules and regulations in this world. I blew up a shipment of weapons her family purchased...and now she has come for my blood. I don't know why she didn't just demand justice in front of all of the pack leaders, but maybe she has no proof.

Even though that wouldn't stop any of the packs from voting for my death.

Confusion wages a fierce battle against my growing despair as I collapse in one of the armchairs in the lobby. Johnson and Papa remain upright, their lips compressed into thin lines as they pace.

"...we can't..."

"I don't know why..."

"...so careful."

Their words reach me like I'm at the end of a very long tunnel. They seem to reverberate through my skull like a pinball, sending a searing pain throughout my entire body.

I'm distantly aware of Papa putting something in my hands—a glass of whiskey, despite knowing I don't usually drink—but I'm shaking too badly to even take a sip. Instead, the brown liquid sluices over the edge of the glass as a delicate tremor overtakes me.

Fuck, what can I do? Can I really be selfish and deny the Davenport family's offer? Would I even want to?

What they're offering...

It's everything we've been fighting for over the years. For decades, even.

And if my death is the price, then maybe it'll be worth it. After all, I'm only one girl. The bitten wolves are my family, and I know that if the situations were reversed, not one of them would hesitate to do what is right. They would throw their heads eagerly on the chopping block if it meant peace between our packs.

It's not like Valentina could rescind her offer of protection. Not after her public declaration.

Now that she has presented the offer in front of all of the wolf packs, she must uphold it or face execution. The Bloody Skulls and Totemics would have no choice but to back us if we chose to pursue justice if she broke her oath.

"I can see your wheels turning, kid," Papa Gray snaps sharply, pulling me from my thoughts. I blink at him. "Don't even fucking think about it. You're not sacrificing yourself."

"This is what we came here for," I begin slowly, carefully, gauging his reaction. His lips are puckered like he just ate something sour, and his eyes are as hard as granite in his wrinkled face.

"I'm not sacrificing any of my wolves. Especially not to become the Davenports' bitches."

"I'm shocked you would think so little of my family." Valentina herself descends on us like a vulture searching for decaying meat. Her smile reminds me eerily of a razor blade, her red-painted lips curving at the corners.

"We're not allowing you to kill Blair," Papa growls, his eyes turning amber and his teeth elongating into fangs. I can sense how close his wolf is to the surface, and a part of me feels warm and fuzzy that he would be willing to go to war for me, that he loves me that much, while the other just feels gripping despair.

We can't win this.

I don't know why we would even try.

I can see similar defeat etched onto Johnson's haggard face, the man suddenly looking years older than forty-five. Is it possible for someone to gain gray hair in the span of minutes? Because I'm pretty sure that's what happened to him.

"Who said anything about killing?" Valentina queries, already turning her attention back towards her phone, as if we're not worth her complete attention. Her long red nails dance across the screen before she glances up and smiles. "We want Blair to marry into our family. What better alliance is there except one made from marriage? Especially to a man like my brother?"

Her words are a metaphorical bucket of ice water being dumped over my head, drenching me from head to toe and leaving me shivering.

"Marriage?" My shrill voice is loud enough to garner the attention of all of the other wolves present. Or maybe they've been listening this entire time, as entranced by our conversation as I am.

Grim's face turns stony as he turns towards his son, Bullseye, and whispers something in his ear. The VP's face is carefully blank, almost impossible for me to read.

Tai and Sarai are also staring in our direction, the former shooting glares at Valentina's scalp while the latter appears contemplative.

"Just give it a thought." Valentina's husky voice pulls my attention back towards her, and she chuckles softly. "I dunno, Blair Windsor. Maybe you can actually find a way to be happy."

WHEN THE MEETING RECONVENES ONLY A FEW minutes later, I know immediately that something has changed. Instead of dealing with territory disputes and attacks, the wolves are focusing on one thing and one thing only—me.

Now that the totemic wolves and the Bloody Skulls know about Valentina's interest in me, they're more determined than ever to keep me for themselves.

"I have a proposal to make as well," Grim says as soon as we're seated around the table. Where I once thought the ballroom was beautiful and elegant, it now seems dangerous and malevolent. Too many shadows. Too many places for monsters to hide. The five-tiered chandelier almost feels like a spotlight, illuminating me for the entire world to see.

Or maybe that could just be the eyes penetrating my scalp.

I try to pull a page out of Papa's book and keep my face carefully blank, but it's hard when all of the men are staring at me like I'm a commodity.

Grim casually slings an arm over the back of Bullseye's chair, and I watch the once smiling man wince almost imperceptibly. He hasn't met my inquiring gaze since we reentered the room, his eyes downcast and his hands curled into tight fists. His father, on the other hand, is positively beaming, the jubilant expression taking years off his age.

"We would like the girl as well. For my son, Mason," Grim continues, and his words quite literally steal the breath from my lungs. I wonder if this is how a fish feels when it's brutally wrenched from the water, flopping on dry land as the searing sun beats down on it.

But I refuse to be fucking weak.

"I'm not for sale," I manage to bite out through

clenched teeth, my stomach churning. Grim actually throws back his head in hearty laughter, the deranged bastard.

Bullseye—or Mason, apparently—blanches.

"Everyone is for sale," Grim manages to gasp out, slapping his hand down on the table in mirth. "We just need to find your price."

Valentina's lips purse with irritation as she taps her manicured fingers against the armrests of her chair.

"Is this really necessary, Fergus?"

Grim visibly scowls at the usage of his real name, but he ignores her, turning to pierce Papa with a cold look.

"We would like to offer a similar deal that the Davenports made you." His cruel lips curl into a conniving smile, one that puts me instantly on alert. He's the type of man who would smile to your face and then stab a knife in your back, laughing gleefully while you bleed out. There's something savage and fierce in his expression, something that speaks to years of getting what he wants, when he wants, regardless of who he hurts.

And what he wants right now is me.

"No deal," Papa Gray grits out, anger emanating from his frosty gaze.

Grim ignores him, squeezing Mason's shoulder

with another gleeful cackle. "If a marriage is what you want, a marriage is what you'll get. Bullseye, you can handle some bitten wolf pussy, can't you? After all, you spend a lot of time with that one mute wolf." He throws his head back in laughter, ignoring the way Mason's face takes on a green quality. "Unless you prefer bitten cock over bitten pussy."

At this, all of the representatives for BS guffaw, the noise grating on my nerves. A low growl builds up in my throat, but I tamp it down before it can escape.

"You want me to marry the bitten wolf?" I can't quite read the inflection in Mason's voice. All I know for sure is that his green eyes have lost their luster from earlier and his skin is ashen. For a brief, *brief* moment, I think I spot shame and guilt in his gaze before he smothers those emotions, replacing them with a calm, calculating look. "Are you out of your fucking mind?" He finally lifts his head and turns towards me, a sneer contorting his pretty boy features. He leans back in his chair, his movements unhurried and almost indolent in nature, and forks his fingers together on his chiseled chest, his eyes roving over my body. That sneer remains firmly in place when he finally rips his gaze off of me. "No way in hell am I marrying some bitten slut."

His words are a kick to the gut, though I don't

know why they affect me the way they do. Out of everything that has happened in the last hour, Mason's words are what nearly break me.

But I won't let them. I fucking refuse.

I mask my expression carefully and give him a narrowed-eyed glare. "As if I would want to be married to a disgusting, sexist not-wolf," I hiss, hurling the common fenrir insult at him. I know that it's a sore point that they're not able to shift into wolves, and right now, I want Mason to bleed. I want to flay him open and see everything that makes him who he is.

He doesn't react to my words, his gaze cool and indifferent as he stares at me. Only his lips give him away—they curl slightly downwards, half a frown and half a scowl. It doesn't look right on his face. Too practiced. Too cold. Too empty.

"You can't be fucking serious!" Tai roars, pounding his hands on the table until he's able to garner the group's attention. "You're really talking about marrying a bitten wolf?" He doesn't look at me as he says that, but I can hear his disdain from miles away. It drips like acid eroding rock, demolishing everything it comes into contact with.

Like with Mason, Tai's derision hurts me. It's a brief pain—there and gone in less than a second—but I can feel the lingering effects in my chest, almost like a bowling ball is resting on my rib cage and continuously providing pressure.

"And of course, if Bullseye and Blair are married, the Bloody Skulls will provide protection to all of the bitten wolves," Grim continues, ignoring all of our outbursts. He smiles smugly at Valentina, and it's then I recognize this for what it is—a power grab. Grim hates the bitten wolves, but he hates the Davenports even more, mainly because he knows that they're a threat to his empire of bikers. If building an alliance with my people pisses off the Davenports...

Then it's a sacrifice he's more than willing to make.

"I would also like to throw my hat in the ring," Sarai interjects, and Tai's head whips so fast in his father's direction, I'm afraid he got whiplash. His dark, slashing eyebrows pull lower over glowering eyes as a growl rumbles through his body.

"You can't be—"

Tai's protest is interrupted by Sarai waving a hand in the air. "If you're not interested in marrying the pretty bitten wolf, I'll ask one of your brothers," Sarai exclaims dismissively, and Tai's mouth snaps shut. The tattoos on his neck begin to flex as he levels a ferocious glare at the side of his father's head. I expect him to argue, to push me off onto one of his brothers, but instead, he deflates in his chair, his arms crossed over his chest as he stares moodily ahead.

"The little she-wolf can't very well marry three different guys," Grim says, his voice heavy with amusement. I swear Valentina looks as if she's seconds away from jumping across the table and cutting his head straight from his shoulders. Her golden-brown eyes flash dangerously. For once, she doesn't have her cell phone out.

Apparently discussing my eventual demise is enough to hold her attention.

And rest assured—no matter what I do or say, this game only leads to my death.

All three of the men they want me to marry have reputations of being cold-hearted, murderous assholes. Sure, maybe at first, they'll enjoy having a little bitten wolf to do with as they please, but that mentality won't last long.

They'll torture me. Rape me. Probably kill me.

It'll be worth it if you're able to protect the people you love. Martha. Papa. Johnson. The children. They're your family.

When my biological family was murdered, I thought I would never find that love again. It was only when Papa plucked me from the streets—a scared, bitten wolf with no idea of what she was or how to control her primal urges—that I finally begin to feel safe and complete. I'll do *anything* for my family. Give up anything…including my life.

"We'll allow the wolf to choose," Valentina says, straightening in her chair. There's a tiny, secretive smile on her face, almost as if she knows something the others don't. I would almost describe the expression as…smug.

Grim scowls. "Why would we do that?"

"Why, Fergus." Valentina places a hand to her chest in horror. "I didn't know you were afraid of a little competition. I suppose I'm not surprised that you have no faith in your son's seduction skills. He seems a little…" She gives Mason a dismissive once-over while he returns the favor. Immediately, my hackles raise, and I have the irresistible urge to lunge across the table and claw out Valentina's pretty eyes. I only feel marginally satisfied when Mason looks away from her in disgust and Valentina rolls her eyes heavenwards with a sneer. "Boring," she finishes at last.

"So the little she-wolf chooses who she wants as her husband?" Sarai taps a finger to his chin in mock contemplation.

"One month. Thirty days." Valentina clasps her hands together on the table. "She'll spend thirty days with each of them, and at the end of the ninety days, she'll choose a husband."

I can't take it anymore. I refuse to allow them to talk about me as if I don't exist or if I'm not worthy of having a voice. As if I'm simply a fancy, glittery coin that they can trade in for new shoes. I've experienced a lot of demeaning shit in my life, both because I'm a woman and a bitten wolf, but this takes the fucking cake.

Placing a hand into the air, I begin speaking before anyone can talk over me. "If I do this, I'll need a written contract stating that the pack of the man I choose will support the bitten wolves and will provide protection and economic assistance." Grim opens his mouth as if to protest, but I shoot him a vicious glare. "That's not a request."

"Blair..." Papa warns me, his face draining of all color. He knows what I'm doing, and though he doesn't like it—hell, he fucking *loathes* it—he also knows it's the only option. They're going to take me regardless, so if I can carve out some rights for my people in the meantime, then this will all be worth it.

I hope.

"And I also need a written agreement from everyone that no matter who I choose, the other two packs won't declare war on us." I level them all with a stern glare, letting them know that I won't compromise on this.

Sarai and Grim both look annoyed, their faces grave, but Valentina bites down on her lip to contain her smile.

"And finally, I want you guys all to agree that you will stop hunting and harming bitten wolves. Starting today. Starting right this damn minute. I won't agree to anything until that happens." I fold my arms over my chest as once more, all of the wolves exchange a glance.

I know they're going to agree to my terms. Despite killing us for sport, they actually don't give a damn about us. If they can't kill us, then they'll just find another group of people to target.

They're too fucking competitive not to agree to my terms.

"Fine," Grim states at last, nodding towards one of his representatives. Immediately, the man grabs his laptop and begins to type something out.

"Agreed," Valentina says primly.

Sarai's voice is bitter and full of loathing as he grits out, "Agreed."

"Little she-wolf." Grim's smile is the embodiment of nightmares, all sharp edges and keen points, shadows and monsters. "Aren't you going to add anything about your own safety?"

I'm aware of both Mason and Tai staring at me, expressions unreadable, but I ignore them and shake my head.

"As long as my people are safe, I'll handle whatever comes next."

Fear sluices inside of my stomach when Grim throws his head back in laughter and Sarai chuckles. Even Valentina looks amused, though there's a darkness inside of her gaze that hadn't been there prior.

I just made a deal with three devils to save my people.

But if I'm going to hell, I'll be damned if I don't drag them with me.

THE DAVENPORTS

9

BLAIR

DAY 1

One month.

I have to stay with the Davenports for one month and date the man I shot at and almost blew up.

It's been a week since the summit ended, a week since I've traded my soul to ensure the freedom and safety of my people. A week since I've begun dating three men I barely know...and who no doubt want nothing to do with me.

My stomach is a tumultuous mixture of dread and anxiety as I wait near the entrance to the camp for the Davenport limo to arrive and bring me to their mansion.

"You shouldn't have to do this," Papa murmurs

from beside me. When I glance at him out of the corner of my eye, it's to see his face grave and his expression solemn. I yearn to comfort him, but I don't know what the fuck I can possibly say. No words can fix this. Not mine. Not his. Not anyone's.

The only thing that has brought me even a sliver of comfort is since the wolves made their little sadistic bet and accepted my terms, no bitten wolves have been killed. Not one.

The immense weight that had once been pressing down on my shoulders, shoving me into the ground, has now abated. My people are safe, and that's worth any torture the Davenports wish to bestow upon me.

"Maybe people in this world should stop being pieces of shit. *Pezzo di merda*," I respond softly as Martha moves to stand on the other side of me, interlocking her fingers with my own. "Maybe then human decency would win out."

"I'm gonna miss you, kid," Martha says with a sniffle, brushing away a stray tear with the hand that isn't holding mine in an iron vise.

"I'll be back before you know it."

If I'm not in a body bag before then.

The Davenports.

The Bloody Skulls.

The Totemic Tribe.

And then, I'll choose a man to marry.

Maybe I'll get lucky. Maybe not all three of them will be worthless pieces of shits. Maybe I'll find someone who'll allow me to live and visit my family on occasion, who'll uphold his promise to protect my people. I wouldn't even care if our marriage is a sham—if they despise me or sleep around or ignore my existence. All I want is for my people to be safe… and maybe for them to extend that same protection to me.

I've already accepted that I'm going to be living a life devoid of happiness, never finding true love or my fated mate. But for the bitten wolves? My family? It's worth it.

"You're gonna be okay, girly," Papa says out of the corner of his mouth just as the black, gleaming limo crawls up the road. "You're strong…stronger than any of us. You'll survive this."

But how broken will I be afterwards? How broken will I become?

Will my family even recognize me after all of this is said and done?

"Maybe I'll stab a few fuckers along the way," I murmur back, flashing him a smile. Papa's watery eyes travel to the duffle bag slung over my shoulder…which contains nothing but weapons. Not my favorite blades, of course, because I can't risk those being confiscated, but enough to protect me if the need arises.

"You stab *all* the fuckers," Papa retorts with a cheeky grin. But that grin slides off his face, becoming replaced by a scowl, when the limo pulls to a stop in front of us and a red-faced driver hurries to open the door for me and collect my suitcases.

Despite planning on living with the Davenports for a month, I only brought two suitcases—one containing only my weapons, and the other consisting of…everything else. It's not like I had a lot to begin with.

"Blair!" Valentina smiles brightly at me from where she sits in the back of the limo, her fingers dancing across her phone screen. This time, her nails are painted a hot pink that matches the pink of her lipstick. Her dark hair has been meticulously straightened, not a strand out of place, and she wears a white blouse and black pencil skirt that shows miles upon miles of bronze legs I'm instantly envious of.

She makes me look like an Oompa Loompa in comparison. Because makeup? Nah. Hair? A messy bun will work. Clothing? I'm pretty sure this shirt doesn't have a stain, so I'll call it a win.

It's not like I'm against makeup or anything. I'm not one of those girls who believes she's too good to spend time on her appearance. I actually love dressing up, putting on sparkly pink nail polish, curling my hair.

But when you're poor, you learn to prioritize things, and if it's between looking good and eating, I'll choose eating every damn time. I know what it's like to go hungry, to not have enough food on your plate, and I'll do my damnedest to never experience that crippling sensation again.

Ignoring Valentina, I turn towards Martha, and she wraps her arms around me, squeezing tight.

"You're gonna make me cry, you bitch," Martha says with a sniff as I tentatively hug her back.

"Look after the kids for me, will ya?" I pull away to flash her a watery grin.

"You look after yourself, okay?" she counters immediately. "Don't let this world of politics and beasts get to you."

My throat closes with emotion, so all I manage is a tiny dip of my head in lieu of a nod.

Turning from one of my oldest friends, I peer into Papa's wrinkled face. His eyes glimmer with unshed tears as he pulls me into his arms. He doesn't speak, but then again, he doesn't have to. An entire wordless conversation is exchanged just through that menial touch. Warmth migrates from where his hands rest on my back, and when we finally pull apart, he has tear tracks down both of his cheeks.

I'm grateful he doesn't try to say goodbye. If he did, I might just fall apart, and that's the last thing I want to do in front of Valentina Davenport. Instead, I nod at him curtly before turning towards Johnson and giving him the same treatment. He places a hand on Papa's shoulder in a silent promise to protect him and our pack in my absence.

Warmth fills me at the gesture, but I freeze the emotion before it can boil over. Adopting an icy mask, I turn away from my pack and walk towards the limo idling at the curb.

Valentina is watching us all with a curious expression, her perfectly manicured brows furrowed, but she doesn't make a comment as I slide into the limo seat opposite her.

Her pink lips push out as her golden eyes travel over my outfit, frowning at a spot on my shoulder. I tilt my head down to follow her gaze, and...oh shit. Yup. This shirt does have a stain. Dammit.

"I'll need to fix this," she murmurs, her voice almost too soft for me to hear. Without waiting for a response—if she was even waiting for one—she begins to type away on her phone again, seemingly deep in thought.

I relish the silence though, allowing it to cocoon

me in warmth and security as we drive farther and farther away from the one place I actually considered home.

Valentina remains silent the majority of the drive, and I watch through the window as the trees transition into houses. And then those modest, two-story houses transform into mansions and castles as we reach a section of the city that only the immensely wealthy individuals can afford to live in.

So of course, that means the Davenports live here.

My eyes practically fall out of my head as the limo pulls up to a silver fence surrounded on either side by meticulously groomed trees. The driver pauses to say something to the guard manning the entrance, and before I know it, the gate is open and we're rolling up a curving driveway. Perfectly planted flowers line either side of the driveway, creating a gorgeous aperture of ruby red and bright pink. It feels as if we drive for miles, but when I blink next, it's to see the trees disappear and a glorious mansion replace them.

It's unapologetically modern. It stands amidst the manicured lawn as if it's an extension of the property, poking through the grass. The mansion is unsurprisingly massive and made of shiny marble, with over a dozen windows displaying a copious amount of golden light. The roof is flat, and from what I can see, there is no visible chimney. Every line is clean and straight, the color scheme a light, pearly pink and white. It's the type of house that fulfills the idyllic notion of wealth and prosperity.

The thick foliage allows only small streaks of sunlight to break through, bathing the property in a burnished red-gold glow. I notice that the driveway splices in two and reconnects near the front entrance to make room for a stone fountain displaying a topless mermaid.

"I thought they only did that in movies," Valentina muses, not pulling her eyes away from her phone. But why should she? She lives in this fucking place. She doesn't realize how opulent and ostentatious it would appear to the outside observer.

"What do you mean?" I turn towards her just as the limo pulls to a stop directly in front of the mansion. Twin pillars, each constructed of hundreds of mismatched stones, erupt from the ground, holding up a circular balcony that overlooks the driveway and front yard. Beneath it rests the largest door I've ever seen, with an actual, honest-to-God golden knocker directly in the center.

"You know." She waves her hand at me dismissively. "The whole mouth dropping open thing. I thought they only did that in movies. You looked like you were waiting to receive a cock."

"Sorry," I retort, climbing out of the limo before the driver can open the door for me. "I wouldn't suck a Davenport cock, even if all of the other cocks in the world have shriveled into gray elephant trunks."

She makes a face, her nose wrinkling slightly. "Considering the fact that the only male Davenport cock belongs to my twin brother, I'll have to say thank you." She primly slides out of the car, running her hands down her pitch-black skirt and ensuring that there's not a wrinkle in place. "Though maybe that would stop him from being such a moody, PMS-ing bastard." Her heels clack against the pavement, the sound almost rhythmic, as she moves towards the entrance. "Come."

I grumble beneath my breath as I turn towards my luggage, preparing to take it.

Only to see that it's already gone.

"Valentina," I call, feeling a strange mixture of agitation and worry. Did they take my weapons? Am I going to go into the lion's den unprotected? "Where did my suitcase and duffle bag go?"

She twists her head slightly, her lips pulling away from her teeth in a move that is more predatory than comforting. "Fabio brought them to your room." She indicates where the driver was less than a minute ago. "Don't worry, baby wolf. We're not going to take away your weapons." She shudders delicately, as if the thought of someone carrying ten knives, thirteen daggers, two handguns, and five grenades is disgusting.

But then again, her palms are clean—quite literally. There's not a single callous or blemish on her dainty hands. She can't know what it's like to constantly fight for your life in a world that is trying to suppress you. She's lived in an isolated bubble, only seeing what she wanted to see. That was made clear at the warehouse during the shooting, when she cowered and ducked instead of standing up to fight.

She doesn't know the steps one would need to take in order to survive.

How the fuck did she know about my weapons anyway?

My spine quite literally prickles at the knowledge she's been watching me.

Feeling like a prisoner facing her execution, I follow Valentina into the mansion, willing my mouth not to pop back open as I glance around the foyer in wide-eyed amazement.

What does someone even need with all of this space?

The foyer itself is size of my trailer, and it's furnished with a simple table. That's it. A table.

Fucking rich people.

As we move farther into the house, I allow my eyes to categorize every door and window. Every hallway and staircase.

But fuck, there's a lot.

We reach a section of the mansion that consists of white marble flooring with a decorative, circular rug in the center. A single podium rests directly in the center with a vase on top. On either side of the room, tiny white tables stand, each one holding a marble head. And then there's a staircase, easily the width of my trailer, that has intricately carved railings that sweep upwards, leading to a second level before branching into two separate staircases that ascend to a third floor.

This time, I don't bother to keep my thoughts to myself, bitterly exclaiming, "Fucking rich people," much to Valentina's delight.

"I mean, seriously," I stress as she leads me up the staircase. It's so large, we're easily able to walk side by side, with room for three more people on the other side of her. "What do you even do with all of this space? That room was nearly empty, for fuck's sake."

Valentina rolls her eyes into the back of her head

as she ignores me, leading me towards the first door on the second floor.

My feet stumble when I set eyes upon a painting hanging on the wall opposite my bedroom, on the other side of the mezzanine. It depicts a man with a cruel, arresting face and brown hair, the exact same shade as Valentina's and Vincent's. His eyes are cold, nearly black in the artificial lighting, and somehow, the artist was able to capture the malice in them perfectly. A cold spark shoots through me as I stare into his beady eyes, losing myself to the memories, before I force myself to look away and focus on Valentina, who is fortunately oblivious.

"This will be your room while you stay with us," she states, pushing it open with a dramatic flourish and watching my reaction.

And fuck if I don't give her one.

It's easily the size of our recreational hall with an elegantly furnished sitting room and three doors branching off from it. The first door leads to my bedroom, consisting of a fluffy king-sized bed, over a dozen pillows, three dressers, and a walk-in closet. The other doors prove to contain a bathroom and tiny kitchen. Everything is decorated in shades of pale pink and white, giving the rooms a feminine flare.

It's fucking gorgeous, and I hate that I'm in awe. I

hate that I have the irresistible urge to dive onto my bed like a toddler and then jump up and down.

Valentina smirks, pleased with whatever she sees on my face, before stepping back and glancing once more at her cellphone. "Dinner will be at six. Don't be late."

With that, she closes my bedroom door, leaving me to explore and ogle.

I find my luggage beside my bed, and I'm relieved to see that they haven't taken any of my weapons. I begin to systemically hide my weapons throughout my room, just in case Valentina changes her mind and deems me a threat.

Because I am one.

A threat, I mean. A cornered animal who will bite if she or her pack is threatened.

For now, I'll play by their rules, adhere to their sick game, but the second my people are put into danger, all bets are off.

Once all of my weapons have been hidden, I move to put my clothes away, desperate to explore the rest of the house.

House. I scoff at the notion that this place is anything less than a fucking palace, befitting the ice queen and her equally icy king. Even the color scheme—whites and peaches—denotes coldness.

Fucking. Rich. People.

As I move to put my clothes away, I'm startled to see that my closet is full of clothes. For a moment, I believe that they're hand-me-downs from Valentina, until I see the tags.

I grab a shirt at random and run my fingers over the satiny texture, pleased to see that it's something I'll actually wear.

Did Valentina buy me new clothes? Simply because she hated the ones I have on now?

I glance down at my stained shirt before flicking my gaze back to the new one.

It's completely possible that these clothes are hers, but then I remember that we're definitely not the same size. For one, she's shorter than me, and for two, my breasts are easily twice the size of hers.

No, the sly bitch must've had these clothes bought and brought to the mansion before we arrived.

I want to resist out of principle—and even more so when I see the price of the violet shirt, easily worth three weeks of tips when I waitress—but I can't resist. And maybe I shouldn't. After all, there's nothing more satisfying than knowing an esteemed Davenport spent money on a poor little bitten wolf. Besides, I'm not one to turn down free clothes, especially knowing I could give them to the children of my pack when I return home.

Pulling my old shirt off, I slip on the new one, loving the way the fabric seems to float around my body, caressing the skin of my stomach. The style of this shirt makes my black lace bra clearly visible, but I can't be bothered to change *that*. I mean, it's not like I have a shit ton of bras to change into anyway. Bras are ridiculously expensive, because society seems to think that things that are necessary for women—like undergarments and period supplies— should have elevated prices.

And it's not like Valentina would buy me—

I pull open one of the drawers and gasp when I spot brand new bras and underwear. Some are plain cotton, while others are lacy and colorful, and a few are…risqué, to put it mildly.

All of them are in my size.

How the fuck did she know that? Is she some sort of clothes wizard or something?

I close the drawer before I can develop an eye twitch and choose instead to explore the rest of the mansion. Valentina didn't say I needed to remain in my room, so I'm assuming I'm free to walk around, right? After all, if I'm to be "married," then I can't be a prisoner, right? *Right?*

I don't believe my own logic even for a second, but fuck them. And fuck this place.

Grabbing a dagger from where I stored it inside

of a lampshade, I tiptoe to my bedroom door and press my ear to the white-painted wood. Silence greets me as I tentatively push it open.

With bated breath, I glance in both directions, ensuring the halls are empty, before sneaking towards the railing that looks over the first floor. Empty as well.

Now where would the Davenports keep their big, juicy secrets?

I smirk at the thought of a large arrow pointing down the hall with a sign that reads, "ALL DIRTY SECRETS HERE!"

Unfortunately, my job has never been that easy, but that's what makes it fun. You need to know what doors to open, what drawers to peek inside, what people to whisper secrets to. The gardener, for example? He's on my payroll. I can't offer him much, but I don't need currency to get what I want.

I just need secrets.

It's a never-ending cycle. When I receive secrets about the Bloody Skulls, for example, I'll whisper them into the gardener's ear in exchange for information about the Davenports. And then I'll take that information to the man who handles the trading with the Totemic Tribe. And so on, and so on, and so on.

I know I'm not always getting reliable information, but at least it's *something*. It's more than we could've hoped for in a war that we're always losing.

I've just made it to the grand staircase, my hand trailing over the marble railing, when I feel a presence at my back, followed by a waft of hot air. Pine surrounds me from his body wash, and I squeeze my eyelids shut, my heart racing in my chest. A second later, a knife is pressed to my throat, digging into my skin.

"What the fuck are you doing here?"

10

BLAIR

DAY 1

"**D**rop your dagger."

I can sense him behind me, his presence a freezing gust of wind, one that blows strands of hair away from my face and encases my entire body in ice, but I don't dare turn towards him, not with his blade so close to my neck. One swipe of his hand…

It's funny how we never comment on the fragility of life until there's quite literally a blade pressed to your jugular, threatening to end you completely. It's something we whisper about in hushed tones or comment on at funerals, but it's not something that fills our thoughts. Until you're face to face with your own mortality, you don't think twice about it.

"I said, drop your dagger," he repeats as I weigh my options.

I make a move as if to comply, slowly lowering my hand and making a show of unclenching my fingers, but when his grip relaxes...

I strike, whirling around so fast that he doesn't have time to blink. With my free hand, I grab his wrist, twisting until he releases a grunt of pain.

But he doesn't drop his knife.

Instead, he kicks his leg out with a fluidity and gracefulness that eludes me and sends me staggering back a few steps. It would've taken me to the ground if I hadn't been aware.

I lunge again, swiping with my dagger, and manage to nick his arm before he dances away on the balls of his feet. His eyes widen comically as he stares at his suit, now sporting a long rectangular hole, and he bares his teeth in warning.

"Is that any way to treat your potential fiancée?" I spit out, suddenly furious with him. With Valentina. With this entire fucked-up world. Because the universe? Yeah, it let me down big time, and it'll continue to do so until the day I die. "I mean, I like knife play just as much as the next gal, but not in any non-sexual context."

"What?" The hand holding the knife out in front

of him momentarily falters, though his voice is sharper than the crack of a whip hitting flesh.

"Vincent," a breezy voice interrupts before I can answer, accompanied by the now familiar clack of heels against the marble flooring. Valentina clicks her tongue as she moves to stand beside me, placing her hands on her hips and leveling her brother with a half-amused, half-annoyed glare. "You're being rude to our guest."

"Guest?" Vincent glares at me as if my mere presence is toxic, as if my poverty is capable of seeping through his two-thousand-dollar suit and poisoning him. Asshole.

"Guest." Valentina nods her head curtly as Vincent circles me, his eyes narrowed. I don't allow myself to think about how attractive he looks, even with his features hardened in anger.

Like when I saw him in the warehouse, he's wearing a three-piece suit with cufflinks and a red tie that's been tailored to fit his slim form perfectly. The muscles of his biceps look particularly enticing as he flexes them, crossing his long arms over his chest. His brown hair is carefully styled away from his face, framing the aristocratic features I found so attractive when I first laid eyes on him, and his black eyes are glacial, carved from granite. Icy. His skin, colored by the sun, is shaded in warm tones that belie the coldness emanating from him in nearly palpable waves.

His dark glare volleys between me and his sister, but I refuse to cower when I receive the full effect of that intense, penetrating stare. That only seems to piss him off further...much to Valentina's amusement. Her pink lips pull away from sparkling white teeth as she smiles—a genuine smile, one devoid of malice or cunningness.

One thing becomes painfully clear—Vincent didn't know I was coming to the mansion.

Which means he more than likely doesn't know about the deal his sister made on his behalf.

I begin to fidget from foot to foot as awkwardness engulfs me. Instead of a gentle hug, it's an iron vise that squeezes my lungs until I'm gasping for breath, struggling to replenish my air supply.

Why would Valentina do this? Why would she offer her brother's hand in marriage? Was it simply a power play?

I dart my eyes between the siblings who are currently engaged in a silent standoff, his pitch-black eyes locked with her golden ones. The similarities between their features are striking. All bronze skin and dark brown hair and perfectly symmetrical features.

But their beauty hides a wickedness that runs soul deep.

Just like their father.

Just like that *stronzo*.

"Blair," Valentina says in that same airy tone from before. Vincent winces almost imperceptibly before running a hand down the front of his suit and removing a crease from his jacket. "If you'll excuse me and my brother for a moment."

"Oh...um...sure," I murmur like an imbecile, practically sprinting towards the staircase. I'm desperate to escape the tension contaminating the room, polluting it.

But instead of entering my room, I hover near the rail, far enough away to remain out of sight if the twins decide to look up.

"Why did you bring her here?" Vincent's voice is glacial, laced with agitation and annoyance.

"Why do you think I brought her here, dear brother of mine?" Valentina singsongs.

There's a moment of silence, and I can't help but inch closer to the railing in order to see their faces. As expected, Vincent is standing directly in front of a smirking Valentina. From this angle, I can only see his profile, but his lips are clearly lowered into a severe scowl. His harsh eyes, chips of obsidian in his arresting tan face, narrow when Valentina's smile simply grows.

"Sister..." There's a warning in that one word, but she ignores it.

"Brother." She mimics his tone, placing both hands on her hips and canting them to the side. "Maybe I was just sick of you moping all the damn time."

"I wasn't moping," he responds immediately, forking his fingers through his dark brown hair. The strands move in every direction, a few of the longer ones flopping in front of his eyes. For some reason, I find that ridiculously attractive, but I push those lust-filled thoughts to the back corner of my mind, refusing to give them leeway. I'll fucking murder those thoughts if I have to.

"You were totally moping." Valentina removes her phone from a pocket in her skirt—seriously the coolest invention ever—and begins to type away absently. "You worry too much, brother. I have everything under control. Smith and Dalley are watching the camp as we speak. There'll be no attacks, not on our watch."

Smith? Dalley?

Camp?

She doesn't mean the bitten camp, does she? Why would she be watching there?

My suspicion ratchets up a dozen notches when Valentina adds, "Bartley as well. I just added him." She slides her phone back into her skirt and raises a perfectly manicured brow. "Your fears are unwarranted, brother. Besides, we both know there's only one bitten wolf you're actually worried about." She sighs heavily. "Pussies. The leading cause of death in men, according to WebMD. Wouldn't you agree, brother?"

Vincent growls sharply, the noise more wolf than human, before pushing past her and stalking out of the room. His muscles are taut beneath his black suit coat, and his hands are clenched into fists.

What the fuck did I just overhear?

Who is this bitten wolf that Vincent cares about? And why does Valentina have her wolves watching our camp—assuming that's what she even meant? For protection? That doesn't seem right, the Davenports hate us, yet I can't help but feel like I'm missing something immensely important. A puzzle piece that would help complete the image.

I bite on my lower lip to keep myself from asking one of the thousands of questions running rampant and unattended through my head. Instead, I simply stare in the direction Vincent disappeared down, wondering what he's thinking. Is he pissed that I'm here? Am I in danger?

Is this going to be one of those goddamn horror television shows where the leading lady is murdered by the sexy, dark lord of the creepy manor at the end of season one? Because let me tell you...

I am definitely final girl material. You know, the pretty brunette in every horror movie who miraculously makes it to the end credits, despite being plain in every which way and having no life skills whatsoever to survive a crazed, psycho murderer.

What is Valentina's endgame? What is Vincent's? And where do I come into play?

Almost instinctively, my eyes drift to the portrait of their father. Why do Vincent and Valentina have to look so much like the haughty man? Why do they have to have his cruel eyes and cunning smirk?

A throat clears from down below.

I snap my gaze towards Valentina, only to freeze when I meet her amused, golden stare. Her lips twitch as my hands clench and unclench by my sides, but instead of reprimanding me for eavesdropping, she simply turns on her heel and exits the room after her brother, calling flippantly over her shoulder, "You're not a prisoner here, despite what my brother would have you believe. Do what you will. As you just did when you listened to our entire conversation."

Did she...?

Did she want me to overhear their conversation? Why?

The more I'm around the Davenport siblings, the more I realize that there is still so much about this world I have yet to learn. And the more I learn, the more confused I become and the more questions I gain.

VINCENT

DAY 1

The limo pulls to a stop in front of a nondescript building with a slated gray roof and graffiti-covered walls. From the outside, it appears rundown and abandoned, the street littered with fast-food wrappers and crawling with homeless people.

But the inside...

The inside, it's paradise.

Once the bouncer—disguised as an unassuming homeless man with a haggard beard and tired, wrinkled face—allows me entry, the pungent stench of sweat and blood assaults my senses. I pause, breathing deeply, as the other wolves give me a wide berth, staring at me with fearful eyes.

They all know that when Vincent Davenport arrives, shit is going down.

My frustration and rage are living entities inside of me, a beast that wants to be set free on the world and destroy everything in its path. It curdles deep in my gut, oddly resembling a ball of yarn encased in fire, but I don't allow it to show on my face, keeping my features perfectly blank.

Why would Valentina bring her to my home? The answer is simple, but I refuse to look at it longer than a second. Maybe if I bury it, fucking demolish it, then it won't be true.

It *can't* be true.

Every time I blink, Blair's features consume my vision. Those brilliant aqua eyes, the color such a striking shade of blue that it resembles sunlight reflected on the water's surface. Her abnormally long brown hair with those golden highlights. A body men would kill for. Correction—die for. And then there's me.

I'd kill any motherfucker who even looked at her.

When I first saw her at the warehouse, my wolf had howled his excitement, demanding to lunge at the wide-eyed, ethereally beautiful female. At first, I thought he wanted to stick his teeth in her delicate neck and pull until her blood splattered us both.

Don't get me wrong—he *does* want to stick his teeth in her, but not to kill her.

No, apparently, my wolf has nefarious intentions when it comes to the pretty bitten wolf.

I growl under my breath, causing the wolves nearest to me to scatter like their asses are on fire. The sight would've been comical if I wasn't in such a sour mood.

Wolves Den is exactly what you would expect from the title—a sleazy bar and fight club that caters exclusively to wolves. It rests smack dab between all four territories, and everywhere I look, I see a combination of lycan, fenrir, totemic, and bitten wolves. Some are in passionate embraces, uncaring of their standing in the world, while others are glaring daggers at anyone who gets too close. I spot a female fenrir with her shirt unbuttoned, revealing a lacy red bra pulled down and her beaded nipples, being fucked by a totemic wolf.

In here, it doesn't matter what type of wolf you are, only that you *are* one.

And that you're willing to get dirty.

It's the only neutral zone in the entire city, but even that protection is feeble at best. Bitten wolves, particularly female, still need to be aware of their surroundings when they enter.

I move over the distressed wooden floor boards until I'm at the bar, tapping my fingers against the countertop until the bartender hands me my usual glass of whiskey. Without bothering to thank him, I turn in the direction of the fighting ring, located in the center of the room and separated from the cheering crowd by flimsy rope. Two wolves—one who I recognize from my own family and the other a stone-faced fenrir—engage in a fierce battle, blood flying in every direction as they beat the ever-loving shit out of each other.

The familiar tendrils of blood-lust rise up my throat as Jacob, who serves as part of our security team, lands an uppercut to the fenrir's throat. The bald biker collapses to the ground, blood pooling around his body, as the crowd goes wild.

I don't bother to clap as I down the remainder of my drink. I'll only begin to feel more like myself after I effectively beat someone's face into a bloody, unrecognizable pulp.

"Vincent Davenport."

The growl behind me has me straightening my shoulders and casually flicking imaginary lint off of my jacket's sleeve. I don't need to look over my shoulder to know who would be baring down on me, his lips pulled away from his teeth as a growl rumbles through his body.

"Tai. What an unpleasant surprise." Turning on my heel, I meet the totemic's eyes with a defiant arch of my brow. He's shirtless, his tattooed chest covered in sweat and dried blood, no doubt from a fight he just took part in. There's something near manic in his brown eyes as his teeth elongate, turning into dangerously sharp fangs.

"Where is she?" I barely recognize his voice around the ferocious growl. Wolves stare at him with wide, fearful eyes—the same look they always give me whenever I enter a building. They know innately that Tai is a man to fear.

But he doesn't scare me.

He may be a totemic wolf and a member of the Totemic Tribe. He may be able to shift into a wolf while I'm forced to remain in my human form until the full moon. He may be an alpha at heart.

But to me, he's just an overgrown man-child who blindly follows his daddy's rules and requests, regardless of who he hurts in the meantime. Men like him—puppets, in a sense—disgust me. Maybe because I was one not too long ago.

"Where is who?" I quirk a brown brow as he practically trembles with fury. Does he mean my sister? I can feel my lips curling downwards at the thought of Valentina with this Neanderthal, but I don't know who the fuck else he could—

"Blair," Tai grits out, his eyes flashing a moonlight yellow as his wolf rises to the surface.

His words cause my entire body to freeze as if I've just been struck by an electrical current. Anger percolates in my gut, combined with...jealousy. Why would he be asking about Blair?

I suddenly wish I had stayed longer and demanded Valentina give me more information about the summit meeting. But the second I saw Blair, felt her smooth curves pressing against my rapidly hardening cock while I held a knife to her pale throat, I knew I needed to get out of there. I needed to fuck or fight this frustration out of me.

And since I can't do the former, I'm here, ready to kill someone.

Even if that someone is the son of the Totemic Tribe's alpha.

The cold-blooded werewolf prince everyone fears.

I keep my eyes impassive, even as my lips morph into a rictus grin.

"Why are you asking about the little wolf?" I query, desperate to get a rise out of him...and discover the truth about his inquiry. Why would he ask about her? Why would he care? "Are you jealous that I'm engaged to her?" My voice is light and taunting, a direct contrast to my apathetic features and cold, deadly stare. I can feel my hand jerking towards my concealed weapon, located in a holster underneath my suit jacket, but I tamp down the urge to blow his fucking head off.

Later.

In the ring.

But instead of getting upset by my words, Tai throws back his head and laughs. The sound makes me want to stab someone, preferably him, in the balls.

"If she chooses you." Tai's face contorts into a sneer, even as his eyes radiate smugness.

I try to school my expression, but I know I don't do a good job of it when Tai begins to laugh harder, the sound garnering the attention of everyone in the vicinity. The looks tossed his way range from anxious to horrified to aroused.

"Your sister didn't tell you?" Tai laughs again, but this time, the sound holds very little humor. There's a cruel edge to it, like a razorblade peeling away layers of skin and baring the flesh underneath. "She spends one month with each of us, and at the end of the ninety days, she'll choose a husband."

"Us," I repeat lazily, not allowing him to see the turbulent anxiety rumbling through me. Blair gets to choose? I don't even understand my own emotions. Just a second ago I wanted nothing to do with her, but that was when I thought I already had her. "You and me?"

"And the 'choir boy,' as I heard Blair call him. Fucking Mason." Tai makes a face at the mention of Mason, though I want to point out that they have very similar facial structures. If Mason's an angelic little choir boy, what does that make him? A priest?

I hold in a snort. There's nothing remotely priestly or godly about Tai.

So apparently, my sister decided to wager a little bet with the other packs. Interesting. And despite the growing unease I feel at the thought of Blair with the other packs, at the thought of her *dating* Tai and Mason, I'm not worried.

Inevitably, she'll choose me.

Even if I don't want her to.

The thought only exacerbates my rage, and I level Tai with a glare capable of freezing over lava. He simply smirks at me, the cocky shit, and flexes his arm muscles. He's bulkier than me, taller even, but that doesn't mean anything. Not between two wolves.

Everyone knows that lycans are immensely stronger than any of the other breeds.

Keeping my voice cool and level, I spread my

arms wide to encompass the entire room and scream out, "I challenge you to a fight."

The response is instantaneous. Wolves begin smacking their hands against the sticky tabletops and howling towards a moon that isn't full yet. I allow the noise to soothe me, caress my frayed nerves, as I resist the urge to howl as well.

But Vincent Davenport *doesn't* howl in a bar like a fucking Neanderthal.

Tai's grin falls from his face, replaced by something darker and infinitely more dangerous.

"You're on, stiff," he hisses, shouldering past me to enter the ring.

Cracking my neck from side to side, I systematically remove my suit jacket and drape it over one of the few chairs not covered in splashes of blood. I unbuckle my holster and gun and drop both of them on the table. Instead of removing my dress shirt, I simply roll up the sleeves until I have full movement of my arms.

And then I duck into the ring, watching Tai with narrowed eyes as he circles me.

I'm vaguely aware of the referee counting down, but I'm no longer simply Vincent Davenport. I'm a predator, and Tai is my prey. I can't kill him, unfortunately, without starting an all-out war that we're not prepared to win yet, but I *am* allowed to maim him.

And if he thinks he can steal Blair from me, he has another thing coming.

When the cheers grow louder, I realize that the referee has finished his countdown and Tai is waiting for an opportunity to strike. We circle each other, our lips pulled away from our teeth as our wolves rush to the surface.

A sick excitement flashes in his eyes as he runs at me, choosing to use brute force instead of stealth. It might've taken a normal wolf by surprise, but I'm *not* a normal wolf.

Just as his arms would've wrapped around me, I swiftly step to the side and aim an uppercut at his jaw, watching as blood spurts from his nose. That doesn't stop him, though, as he clamors back to his feet, his hands raised into fists.

Unfortunately, my momentum put my back against the rope, and Tai uses that to his advantage, coming at me and pounding me repeatedly in the stomach. I hear something crack, but I don't pay it any mind as my own fist slams into his chest.

I've never been the type of man who runs from a fight. Instead, I'm the asshole who sticks around to see how many bullets I can shoot into someone's head until their skull is nothing but fine pieces of dust.

Death...

I crave it.

Maybe it makes me a psychopath, maybe not, but there's nothing more satisfying than watching the life drain from a bastard's face.

I dance back on the balls of my feet, frowning when I spot a speck of blood on the collar of my white shirt. Fuck. I'm gonna have to throw it away or face Valentina's wrath. She always gets a brain hemorrhage when I ruin the clothes she buys for me.

Tai comes at me again, pounding into me with ruthless abandon.

I feel a sick thrill worm its way through me.

This...

Fighting...

It's what I live for.

We exchange blow after blow, and I have to admit that we're evenly matched. For every punch I land on him, he returns it, and vice versa. I can feel my face swelling as the fight continues, as anger pumps blood through my veins. My rage is the only thing keeping me upright through the crippling exhaustion that threatens to creep up on me.

When the referee finally calls the fight—to the shouts, hollers, roars, and growls of the crowd—Tai's face is mottled and discolored in hideous bruises. I can barely see any of his tattoos around the myriad of bruises on his torso. I imagine I look similar, blood molding my dress shirt to my pecs

I'll have to burn it before I get home. Fortunately, my healing will kick in before anyone notices what I've been up to.

"Good fight," I say casually, ducking underneath the rope and grabbing my jacket. No one is stupid enough to even attempt to steal it from me. Not here. Not when they know who the fuck I am. I place my holster back on and check to make sure my gun is secure. "You heading home?" I continue when he doesn't immediately respond. "I know Blair's probably waiting in bed for me."

He growls harshly, the reaction seemingly instinctive and primitive, but doesn't rise to the bait, much to my disappointment. Maybe he got all of his anger out in the ring, unlike me. Or maybe he truly doesn't care that I could be potentially fucking the pretty bitten wolf.

But no. One glance into his dark brown eyes shows an almost elemental level of fury and hate. Pure malevolence shoots from his eyes like laser beams as he sneers at me.

"Enjoy her while you can, stiff," he rasps, as if I'm honestly offended by the nickname. Stiff. It fits me, I suppose. And my cock when I'm around Blair. "You only get thirty days."

Without waiting for me to respond, he turns on his heel and stalks down the hall that houses the bathrooms, ignoring the female wolves touching his arms and propositioning him.

I glance at the face of my Rolex, frowning when I notice the screen is cracked, and curse venomously when I realize the time. Valentina is going to be furious with me for staying out all night.

"Hey, handsome," a sultry voice says from beside me. I turn only my head to see the female wolf I noted earlier—the one being fucked by a totemic—sauntering towards me, her hips swaying. She's pulled her bra and top up, once more concealing her breasts, though the outfit she wears leaves little to the imagination. She runs her fingers down my arm. "Why don't we celebrate your win, handsome?"

"It was a draw," I answer tiredly, shoving her hand off of my arm and shrugging my jacket back on.

"Maybe we could—"

"Not interested," I cut in briskly, already storming towards the exit. I tell myself that I'm not interested merely because I'm desperate to get home and see my sister, but I know that's not true. I also know that it's not Valentina I want to see, but the beautiful she-wolf with eyes that seem to sparkle like the fathomless depths of the deepest ocean.

Blair has ruined me, and I haven't even had an honest-to-God conversation with her yet.

But maybe…

Maybe some people are worth being ruined for.

BLAIR

DAY 4

It's been three days since I arrived at the Davenport mansion.

And three days since I last saw Vincent Davenport.

Even though I explored every inch of the house, every closet and every room, every bathroom and every kitchen—because rich people need more than one—I still have yet to set eyes upon the striking, impassive man.

His sister, however, has been a constant thorn in my side since I arrived.

She's currently perched on my bed, her back ramrod straight despite her relaxed features. Today, she wears a dark purple dress that crisscrosses at her chest before flaring out at her waist. A smart suit jacket completes the sexy business woman look. Her brown hair is carefully fishtailed away from her face, cascading down her right shoulder without a single strand escaping. Her ruby red lips are pursed as she sends off text after text, the jabbing motion of her manicured fingers betraying her impatience.

I watch her warily, unsure if I should fear Valentina Davenport or be in awe of her. There's something so cold in her gaze, but at the same time, she's been nothing but friendly with me. I don't know if she's playing some sort of sick, sadistic game, or if...

Or if she's just lonely.

One thing is certain—her makeup game is *strong*. I'm honestly kinda jealous.

"He's going to be here in five minutes," Valentina declares at last, dropping her phone onto her lap and crossing her ankles. It's a pose I've dubbed her "power pose," much to her amusement. With the imperious set to her chin, she could be a queen on a throne, overseeing her wayward subjects. Unfortunately, I'm the only subject in the vicinity.

"He?" I can't ignore the way my heart skips a beat and then flutters madly or the way hope flares in my gut like an errant firework. When Valentina's lips quirk in a mischievous smirk, I know I didn't do a good job of hiding my emotions.

Though why the fuck I feel hope at the thought of seeing Vincent remains a mystery.

I'm not one of those girls who claims to hate a man but instantly becomes enamored by his sexiness. I *do* hate Vincent Davenport.

But I'm also enamored by his sexiness.

Dammit.

It doesn't change the fact that I want to see his head on a spike and his body buried six feet below beside the despicable lycan he called a father.

"Johnathon," Valentina corrects, deciding to spare me. When I simply stare at her, waiting for her to explain, she sighs, the sound way too pretty when compared to the annoyance etched onto her face. "You're living in the Davenport mansion, my dear friend, and are technically dating the Davenport heir. You need to...look the part." She gestures towards my too-large pink top and ripped skinny jeans with a sneer of disgust.

"Are you saying I need a makeover?" I don't know whether to be horrified or amused. Maybe a mixture of both?

Or maybe...?

Maybe excited?

I really like clothes and makeup, dammit.

Valentina purses her lips and rises gracefully from the bed. Despite her heels being inches off the ground, she moves towards the desk chair I'm sitting on and circles me like a lion preparing to devour a gazelle. Her eyes flash amber in the dim lighting of my bedroom as she pulls her lip between her teeth.

"The hair…" she mumbles, picking a strand of my brown hair up and holding it between her fingers. At this point, I'm not even sure she's talking to me. She sorta seems like one of those crazy cat ladies who hides in a bunker cackling gleefully while she ties the hair of her enemies together. "It can be cut a few inches. Get rid of those hideous split ends." She resumes her pacing, stopping only when she's able to bend in front of me, staring intently at my face. I wet my lips self-consciously, because come the fuck on. What's wrong with my face?

"Do you even own makeup?" she demands, straightening and crossing her arms over her chest.

"Um…I have mascara. But it's expired. Honestly, I didn't even know mascara *could* expire. You learn something new every day, I suppose." I laugh awkwardly, even as her eye fucking twitches.

"I'll send for Carina as well," she states, whipping her phone out and shooting off yet another text. "And don't you dare complain. I won't have you—"

"Okay," I reply easily, and she glances up from her phone, her eyes narrowing suspiciously.

"Okay?" Her lips purse together as those golden eyes of hers thin into slits. Yeah. I can't entirely blame her for being suspicious. I haven't exactly been a compliant prisoner since I've arrived here.

I shrug half-heartedly. "It's not like I don't like new clothes or a haircut or makeup, Valentina." I can feel my face twisting into a grimace as I stare around the opulent room with the same distaste and derision she gave my clothes just a few seconds earlier. "Sometimes people just can't afford the same things you can."

"Like the people in your camp?" Though she phrases it as a question, I can see that she already knows the answer. Her brows crease as something flickers in her gaze.

Still, I answer as if she doesn't know, as if she isn't aware of the hold poverty has on all of us. "We're lucky if the children are able to have warm clothes over the winter," I confess, unsure why I'm telling her this. I hate her, but it's not as if the circumstances surrounding our wealth—or lack thereof—are a closely guarded secret. All of the wolves know that the bitten wolves live in squalor.

Valentina frowns, golden eyes glimmering

dangerously, before she grabs her phone once more, her fingers flying across the screen.

"What are you doing?" I ask tiredly, unsure if I should be offended or not that Valentina is always on her phone with me. I settle on *not*.

When she finally looks back up, her grin resembles the cat who captured the canary. Pride and satisfaction emanate from her gaze as she tosses her dark brown hair over her shoulder. "I just talked to a few of my contacts."

And...that wasn't cryptic whatsoever.

Crazy bitch.

"Come. Let's behave like normal women and go get our nails done, gossip, and then cut bitches who look at us funny."

VALENTINA IS SURPRISINGLY NOT BAD COMPANY. I would never admit that to her face, but she's quick-witted and sarcastic as fuck. I don't necessarily like the way she treats the workers, but when I call her out on it, I receive a glare so vicious, I hold my hands up in a placating manner and surrender.

Johnathan, a handsome man in his mid-thirties, has me sit down in a chair in the middle of my bedroom. Because yes, Valentina is apparently able to have the stylists come to her instead of having to go to a salon.

Fucking rich people.

He agrees with her that it needs a trim, but when he asks if I want to cut the length, I shake my head vehemently. It seems silly and irrational, but for some reason, I associate my hair with the life I had before—before the wolves attacked my family and killed them. Before I was turned into this beast. Before I was thrust into poverty and homelessness, living on the streets. The long strands of hair have been with me since I was a child, since I held my father's hand and stared up at my mother with the blinding love only a child can possess. Since I teased Percy mercilessly and jabbed my elbow into Brett's stomach.

Getting rid of my hair feels like losing the last piece of my family I possess.

As Johnathon—or John, as he insisted I call him—begins to brush through my brown-gold locks, praising the color and texture, Valentina suddenly cackles. I turn towards her and see that she has her phone out, no surprise, and is snapping picture after picture.

When have I ever heard her laugh before? The noise, honest to God, takes me by surprise and makes me blink at her like an imbecile.

"What are you doing?" I ask as John finally begins to cut. A piece of my soul shrivels into dust when I spot strands of my hair on the marble flooring, and I have to rein in the growing panic and terror I feel. I tell myself that it's just hair, that just because it's gone, doesn't mean I lost my family all over again, as I wait for Valentina to stop laughing long enough to respond.

"Just sending my idiotic brother some pictures," she says ominously, smirking first at me and then at John, giving him a sultry once-over. There's no doubt that John is an attractive man, with golden blond hair and a sweet smile. But why would Valentina send a picture—

On the level below us, I hear something crash against the wall followed by a fierce, threatening roar. John and I both jump while Valentina crosses her legs, looking completely unperturbed by her brother's temper tantrum.

"What the fuck was that about?" I demand as her smirk grows to epic proportions.

"Oh, you know, the usual. Trying to convince my brother to get his head out of his ass." She pauses, finally peeling her gaze away from her phone to spear me with an indecipherable look. "He's not a bad guy, you know. My brother," she clarifies when I remain silent.

I don't bother to hold in my snort of disbelief.

"He's not!" she protests. Lowering her gaze back to her phone, she slides her finger rapidly across the screen before she triumphantly throws a fist in the air. "Ha!" She moves so she's standing beside me, shouldering one of the women doing my nails out of her way, and thrusts her phone in my face. "Isn't he the cutest?"

It's a picture of a younger Valentina and Vincent with a gorgeous woman standing between them who must be their mother. Valentina is wearing a pure white dress and red headband, while Vincent has on a bright purple baseball jersey and carries a catching mitt.

"What am I looking at?" I inquire as John pulls at my hair, eliciting a pained gasp from my throat.

"Snarl," he explains sheepishly as he continues combing through the long strands.

"You're looking at the T-ball state champion," Valentina announces proudly. She tilts her chin up ever so slightly, the move somehow both condescending and vulnerable at the same time. "We were six in this picture, and Vincent actually threw the damn baseball for an out instead of eating it like the rest of the kids. Because of that throw, his team won."

I focus on the picture once more.

It's strange to see him like this—full of life and innocence, a jubilant smile splitting his face in two. His eyes are just as dark as they are now, nearly black, but there's a ring of gold around his irises that I don't see in the older version. He looks so...happy.

An ache starts up in my chest.

What happened to him?

"Did you do sports too?" I question Valentina, and she stares at me like I'm crazy.

"If you call finding the television remote before your twin brother a sport, then yes. Yes, indeed. Won about fifty percent of the time. I also got a trophy in second grade for catching the most cheese puffs in my mouth." She smooths a hand down her pencil skirt before reclaiming her seat. I watch her with wide eyes, my mouth agape, before I snort out a laugh.

"I literally cannot picture you watching TV or eating cheese puffs," I manage to say. Valentina is the epitome of dignity and grace. It's comical to believe that at one point of time, she was a child. A dirty, smelly, misbehaving child.

She eyes her fingers as if she's remembering the cheese smudges that once stained them. A shudder works its way up her body.

"That was a dark time, Blair. A dark, dark time."

I giggle again, and this time, she joins in with me.

After John finishes cutting my hair, only taking a few inches off the bottom, Valentina instructs two females to begin work on my nails, much to my displeasure. A third female, who introduces herself as Carina, starts layering makeup on my face, all the while writing notes in her tiny book of colors she thinks looks good on me. While the three women work, Valentina talks in hushed tones with a woman who identified herself as Genieve. The two of them cast furtive glances my way before Genieve finally nods, disappearing out the door to reappear a moment later with a rack of clothes. Valentina squints at the collection, taking a few dresses off the rack, before she smiles in satisfaction.

"Perfect," she purrs.

And that's how I find myself less than two hours later standing in front of a mirror, unable to recognize the reflection staring back at me.

I mean, sure, I look like me, but something fundamental has been changed within me. My hair appears more vibrant than ever before, healthier, and tumbles down my back in shades of forest brown and radiant gold. The makeup Carina painstakingly applied makes my blue eyes even brighter, my cheekbones sharper, and my lips fuller. Genieve has given me a pair of skinny blue jeans to wear and a bright pink sweater that slides off one shoulder stylishly. There are no holes distorting the fabric, no stains that I can't scrub clean, no awkwardly fitting bras that are too tight on my shoulders.

"I look... I mean, you are..." I trail off, unable to encapsulate all that I feel with words. Is it wrong that I feel grateful for my captor? I imagine it is, but I can't find it within me to give a flying fuck. If I were lesbian, I would totally wife the shit out of Valentina. It's funny how only a few days ago, I feared her. She was the boogeyman whispered about around the campfire, the scary story we told misbehaving pups. But the truth is, she's fiercely loyal to the people she cares about and willing to raise hell to protect them. I don't know if I fall into that category yet, but I know that I enjoy my time with her. And I don't believe she'll murder me and use her connections to hide my body. I call that a win.

"You're hot as fuck? And I'm a goddess? Yes, you would be correct," Valentina says cockily, flashing me a cheeky smile as she tosses her hair behind her shoulder. "But now for the real test..." She all but wrenches my arm out of my socket as she pulls me away from the mirror and out of my room.

Automatically, my eyes flash to the picture of Bellamy Davenport before I force them away, allowing Valentina to drag me down the huge staircase—I notice almost absently that one of the marble heads I spotted when I first arrived is now destroyed —and towards a hall I've ventured down only once before. There's nothing down here besides a den furnished with a pool table and bar that reeks of cigar smoke, and a second room that must be an office of some sort. It has a large mahogany table, three cozy armchairs, a hearth against the far wall, and a glorious bookshelf that rests in between two of the chairs.

It's the second room that we head to, Valentina barging inside without bothering to knock. I'm confused at first, until I spot the man sitting comfortably in one of the armchairs, reading a book.

Vincent's head snaps up when we enter, his eyes landing on me instantly. He gives me a slow, almost lazy once-over as his eyes turn hooded. Slitted.

Dangerous.

"Well?" Valentina snaps, placing one hand on her hip and cocking it to the side. She steps away from me to stand by her brother. "How does she look?"

Vincent very, *very* slowly closes his book—I recognize it as *Moby Dick* by Herman Melville— while his eyes remain fixed on me.

He looks ridiculously sexy in the comfort of his office. His suit jacket has been draped over the arm of the chair, and the sleeves of his white dress shirt have been rolled up, displaying impressive forearm porn. His brown hair is uncharacteristically tousled. I might even call it bedroom hair, if the thought of him fucking some skank didn't send me into a murderous rage.

"She looks...radiant," he decides on at last, almost appearing pained by his confession. I wonder if he planned on lying, if he planned on dismissing me or calling me a hag. I wouldn't have believed him either way. The heat in his eyes begs to differ.

"I'm amazing, I know," Valentina singsongs, and he finally drags his eyes away from me to give her a cold look.

"And very humble, sister," he responds dryly, to which she shrugs.

"There are many things I'm good at, brother of mine, and styling is one of them."

"Maybe next time we have a girl's day, I could teach you how to fight," I interrupt, not thinking my words through before I say them. Immediately, they both turn to stare at me, Vincent's expression carefully blank while Valentina just appears intrigued. I refuse to blush beneath their intense scrutiny and instead raise my chin defiantly, choosing to test the waters, so to speak. "For example, if you're being shot at in a warehouse, it would probably be good if you knew how to defend yourself. Cowering isn't always the right option."

I wait with bated breath, desperate to hear their response. I'm positive that they know about my involvement in the explosion, but they also haven't brought it up. What are they waiting for?

Why does my unease grow every second they remain silent?

I expect them to be furious, but instead, Valentina throws her head back in laughter and Vincent flashes me a look of wry amusement, one that appears in his eyes rather than on his lips.

"I might have to take you up on that, wolfie," Valentina says flippantly. "But I'll have you know, I'm an expert already."

"You can't really kill someone with sparkles," Vincent points out, and she swats at his shoulder.

"I can't...but that doesn't mean I'm not going to try. Besides, I don't need to learn how to kill someone when I can just hire other people to do it for me." Without waiting for her brother's response, she stalks back towards me and relinks our arms. "Come, my new best friend." Her grin turns sinister as she gives Vincent her back. "Let's show *Johnathan* your finished look."

Ignoring Vincent's vicious and sudden growl,

Valentina leads me out of the room, slamming the office door shut behind her.

I can still hear Vincent fuming, even when we leave the hall, and I can't help but wonder what he's going to break this time.

13

BLAIR

DAY 6

I don't see Vincent or Valentina for two days. Valentina entered my room only once to tell me she was going out but refused to tell me where. And Vincent...

He's an enigma. A monster hiding inside of a sinful body and expensive suit. The one time I saw him, in the dining hall last night, he snapped his book shut, jumped to his feet, and stormed from the room, his plate of food forgotten.

I don't know why I'm even bothered by his behavior.

Everything about Vincent is an enigma. Why wasn't he pissed when I basically confessed to being the one to blow up the shipment of weapons? Why did he seem almost amused? And why the fuck do I care so much about his opinions?

One thing is clear—Vincent Davenport has gotten in my head.

I huff out a dry laugh as I grab a bar of soap and lather it over my breasts. The one benefit of being the Davenports' prisoner is that I get a huge bathtub all to myself. It's claw-footed and so white, I can see my reflection in the meticulously polished side. It comes equipped with soaps of all scents and various shampoos and conditioners. And something called a bath bomb. There's even one labeled "Blood." A blood bath bomb. Apparently, it's a thing.

My lips twist into a devilish smirk as I picture Valentina lounging in a bath coated in dark blood. She's just twisted enough to enjoy something like that. Of course, in this fantasy, she's cackling malevolently as she plans world domination, the crazy bitch.

The vision shifts, and instead of Valentina, I see Vincent himself in the red water. As he flexes his naked muscles, blood slides down his impressive chest and to his enticing hip muscles. Does he have any tattoos on him? I can't imagine he would, considering what he wears and how he acts. And is his cock pierced?

Biting my lower lip, I allow my hand to caress

first one of my achy breasts and then the other, stim-
ulating my nipples into sharp, beaded points. I
continue squeezing my tits as a low moan leaves my
throat. My other hand travels down my stomach,
across the tiny section of pubic hair, and into my
slick channel.

"Touch yourself." Vincent's voice is a sinful purr in
my ear, and I throw my head back against the rim of
the tub as I place one finger in my dripping pussy.
But I quickly realize that one just isn't enough, that I
need to feel fuller, and add a second digit to join the
first. My thumb rises to circle my clit as I squeeze
my nipple to the point of pain.

And then I hear a quiet voice, directly outside my
bathroom window, and the lust dissipates like a
storm cloud moving in front of the sun. Irritation
crashes over me like a tidal wave as I take my fingers
out of my pussy and push myself out of the tub, soap
cascading down my pale body, before stalking
towards the bathroom window. It's small enough
that if someone were to look up, only my face,
shoulders, and breasts would be visible.

I can feel my eyes narrow suspiciously when I
spot none other than Vincent Davenport walking
briskly towards a parked limo, not a hair out of place
and dressed in another expensive suit. The driver
opens the door for the pretentious prick, and he

slides inside, smoothing out a crease in his dress pants.

Where the hell is he going?

My curiosity piqued, I slip a robe on and hurry out of the bathroom. I won't be able to make it in time before the limo leaves, but I'm prepared for that. I'm prepared for anything when it comes to this man and his family.

Tugging on a matching bra and panty set—courtesy of Valentina—I grab my phone out and pull up a map. The red dot blinks intermittently as it travels down a road, driving away from the rich section of town and towards the center.

The fuckers didn't even consider searching for tracking devices on their vehicles.

Smirking at my own creativity, I slip on a pair of jeans and a loose black sweatshirt, pulling the hood up to conceal my brown and gold hair. I slip a knife into my sweatshirt pocket before staring back down at the map on my phone.

Where the fuck are you going, Vincent?

THE PARKED RED DOT LEADS ME TO AN inconspicuous bar in the center of town. I've heard about it, of course, but haven't visited. It's too dangerous for bitten wolves, particularly females.

Now, I don't hesitate, slipping past the werewolf bouncer posing as a homeless man. He gives me an appreciative once-over, his eyes flaring with lust, but whatever he sees in my expression has him backing away, his hands held up in mock surrender.

Ignoring him, I enter Wolves Den and scrunch my nose in disgust at the smell that immediately barrages me. Sweat, stale beer, and blood.

The staples of a wolf's life.

There are wolves of all types mingling—fenrirs from the BS MC, totemics from the Totemic Tribe, lycans that belong to the Davenport family, and even some bitten wolves I recognize from home.

But with my hood pulled over my head, none of them recognize me, and that's the way I need to keep it. At least until I find Vincent. They may be able to smell I'm a bitten wolf, but unless they're intimately familiar with me and my scent, they won't recognize me.

My first glance around the room proves to be futile, so I move away from the fighting ring where two wolves are beating the shit out of each other and head towards the bar. Pushing back my hood, I shake out my long hair, ignoring the hungry gazes from the wolves beside me.

"What can I get for ya?" The bartender gives me a grin that's probably capable of getting into most girls' pants. It's sultry and genuine, revealing twin dimples on both of his cheeks. That, combined with his russet hair makes him an enticing package.

Unfortunately for him, he's just not my type. Too...sane.

I never said I didn't have problems.

"Whiskey," I answer automatically, and his grin widens.

As he turns away from me to prepare my drink, I risk a sniff. Fenrir. When he reappears a moment later, I spot the bloody skull tattooed onto his bicep, which he flexes invitingly. How bad would it be if I accepted what he was so graciously throwing my way? If I took him to bed and blew his fucking mind? The terms never stated that I couldn't have any outside relationships. They never said I couldn't fuck men on the side while dating their beloved princes. All I need to do is ask him when his shift's over, give him a flirtatious wink, and flash him a hint of cleavage. By the end of the night, he'd be mine.

But instead of doing any of that, I accept the drink gratefully and move towards the fighting ring. It's almost as if I'm not in control of my body, as if there's an invisible string connected to my stomach, propelling me forward. I can't help but think of that stupid dance move, where someone pretends to lasso a stranger and then "pulls" her to him.

A marionette with its strings cut.

I move like a woman possessed until I'm near the edge of the ring. Quickly, before anyone can make note of me, I toss my hood back up over my hair and slink towards a dark corner.

I learned at a young age how to become one with the darkness. How to dematerialize into nothing but a misty shadow. How to watch everyone while no one watches you. How to be the lurking predator hiding behind tall, spindly grass instead of the prey waiting to be pounced on.

It's not just because I'm a bitten wolf, though that does factor into it. It's because I'm female in a society that demeans and targets them. I received my first lust-filled stare when I was only eight. Eight. I didn't even have boobs at that age, yet men still stared at me as if I was something they could own and possess.

The light is nothing but a trick. It shows pretty smiles and pretty faces, but the darkness highlights all of the monsters lurking in plain sight. In order to survive in the light, you need to be apt at fighting in the dark.

Wrapping my arms around my waist, I watch as Vincent strolls into the center of the ring as if he doesn't have a care in the world. He's missing his suit jacket, and his white shirt is pushed up to his elbows. His eyes resemble flinty chips in the darkness.

His opponent isn't someone I recognize, but one smell confirms he's a totemic wolf. His dusky skin is lathered in a copious amount of sweat—more sweat than I thought a man could possibly excrete. It's obvious he's been fighting for quite some time. Still, his smile is smug as he lifts both arms into the air, attempting to garner the crowd's support. He receives a few cheers, though the sound quickly tampers off when they flicker their eyes towards his stone-faced opponent.

Vincent may be smaller than him, he may be skinnier, he may be wearing dress clothes fit for a banker—a *mobster*—not a fighter, but there's no hiding who the true predator is.

My tummy flutters as I stare into Vincent's cold face, crafted by the gods themselves and made to ooze sin.

The referee begins to count down from three, but Vincent barely spares him a glance, his eyes glued to his opponent with unwavering intensity. Pure focus. The coldness in his gaze is capable of freezing molten lava, of shattering hearts into thousands of diminutive shards, each one sharper than the last.

I can't believe this is the same man who spends

his days in a chair, reading. Or writing in a leather-bound notebook, lost in his own head. Then again, the first time I saw him, he shot multiple men in the skull without breaking a sweat.

He's a monster, the perfect dichotomy of light and dark. I can't say for sure if it's good and evil as well, but I know that he has layers—layers that I wish I could peel away to see the vulnerable man underneath.

But the thought of Vincent being even remotely vulnerable is comical.

He's dangerous, Blair. Both to you and your people.

Remember that.

And...

You hate him.

The referee counts down to one and then steps to the side, just as the large totemic rushes at Vincent.

The stoic Davenport doesn't step out of the way as the totemic wolf barrels down on him, wrapping his meaty arms around his middle. But then again, he doesn't have to. While Vincent may appear smaller than the other man, all of the wolves here know that he's significantly stronger. All of the lycan wolves are.

Instead of being put down by the totemic, Vincent simply lowers his head and flips the wolf over his shoulder. His smile is like a knife, and it cuts right through my skin, despite not being directed at me.

Seeming almost bored with the entire fight, Vincent lowers himself onto the totemic wolf's chest and lays punch after punch into his not-so-smug-anymore face. Blood squirts from his mouth, and I even spot a tooth flying across the arena. All the while, Vincent maintains an indolent smile, as if this fight is beneath him. And it very well may be. After all, the wolf didn't prove to be much of a competitor, despite his initial swagger.

The referee eventually calls the fight, blowing his whistle and running back into the ring to lift Vincent's bloody hand in the air. There's not a single speck of blood on his clothes, despite the myriad of bruises and cuts covering his knuckles.

When Vincent's eyes slowly travel over the crowd, I swear they rest on me a moment longer than propriety's sake would allow. But it's impossible he could recognize me. Not in the cloaking shadows. Not with the hood pulled tight over my head, obscuring my hair from view. Not with my head lowered slightly and my hands tucked into my pockets.

I only feel like I can breathe normally when Vincent's eyes finally move on to the next person, dismissing me like I'm any other person. And maybe...

Maybe I truly am to him.

When he slides under the rope, exiting the ring, my eyes remain fixed on him like a hawk waiting to devour a flock of innocent songbirds. He moves with the agility of a dancer, even when he's not fighting. There's something so controlled about his movements, something I would almost describe as cautious. It's almost as if he's holding himself back, like if he ever truly let himself go, he would destroy this entire world with his bare hands.

Why does the thought intrigue me the way it does?

I continue watching him until he disappears into the throng of rowdy wolves, his exit syphoning the remainder of my oxygen. The response is instantaneous and foreign, and I don't understand it one fucking bit. I'm not one of those girls you read about in romance novels, who immediately swoons for the bad guy with just one eloquent dark stare and smolder that makes words unnecessary. I'm *not*. Sure, I find Vincent attractive, but I wouldn't hesitate to kill him if that's what it took to protect my family.

Even if the thought of killing him leaves a sour, poisonous taste in my mouth. It's like the apple in

Snow White—the beauty of the fruit hides its wicked intent.

I bite my lower lip, preparing to follow him and see what other secrets I can uncover, but before I can make it more than a few steps, a rough hand clamps down on my shoulder, yanking me to an abrupt stop. A low, threatening growl leaves my lips as I'm whirled around, coming face-to-face with a man easily twice my age.

Besides the glaringly obvious age difference, there's nothing significant about him whatsoever. His hair is thin, revealing a bald spot in the center of his head that he tried to hide with a few wispy strands, and though he's lean, his body is weirdly proportioned. Torso too long, legs too short. He offers me a sleazy smile, one that he probably thinks is attractive but draws attention to the large mole dotting his upper lip.

"Hey, sugar. Where you heading?" There's the slightest drawl to his words, almost like an accent from the deep south. But for some reason, it doesn't seem natural, as if he's putting on an act, faking the accent.

What a pathetic fucker.

"Away." I'm not always a rude bitch, but I can tell from one glance at his face that he's trouble. Danger- ous. There's something greedy and malicious in his green gaze that says he takes what he wants, damn the consequences.

That's only reaffirmed when his hand lowers from my shoulder to my upper arm, tightening.

"What's the matter, sugar?" That horrible endearment spills from his lips like dark tar, coating my skin and making me desperate to wash it away.

In the next moment, he has my back against the wall and his body is hovering over mine. A second fight has already begun in the ring, drawing the wolves' attention away from us. That is, if anyone was even paying us any attention to begin with.

But he's underestimated me, as most men do when they see a small, apparently docile female. Before he can touch me any further than my arms, I remove my knife from my sweatshirt pocket and hold it to his throat.

"Get the fuck away from me."

At first, I think he complied with my request. One second, his body is hovering menacingly over mine, and the next, he's across the room.

But then I see the wolf standing directly in front of me, his face slightly morphed, like an image of a wolf has been superimposed over the face of a breathtaking man.

Tai.

If Vincent is pure ice, Tai is a fire that burns so hot, it steals the very breath from my lungs.

He's shirtless, wearing only a pair of workout shorts that hang enticingly low on his bronze hips. Tattoos cover every bare inch of his torso, except for a single empty space directly over his heart. And though I can only see his profile with the way he's positioned, I can tell his teeth are bared as he glares at the southern "gentleman."

"Get the fuck away from her," Tai growls, and the man holds up both hands with a wry grin.

"Just getting to know the bitten slut. Sorry, Tai. Didn't know you claimed that pussy for yourself." He throws me a wink over Tai's shoulder, and I barely, just barely, stop myself from slashing the knife across his neck and creating a similar smile of blood there to match the one on his lips.

Maybe it's psychotic, to envision slicing his neck from ear to ear, but a genuine smile erupts on my face regardless.

I never claimed to not have a few screws loose.

I never claimed to not be a monster cut from the same stem as the three men I'm forced to marry. Or *choose* to marry, as the case may be.

But while they're covered in prickly thorns, my section of the stem is relatively smooth. At least, it can be, until you reach a particular part that's covered in more spikes than all of them combined. If you touch it, you'll bleed. It's that fucking simple.

"Leave, Billiard." Vincent materializes like a dark angel on my other side. A dark angel dressed in an immaculately-pressed suit with his hair slicked back. "Before I challenge you to a fight and fucking kill you."

Billiard finally seems to realize the severity of the situation. Because apparently, the princes are united in the fact that no one besides them is allowed to touch their property.

"But—"

"Leave!" Vincent snarls.

I watch the wolf scurry away, his metaphorical tail between his legs, just as Tai whirls on Vincent, glaring at him over my head.

"Why the fuck did you bring her here?" Tai's hands clench into fists at his sides, and I can't help but wonder who he's imagining pounding them into —Billiard, Vincent, or me.

Vincent gives Tai an impassive look before he shifts his gaze to me. "I didn't realize I was the wolf's keeper," he drawls, quirking one eyebrow expectantly at me. Despite how much I fucking loathe him, I can read his expression easily enough.

Why are *you here?*

Instead of responding to his unspoken question, I cross my arms over my chest and glare at him.

The bastard doesn't even blink as he meets my fierce gaze, his own eyes resembling flecks of steel.

"Vincent! Baby!" a voice coos.

Vincent keeps his eyes on me as an unfamiliar woman sashays up to his side, wrapping both hands around his arm possessively. Her pink-painted nails dig into his jacket sleeve, creasing the fabric, but he doesn't shake her off.

His eyes remained fixed on me.

But my eyes? They survey the newcomer with abject curiosity and a tiny smidgen of horror.

Her blonde hair has been teased, causing the mane to resemble something from an eighties movie. Her lips are a bright red, but unlike with Valentina, the color causes her face to look sickly pale.

A kernel of jealousy appears in my chest, curling around me like smoke, but I refuse to let it fester. There always seems to be this mentality that women need to go after other women. That we covet what someone else has.

I find it a load of bullshit.

So despite the growing jealousy burning like sparking embers in my stomach, I smile at her cordially, shocking the hell out of both Tai and

Vincent. I don't know how I can tell, only that I can. Vincent's expression doesn't even change, really, except for the slight widening of his eyes. Tai simply appears annoyed, glaring at Vincent with a fury I can almost taste, something hanging heavily in the air like smog.

"Are you Vincent's girlfriend?" I ask the newcomer, trying very, very hard not to get stabby at the way she clings to him. She's wearing a hot pink shirt that allows her breasts to spill over the top. That, combined with shorts so tiny, they could be a pair of underwear, makes me almost blinded with jealousy and rage.

But I don't let that show.

It's what Vincent wants, after all, and I refuse to give him the satisfaction.

"What the fuck are you looking at, bitten whore?" the woman snaps, pushing onto her tiptoes to kiss Vincent's neck. Again, he doesn't push her way, his eyes trained on me. He appears almost...hopeful? But what the fuck is he hoping I'll do?

And what the fuck did she just call me?

"Go home to your mommy and daddy, baby wolf," the woman taunts as she grips Vincent's cheek in a claw-like hand and tilts his face down towards hers. At that, he finally moves, twisting to the side before her lips can touch his. But he doesn't shrug her off of him completely, allowing her to basically grind against his leg.

Deep breaths, Blair. Deep breaths.

Remember you hate him.

And then the woman's next words penetrate my skull, and the jealousy I felt transitions into blind fury.

"Oh wait. You can't go to mommy and daddy, can you?" She places an abnormally long fingernail to her lower lip. "Because they're dead, aren't they? God, your fucking backstories are all the same. Dead families."

I...

I snap.

It's like the leash that has been containing me has been severed in two. One remains wrapped around my neck, steadily squeezing away my air supply, while the other...

The other wraps around *her* neck.

Before I realize what I'm doing, I have her pinned beneath me and am throwing punch after punch into her heavily madeup face. She shrieks desperately, blood flying from her nose, but I don't stop.

And Vincent and Tai don't stop me either.

My father's screams of anguish...

The blood pooling around my mother's head as her naked body lies bent and broken...

Percy's lifeless eyes...

"Run!" Brett screams, fear darkening his features. "Run, Blair!"

When I'm finally pulled off of her by two wolf shifters I don't know, Tai is staring at me with something akin to...respect. Maybe admiration? And a whole fucking lot of lust.

Vincent is as expressionless as always as he wraps an arm around my waist and steers me out of the club. I'm aware of all of that, I honestly am, but it's like a piece of my brain doesn't process it.

I'm still consumed by rage. By an incandescent anger that alights a fiery trail inside of my body.

Tai's voice floats to me as if I'm hearing it in a dream.

"You need to fucking take better care of her," he snarls. "And why the fuck are you touching her like that?"

Vincent's voice is glacial when he responds. "Why do you care?"

I hear something shatter—more than likely Tai throwing a fucking hissy fit—but I don't turn away. I don't look anywhere but directly in front of me.

Deep breaths, Blair.

Deep breaths.

I tried being nice, respectful, but it's women like her...

It makes me want to give up on humanity. To embrace the beast prowling within me and finally set her free.

I'm led to the limo—not that Vincent even asked me if I drove myself, which I didn't, because the fuckers don't let me have a car, and instead, force me to walk when I go on my top secret stealth missions —and slide absently inside. The leather creaks beneath my weight as I stare down at my bloody hands.

The female wolf, a totemic like Tai, will heal. I know she will.

And it's not guilt I'm feeling...

Fuck, sometimes emotions suck. Sometimes, they're confusing and conflicted and muddy and dirty. But other times... Other times, they're fucking amazing.

Today is *not* one of those times.

"I was a boy when I killed my first man." Vincent's monotone voice drags me kicking and screaming out of the spell I found myself in. When I glance at him out of the corner of my eye, his thin lips are pressed together, somehow making the angles of his face even sharper and more pronounced.

Chiseled marble perfection.

I don't answer him, though I have the distinct

impression he isn't expecting one. Instead, my fingers tap against my thigh as I stare pointedly out the window—his handsome face somehow still demanding my complete and utter attention where it sits in my peripheral vision.

"Seven, to be precise. My father—the devil take him—wanted me to be more like him." His upper lip curls away from his teeth. "A killer. A...monster."

Never in my life have I heard any of the Davenports talk about their father with anything less than complete respect. His cold words have me straightening almost imperceptibly, my stomach a tumultuous, explosive mixture of dread and eagerness. Outwardly, my features remain calm, and I absently bring a hand to the window, tracing invisible patterns on the glass.

"He took me to a restaurant where an older gentleman sat in a booth, laughing with his wife and kids. He looked me square in the eye and said, 'Kill him.'" For a brief, brief moment, anguish reflects on Vincent's face, etched into every line of his perfection, before he schools his expression and clears his throat.

He doesn't immediately speak again, and before I realize what I'm doing, I'm swiveling in my seat to face him fully.

"Did you do it?" I ask, my voice barely above a whisper.

His long, elegant fingers tap against his knee. I can't help but think that they're fingers that belong to a pianist. Does he play? It wouldn't surprise me. I can envision Vincent on a piano stool in a four-piece suit, his fingers dancing across the keys as his head sways from side to side. Would his face lose the rigidness and frost constantly plaguing it? Would his eyes flutter shut in pleasure?

"I did not," Vincent responds at last, his haughty tone at odds with the constant movement of his fingers against his knee.

Tap. Tap. Tap.

"So what happened?"

"He punished me, of course," he states, as if that should be obvious. As if all parents should punish their seven-year-old kids if they refuse to commit murder.

If I didn't already hate the dead bastard, I think I would now.

Another silence reigns, though I don't dare interrupt this one. It feels precarious, somehow, as if the slightest amount of pressure applied will send it into pieces.

"He forced me on my knees in the living room and said, 'Bad boys spend their lives on their knees, while the good ones get bowed to.'" He rubs absently at his jaw. "I stayed that way for ten hours. Wasn't allowed to move or eat. And pissing?" An undignified snort escapes him. "Well, let's just say I was happy I never had to take a shit."

"Vincent…" I murmur. I don't know if I want to comfort him or urge him to continue his story. Maybe a mixture of both?

His father…

His father is a complete and utter piece of shit. There are no words capable of encapsulating all that I feel for him.

What type of man does that to his children?

"The next day, he took me to the exact same restaurant and pointed out a different person. Another man. This one was sitting by himself at the bar, sipping a cup of coffee. I remember my father looked at me with his dark gaze and whispered, 'Kill him.'"

"Did you?" I'm enraptured by the story, by the way his cool mask breaks with every word he says, revealing a sliver of the vulnerable man underneath. A man who has been molded by hurt. A man who has faced unspeakable horrors. It's splayed across his face, tattooed onto his body.

"No," Vincent says at last. His jaw clenches so tightly, I'm afraid he'll break a tooth. "No, I did not. I figured any punishment that the despicable man bestowed upon me was worth it to spare a human life." His dark gaze turns distant, shadowed by memories from his past. Haunted by his demons. "But it wasn't me my father made kneel this time. It was my sister. My sweet, innocent sister." His entire body goes rigid, and when he directs his gaze onto me, I'm struck by how cold his eyes have become. Ice. Pure ice. They feel like a spear being thrown across the limo, the keen tip embedding itself in my chest.

"I can't describe the agony I felt when my sister was forced to her knees that day. The way she cried. The embarrassment and shame she felt when some of my father's men wandered into the room." A breath hisses out through his clenched teeth. "The vulgar things they said to her…"

Before I realize what I'm doing, I'm leaning forward and placing my hand over top of his. He startles at the touch, his eyes flickering from my face to my fingers and then back to my face in wonderment, but he doesn't pull away.

And I don't either.

His hands are so…warm. I don't know what I expected. For his hands to be as cold as the blood rushing through his veins? But for the first time ever, he doesn't seem as monstrous to me as he normally does. Maybe it's because for the first time ever, I'm learning the origins of this particular beast, and my heart aches for him.

Warmth migrates throughout my body from where we touch, our eyes still locked together. A surge of butterflies flutters their frail, delicate wings in my stomach.

With heavy reluctance, I remove my hand from his, and it takes him a moment before he can continue with his story. His voice is raspier than before, though, and I swear I can hear his heart hammering like a drum.

"And then I decided, no more. Never again. I can handle any punishment, but my sister? My sister would never kneel for another person. *I* would never kneel for another person. If that meant I had to become the bigger monster, then so be it."

"But you were just a child," I breathe in horror. A small, innocent boy who didn't deserve to have his childhood brutally ripped away from him.

"I was—*am*—a Davenport," Vincent corrects. "And a Davenport doesn't kneel for anyone." He scratches absently at his chin before dropping his hand back to his lap once more. "The next day, my father took me back to the restaurant and pointed to a new man. 'Kill him,' he instructed. I considered, briefly, killing my father. Just briefly. Before the thought could fully solidify, I took the gun he offered and shot the target point-blank in the head." A wry grin plays on his lips. "I didn't feel any remorse. I always thought I would—that my first kill would break me. But I knew it was either that man, that stranger, or my sister." His eyes spear me. "Maybe that makes me a monster...but I'm a monster who will only kill for the people he loves."

Words fail me, and something strange tangles with the ball of nerves already present in my chest. I try to peer at the indecipherable emotion, but it shies away, ducking its face.

"I-I don't know what to say," I decide on at last.

"Don't say anything," he says dismissively. "But just know that some monsters aren't born like that. They're bred. And some monsters will kill for inherently selfish reasons, while others refuse to. Does that make us moral? Just? Or does it just make us stupid?"

There's nothing I can think to say, so I don't speak. Instead, I twist my head so I'm staring out the limo, watching the town's bright lights transition into thick forests.

Vincent's story is a knife twisting in my heart. The pain he felt...

It makes him seem even more human. Not the robot or machine I thought him to be.

And I don't blame him for the life he took when he was a child. He did what he had to do for his family, for his sister, and I know I would've done the same if I had the courage. He was probably scared and confused, groomed by a despicable man to do despicable things.

I wonder what it would be like to be loved by Vincent. To know that he'll be your monster, your sword, your shield. I don't know if anyone ever loved me that much. Maybe my parents? My brothers? But they're gone now.

Would things have been different if I killed the men hurting them? If I did what Vincent did and shot them point-blank?

Vincent doesn't speak the rest of the ride, lost in his own thoughts, just as I am. He doesn't ask what set me off back in the club, what triggered my visceral, dangerous reaction. Maybe he senses that I'm barely holding it together, that I'm a thread on a sweater that is steadily unraveling. Maybe he knows that I'm damaged, that I'll never be whole because the people who made me like that have been taken from me.

He shared something with me about his past, and he didn't ask for anything in return. Didn't demand answers to the questions I can see plaguing that handsome head of his.

What the fuck am I to do with that?

All I know is that when we finally arrive, he helps me out of the limo, still not speaking, allowing me to wallow in my own thoughts and regrets.

I'm aware of a phantom touch on my wrist as he brings my bloody knuckles to his mouth. And then he kisses the bruised and mottled skin there, his lips a mere breath, before releasing my hand and stalking inside.

Vincent Davenport.

An enigma with a beautiful face.

A perfectly wrapped package belying something significantly darker and more dangerous than I could've ever imagined.

But maybe? Maybe that's what attracts me to him, like a moth pulled unwillingly towards a flame.

Maybe I'm beginning to see that the quiet boy who reads and writes and shoots people in the head is just as damaged as me.

14

BLAIR

DAY 7

I don't sleep.

When I close my eyes, my parents' faces bombard me. All I can see is my older brother screaming for me to run. Run, run, run. Because that was all I knew how to do then. Run.

But no more. Never again.

And when I get out of bed the next morning to rapping on my door, I swear I see a shadowy silhouette in the far corner of my room, his face mutilated with twisted scars. He lifts his hand, and I note that he's missing some fingers. His middle finger and pinkie, to be exact. Still, that doesn't stop him from placing his pointer finger to his lips in the universal *shh*.

But when I blink, the mirage of my older brother is gone, and I'm once again in a too-soft bed with too-fluffy pillows and too-warm blankets. Sunlight streaks through the blinds in my bedroom as I patter on bare feet to the door. I don't bother throwing on clothes, knowing that it'll be Valentina on the other side of the door coming to bother me again. Besides, my pajamas are modest enough, considering the fact that they're an oversized T-shirt that reaches my knees and a pair of panties. At least everything's covered, which can't be said for *some* of the pajamas in my room.

Valentina has an entire wardrobe for me focused just on fucking pajamas, but I'd rather be comfortable than stylish. I mean, how many silk clothes can you wear in one sitting? And why the fuck would you wear something so damn tight when you're in the safety of your bed?

I'm still shaking slightly from my dream as I move to the door, though I do my best to quell the trembles coursing through me. The she-wolf's comment...

It stuck with me.

Because it's true, in a sick way. Most of us bitten wolves are victims of brutal attacks that have taken most of our family from us. It's why the mothers and fathers dote on the orphan children in our stead—

because their own children were murdered by the same vicious wolves I'm forced to play housewife with.

Even Johnson's.

Even Gray's.

"What?" I snipe as soon as I pull the door open.

Only it's not Valentina's face staring back at me.

It's Vincent.

He gives me a slow, lazy once-over, his lips set in a taut line. His eyes flicker over my head as he stares at my rumpled bed sheets. He then turns back towards me, eyes guarded and brows quirked.

"What?" I repeat sharply, cocking an eyebrow, easily able to read the expression on his face—one tinged with anger and jealousy that he tries to mask. Understanding dawns when his gaze flickers past me, towards my bed once again. "You thought I was fucking someone in here, didn't you? While I'm 'dating' you?" I say dating as sarcastically as I fucking can, though his eyes do not lose that intense focus they hold.

I imagine I *do* look like I just came from a good and deep dicking. My brown-blonde hair hangs loose around my face, more tangles in the strands than I care to admit. No doubt, violet shadows line both of my eyes, curling downwards like purple crescent moons. Combined with my bare legs and ratty T-shirt that's three times my size…yeah. I can totally see why he'd think I fucked someone last night after I returned home from the fight club.

What I don't understand is why he cares.

"Get dressed," Vincent demands curtly, straightening out the sleeves of his suit. This time, it's not black but gray. A dark gray, with lapels and a white dress shirt. I can't quite decide if the color suits him or not, what with his slicked-back brown hair, tan skin, and cruel black eyes.

His smile is like a knife, and it cuts right through me.

"Make me, Davenport." I fold my arms over my chest, the movement drawing attention to my breasts and raising the shirt so it now caresses my thighs.

I have to hand it to Vincent Davenport. Though he stares at me as if he's in immense pain, as if he needs to pray to a higher power for patience, he doesn't lower his gaze to where I can tell it so desperately wants to go.

"I have a job, and you're coming with me," Vincent states. Yes, *states*. It's not a fucking option. Either I get dressed and go with him…or he'll drag me kicking and screaming in only the clothes I have on.

Fucking prick.

"If you want me to go, Vincent Davenport," I take a step closer until my bare feet are touching the toes of his shiny black loafers, "then you're going to have to carry me."

His eyes are pure fire, burning me in a way I doubt anyone else could. But maybe it's not fire. Maybe it's the type of ice that's so cold, it feels almost blistering on your skin.

"Do." He takes a step closer until one of his loafers is on *top* of my bare feet. He doesn't apply enough pressure to hurt me, but the threat is clear. "Not." His suit coat brushes my chest as he stares down at me, a single wayward strand of brown hair falling in front of his face. "Tempt." His hands rise, touching my hips, before he immediately drops them to his sides. "Me."

My heart's racing, my blood spiked with adrenaline and something akin to arousal. I lick my upper lip, and his attention is automatically drawn to that.

But then I throw my head back in laughter, and like a spell being broken, he steps away from me with fierce, flinty eyes, staring at me like I'm some sort of evil witch.

Huh.

Maybe I *am* a witch. Heaven knows that he looks at me like I'm one. All I need is a black, pointy hat, a wart on my nose, lime-green skin, and to cackle maliciously as I stir a bubbling cauldron and pour children's tears into a potion.

"Fuck you, Davenport," I hiss.

His smile is cold—so cold, my heart freezes in my chest, even as my expression remains impassive. "Never in a million years, bitten wolf slut." He turns on his heel and stalks back down the hall, pausing only when he reaches the staircase. "You coming or not?"

"Not," I reply immediately, instinctively. Because while my curiosity is piqued, every pore within my body is warning me to run. To hide. To escape the wickedly beautiful beast.

"Scared?" He glances over his shoulder to cock a dark brown brow at me. His pink lips twist in a haughty grin, one that makes me want to slap him. In the dick. With a hammer.

He's taunting me, I know he is, yet…

Without giving him a response, I slam my door shut to get changed for the day.

Wherever Vincent Davenport is taking me, I need to be prepared.

He seems unsurprised when I stroll down the stairs thirty minutes later, having purposely taken my time in my room just to piss him off. I wasn't even getting ready. After I threw on a sweatshirt and a new pair of jeans, I sat on the sofa in my bedroom —because that's something rich people have, apparently—and texted Papa Gray.

No new attacks since I began this…

Whatever the fuck this is.

Indentured servitude?

Prostitution?

Wife for hire?

And surprisingly enough, Gray told me that a shipment arrived at the camp a few days ago with over one thousand articles of clothing. Everything from dresses to winter coats to jeans to boots. And makeup. Lots and lots of makeup.

Did Valentina do that? For me?

Why would she do that?

Does Vincent know?

My heart swells, and tears threaten to enter my eyes before I blink them away. Providing for my people…

It's the greatest gift anyone could've given me.

After I finished my conversation with Gray, feeling incredibly lighter than I had felt mere moments before, I simply did a little more research on Vincent Davenport through my trusty friend, social media.

Of course, I researched him and his family one hundred times before, but this time felt different. Maybe because before, I wasn't his slave. I wasn't to potentially be his—gag—wife.

Like I expected, Vincent didn't have a huge social media presence. No Facebook or Instagram or TikTok or anything like that, just websites for his legal companies.

But Valentina…

That girl needs to be taught a lesson on what *not* to post online.

I swear she gives a play-by-play of her everyday routine. From what moisturizer she uses, to what girl her brother's dating—gag again. Since this morning alone, three new Instagram posts have popped up, two new Facebook ones, and four TikTok videos. Honestly, I'm looking forward to the time when social media becomes obsolete. I mean, who has the time to sit at their computer or stare at their phone and *socialize*? I'm shuddering just thinking about it.

As I step down stairs, I find Vincent waiting for me in the parlor, his arms folded over his broad chest. His gaze flickers across my body, a liquid heat appearing in his eyes, turning them molten, and he slowly licks his upper lip. My pulse skitters, my tongue turning to cotton, but before I can comment on the carnal promise splayed across his face, he snaps his fingers, his features hardening.

"Come." Vincent doesn't comment on my tardiness, and I can't decide if that pisses me off or... pisses me off.

It definitely fucking pisses me off, especially since I did it for him. Or maybe I'm more pissed about the fact that I'm panting like a bitch in heat, desperate for him to stare at me with those glazed-over eyes once more.

Asshole.

Bastardo.

Instead of guiding me towards one of the many, many limos waiting in his driveway, he leads me towards a second house I didn't notice when I first arrived.

Though house is too generous of a term for what this is. And it's not like people even fucking sleep in it.

No, the Davenports apparently have an entire fucking mansion dedicated to their cars. Yup. You heard me right. Their. Cars. I count at least five limos, if not more, and a few town cars. In a different section, separated from the modest black vehicles by a garage door, are numerous sports cars. Even motionless, they appear fast. Sleek. Predatory.

Not unlike Vincent himself.

"What the fuck?" I murmur, allowing my hand to caress the hood of a 1967 Shelby Mustang GT500. I almost don't dare to touch it, as if my poverty can somehow tarnish the beauty of the car.

But then I decide, fuck it, and begin touching it like I'm giving it a wash with the palm of my hand.

Vincent watches me with a droll expression, but he doesn't comment on my childish behavior as he moves to a vehicle at the very end of the garage. A Mercedes-AMG Project One.

Holy shit.

It's worth just under three million, give or take.

The silver car glistens in the bright fluorescent lighting of the garage, and Vincent stares at it with pure adoration. A lesser woman might be jealous. Hell, I'm pretty sure he'll fuck the car if given the chance. Maybe put his dick in the fuel tank?

Like a gentleman—I'm puking a lot in my mouth today, aren't I?—Vincent opens the passenger door for me. And like all expensive, fancy cars, the door opens upwards.

I would be impressed if I didn't hate the fucker so much.

But this car?

I can totally see the appeal. I'm half in love with it already, and I haven't even driven it yet.

"Where are we going?" I query as Vincent slides inside the driver's seat.

Instead of answering, the asshole simply twists his gaze my way, his eyes lingering on the seat belt around my waist, before he drives the car out of the driveway.

We don't talk.

Vincent simply taps his long, slender fingers against the weirdly shaped steering wheel as I stare out the window.

We receive a lot of appreciative looks from the humans as we pass by, going easily thirty miles over the speed limit. The wolves who see us take one look in our direction, pale, and then go about their business as if it's any other day.

They know how dangerous Vincent is, and the last thing they want to do is capture his attention.

Like me.

Like the poor, defenseless bitten wolf who has somehow ensnared the three princes.

I don't speak, not even when we pull into a gorgeous, middle-class neighborhood with manicured green grass, carefully planted tulips, and houses that adhere to conformity with their white picket fences and brick walls.

We stop in front of one with its shutters drawn,

but I know it's not the house Vincent wants me to look at.

Instead, his eyes remain glued to the house diagonal from where we're parked. His smile is a slash across his chillingly handsome face, though his eyes are bleak and guarded. He stares pointedly at a man kneeling beside a garden of roses and tulips, a watering can in his hand.

"What are we doing here, Vincent?" I finally find the strength to speak, and I'm pleased when my voice doesn't come out shaky and wobbly.

When he turns towards me, the smile carved into his pretty mouth is weary and grim, the crack in his personality more visible than I've ever seen it before.

Without immediately answering, he leans across me, opens a secret compartment located underneath my seat, and grabs a gun and silencer. My heart hammers wildly inside of my chest as I gape at him, my gaze traveling from the gun in his hand back to his cold, harsh eyes.

"Vincent..." It's a warning, a question, and a prayer all at once.

"That man," Vincent nods towards the figure still watering his plants, utterly oblivious to the monster a few feet away from him, "is going to die today."

"No..." Horror bleeds through my voice, but he doesn't even blink.

When I first met him, I thought he was cruel and callous, but I saw the way he was with his sister. I saw the warmth in his eyes.

Now, I'm wondering if he truly is a psychopath, if he revels in the pain and suffering he inflicts on innocent people.

"Do you trust me?" Vincent questions, still not pulling his gaze away from me. It's unnerving to be the sole focus of his dark eyes, to feel like nothing else in the world exists besides you. Unfortunately, that's not true. Other people *do* exist, including the man he wishes to kill.

"Why are you doing this?" I demand. My anger bubbles to the surface like boiling water. I'm liable to scald, to burn, if Vincent doesn't give me some damn answers. "What did that man do?"

"Do you trust me?" Vincent repeats, his eyes carefully searching mine. For a brief moment, his mask drops, and I see a flicker of hope, of desperation. His eyes beseech me to trust him, to believe in him. It's there and gone in less than a second, but it leaves my head spinning.

I don't have to answer. He can read it in my face, and I watch as the expression in his eyes closes over, just as tightly as the windows of the house we're in front of. His lips cut into a brutal, savage line as he nods his head grimly.

"Okay," he says simply, and I think that's the end of it. I think he's going to drive away.

Instead, Vincent slides out of the car, leaving his door wide open, and stalks down the asphalt like a beautiful, deadly, avenging angel. The man in the front yard of the house, innocently watering his plants, whips his head around in wide-eyed horror. He opens his mouth, and I just know he's going to plead for his life.

But Vincent is ruthless and merciless.

He shoots the man point-blank in the head, lowers the still smoking gun, and walks back towards the vehicle, where I'm shaking and panicking, blinding terror stealing the breath from my lungs. It's not like I'm against death or anything—that would be extremely hypocritical—but I don't just go around killing people for no reason like some goddamn serial killer. Why did Vincent kill that man? Why won't he tell me the reasoning behind his decision? Why does he slide back into the car without a care in the world, dropping the gun into the hidden compartment under my seat, and then drive away like this is nothing more than some weird, daily occurrence? I swear I even see a smile grace his handsome features, though he stifles it when he notices me looking.

We don't speak the rest of the day.

15

TAI

DAY 7

She's not here.

I look everywhere for Blair fucking Windsor in the sleezy club Vincent and I both frequent.

But she never makes an appearance.

My hand clenches around the glass I'm holding as yet another female wolf attempts to capture my attention. They all think they'll be the one to bag me, claim me, tame me.

But I'm a monster through and through.

When the thirteenth female of the night places her manicured hand on my shoulder, I explode, jumping off of the bar stool and stalking into the night.

A cool wind caresses my skin as I fumble in my leather jacket pocket for a pack of cigarettes and a lighter.

I need to...

What, Tai? What do you need to do?

My inner voice is tinged with amusement, if not a little bit of impatience. He's known from the very beginning what we'd need to do in order to regain some semblance of peace.

I need to see her.

I don't care that it's not my fucking month. This entire game is a sham.

Blair Windsor is mine, plain and simple. I knew it from the first moment I saw her, blood coating her naked body as her ire-filled eyes glared up at me.

Mate.

And right now, she's in the arms of my enemy.

Yes, mate, my wolf agrees in my mind, perking his head up. His possessiveness mixes with my own until I'm practically choking on it.

If Vincent Davenport learns the truth about her, about who she is to me, he won't hesitate to kill her in order to destroy me. And her death would definitely have that effect.

I don't even know the girl, and I'm already head over heels for her.

Can she sense it? Can she sense *me*?

Us, my wolf corrects. And though it isn't actually his voice I hear in my mind—more of an innate feeling—I nod anyway.

Us.

I growl sharply, running a hand through my black hair in agitation, as I bring the cigarette to my lips and light it. My momma would beat my fucking ass if she saw me smoking, despite the fact that wolves' bodies can regenerate and heal themselves significantly faster than a normal human's. Then again, she still holds on to that human mentality she was born into.

Frowning, I conjure up an image of Blair's beautiful, heart-shaped face when I saw it last night in the club. The raw, animalistic fury that distorted her pretty features. The hatred brimming in her eyes, remaining suspended there like teardrops. When she looked at me…

It wasn't with recognition. She didn't look at me the way a wolf would look at a mate.

Which means that she doesn't know the truth.

The thought has me throwing the cigarette on the ground and stomping on it, wishing that it was actually Vincent's face I was destroying instead.

If she doesn't know, then that means she won't hesitate to do…stuff with Vincent. She has no obligation to remain true to a mate she doesn't even know fucking exists.

My wolf howls mournfully in my head, pacing with agitation and demanding to be set free to *hunt*.

Red sears my vision as I picture her entangled with the Davenport prick, his name leaving her pouty lips as she throws her head back in pleasure. His hand fisted in her hair as he fucks her into oblivion.

Anger is a tangible entity inside of me, slithering like an angry, venomous snake just waiting for a chance to strike and bite down. I swear my jealousy is going to eat me the fuck alive.

Ours. Claim. Hunt.

I need to see her.

That one thought repeats itself in my head as I stalk towards my bike near the front of the parking lot.

I need to see her, and...

And what?

I can't go all possessive caveman on her perfect ass without invoking the wrath of the other packs. This is a game, one I need to play very slowly and very carefully.

Rabid dogs that bite too quickly are usually the first to be put down.

No, I'll need to bide my time until I can take Blair

for myself. Only then can I show her what it means to be possessed and loved by a totemic wolf.

Ours.

My wolf languidly flicks his tail, one eye open, before he calms down enough to retreat.

Ours.

My cock hardens in my jeans—which will make the ride one hell of a time—but I don't let that stop me as I straddle the bike, zooming in the direction of the Davenport mansion.

Nobody notices me streaking through the night like a dark shadow. A silhouette of vengeance and wrath.

People fear me—fear the cold-blooded prince of the Totemic Tribe with the ancient wolf residing in his body—but they don't know even half of the truth. How far I will go for the people I love, for the people I claim as my own.

A dark smile graces my face as I stop a few blocks away from the Davenport manor, sliding off my bike and then moving it so it's hidden by a row of bushes dotting the edge of a fancy-looking playground. A playground exclusively for rich pricks like the Davenports and their lycan wolves. Once, I took my younger brother and sister here to play on the swings. The swings on our land have become rusted with age, precariously hanging from the pole above.

Sarai—my father—never bothered to update our community or pay for new supplies.

So we arrived at the Davenport playground, and a lycan wolf took one look at us...and laughed in our faces. Called us poor and pathetic. Called us unnatural, since we performed a ritual to become one with our wolves. And then security arrived and forcibly removed us from the park.

I was ten.

The memory has my stomach clenching painfully as the familiar tendrils of white-hot anger unfurl inside of me.

I may be a monster, a beast, but society...

It made me that way.

I truly don't believe anyone is born inherently evil. Even Grim and Sarai were probably normal and innocent at some point in their life. But life has a way of chipping away at you, of destroying what little hope and joy you feel, until you're a husk of your former self, something that the slightest gust of wind can carry away into oblivion.

That's me, a broken, damaged man who's been beaten by life one too many times. No, not just beaten. Life kicked the ever-loving shit out of me, leaving behind a being I don't fully recognize. One who won't hesitate to kill to protect his family. One who's a prisoner to his own father. A puppet with battered and torn strings, dangling from the ceiling and dancing to a tune he can't hear.

Ignoring the direction of my thoughts—since when did I get so macabre and poetic?—I head back towards the sidewalk, attempting to remain inconspicuous. Kinda hard to do when you're well over six feet and stacked with muscle. Still, I know this neighborhood like the back of my hand, having studied it before I even met Blair.

The Davenports always have been and always will be my enemy.

When I reach the Davenports' neighbor's house, I duck into a tiny alcove, holding my breath as I wait for security to pass. They do the same route every ten minutes, patrolling the ground and searching for any wayward strays. Like me.

Only I'm not here to assassinate the Davenport siblings.

When the guards finally turn a corner, I continue creeping farther into the neighbor's yard, past their in-ground pool and towards a fence separating their yard from the Davenports'.

I scale the fence easily, hovering at the top to ensure that they haven't added any extra security or cameras, before jumping down and rolling into a nearby bush. Just in time, because another security guard strolls past, holding a machine gun in his hands.

I wait until he's out of sight, my breath stuttering in my lungs, before I jump gracefully to my feet and inhale the spring air, making note of the various scents assaulting me.

Flowers, Valentina's pungent perfume, Vincent's pine cologne…

And there.

Second floor, fourth window down.

Blair.

Her scent cocoons me in warmth, curling around my body like dark, benevolent shadows. I want to close my eyes and bathe in her scent, to merge myself with her once and for all, the way two mates should be.

Like a thief in the night—or a stalker in the night, as the case may be—I race across the field separating me from my girl. When I reach the mansion, I don't hesitate to scale the wall, using the bricks as foot rests and handles, pulling my bulky body up. It occurs to me that a guard can walk by at any moment and see me, that I could've miscalculated how much time I have between guard rotations. That I could be shot down.

But nothing matters besides seeing with my own two eyes that Blair is okay.

The need is borderline obsessive.

I'm sure a therapist would have a lot to say about me scaling the wall to peek at a girl I haven't even really talked to. Maybe I'm a stalker. Who the fuck knows?

I find that I don't give a single damn about the way society would perceive me if they knew.

Only she matters. Only her perception of me.

My wolf raises his head lazily, opening up one eye and yawning. His ears twitch, and though I can't hear him, I know he's in complete agreement.

The window slides open silently, and I find myself in a fucking sitting room decorated in shades of white and pasty pink. There are two doors to the right of me and one to the left, but I don't need to think about which one I'll open. I sense her, a steady ball of fire and light that takes up residence in my chest.

When I reach the door to her bedroom, I press my ear to the wood and assure myself that her breathing is rhythmic in slumber. And that there's only one fucking heartbeat.

I don't know what I'd do if I found her in bed with another man, let alone a fucking Davenport.

I wouldn't hurt her—not at fucking all—but him? Him, I'd bury.

Kill, my wolf agrees, and I have a vivid image of his canines tearing through the other man's throat.

My heart racing, I tentatively venture inside, approaching her sleeping form the way you might a vicious dog, one that's foaming at the mouth as he desperately tries to escape the chain holding him hostage.

But Blair is no dog, and I have a feeling that no chain is capable of holding her.

She looks peaceful in sleep. Tranquil. The hardness that I usually see on her perfect face is nowhere to be seen. Brown hair highlighted in gold cascades around her pillow as she shifts, her blanket moving to reveal the ratty band T-shirt she wears. At first, I think it's a shirt from another man, but one sniff reassures me that it's her own clothes.

Mate.

The primitive, possessive word plays on repeat in my head, bouncing around my skull like a ping pong ball. The wolf in me wants to pull away the blanket, tug down her panties, and wrap my lips around her clit.

But the man in me knows how fucked up that is, even though we're mates. Even though we're fated to be.

Fuck, this entire thing is fucked up, isn't it? Watching her sleep, like some sort of...stalker.

I suppose I should just embrace it, maybe go to an AA meeting.

Hello, my name is Tai, and I'm a stalker.

I'm being creepy, and I find that I don't give a damn.

But she...

She definitely *will* give a damn if she catches me watching her sleep.

Fortunately, my wolf is wide awake now, his impressive flank battering against my head, and he uses his strength and knowledge and archaic magic to mask our scent. The last thing we need is for her to wake up the next morning and discover our presence.

Because while my wolf and I may be one being, we're two different souls. He's old and ancient, having been sleeping for thousands of years before being thrust into my body.

But we both cry out for this sleeping female.

Need her.

Want her.

Obsess over her.

Ours.

I take one last look at her perfect face, memorizing her features, before I force my gaze away and head back towards the windows.

My feet pause when I hear voices just outside her

bedroom door, my hand stilling where it rests on the windowsill. There's an ancient charm on the walls and door that would prohibit an average wolf like Blair from being able to overhear their conversation while she's in her rooms.

But I've never been a normal wolf.

My ears perk up, straining towards the sound.

"You going to see her?" Valentina. I've had the unfortunate non-pleasure of meeting that shallow viper, and I wouldn't wish her presence upon my worst enemy.

There's no response to her question, but she cackles anyway.

"She's fine, Vin," Valentina continues, apparently speaking to her brother. My lips curl away from my teeth when I think about what she's implying. Was Vincent going to sneak into Blair's room?

What the fuck?

Yes, I understand how hypocritical I'm being.

No, I don't give a damn.

She's *mine*.

The sudden surge of protectiveness and possessiveness I feel isn't foreign, though I can't say I've ever felt it this strongly before.

I suddenly want to bash Vincent's face in, to see him bleed. Honestly, I should've done more to him in the club the other day when we were fighting. I should've fucking ended him, ridding the world of one Davenport sibling once and for all.

I wait, ensuring that neither sibling will enter Blair's bedchamber, and only breathe easier when their footsteps retreat down the hall.

Before either twin can be made aware of my presence, I slip out of the room, closing the window as quietly as I can behind me.

Once on the ledge, I don't bother climbing down. Instead, I jump, landing gracefully and silently on the grass directly below her window.

I don't want to leave my mate, but I don't have a fucking choice.

Not until she finishes this sick game.

Not until she "dates" Vincent Davenport and Mason Bloom.

And then, I'll claim her as mine.

I ARRIVE BACK AT MY MOMMA'S COTTAGE JUST AS THE rising sun paints the sky in shades of fiery orange and a subdued pink. Slipping inside, I'm unsurprised to see my mother at the stove, her hand trembling as she makes pancakes.

"Baby boy!" She turns towards me, allowing me to see the full extent of her injuries. A large bruise rests on her cheek, and there are even more on her arms. I imagine the rest of her body is similarly discolored.

She doesn't bother to hide her bruises as she smiles at me, white teeth gleaming in her tan face.

Anger rises inside of me, as insidious as it always is, but I smother it with the promise of vengeance.

Soon, Tai. Soon.

"Tai!" My younger siblings perk up when they catch sight of me, immediately running forward to wrap their tiny arms around my waist.

"Luna. Dyson. Momma." I kiss all three of them on the head before moving towards the counter and filling my plate with fresh pancakes.

"I really wish you would stop coming here." Momma's lower lip trembles as she attempts to hold herself together. "I really wish you would stop antagonizing him like this. You have an apartment, Tai. Stay there for one week. I don't think I can see you go through it again."

"You know why I'm—"

I don't even get to finish my sentence when the door to the cottage is pushed open and my dad and brothers stumble through. All of them drunk. All of them wearing similarly malicious smiles that are sharper than any blade I'm capable of wielding.

Sarai heads straight towards my mother and spanks her, ignoring the squeak of pain she releases.

Fury burns in my stomach as I slowly get to my feet, moving across the counter until I'm standing directly behind him.

I'm taller than my father, but that doesn't make much of a fucking difference when it's one against five. When it's me against my father and four older brothers.

"Father," I greet curtly, glaring at the despicable man who has driven our tribe into ruin. My grandfather, his father, had been a kind, compassionate man who led our tribe to greatness.

How had his son turned out so...tainted? Wicked?

"Son." Sarai's own gaze is just as calculating, if not more so.

But we both know how today will end.

All of them...against me.

And I'll fight—I always fucking fight—but it won't be enough. We're supposed to fight one on one to become the alpha of the pack, but my father...

He doesn't play by the rules, and the people are too scared to stand up to him.

My wolf growls menacingly inside of me, baring his teeth and preparing for battle.

Destroy.

Kill.

Tilting my chin up imperiously, I say the same thing that I've been saying every day for weeks now, if not months. "I challenge you for pack alpha."

And he laughs as he always does, the husky, dark sound curling around me like smoke.

By noon today, I'll end up right back here, nursing broken bones, with more bruises and scars than I can count. I'll heal in a few hours, head to the club to work out my aggression, and then return home to repeat the process.

One day, I'll win.

One day, I'll defeat my father and brothers.

But until then, I'll do the only thing I can for my mother and younger siblings, for the people of my pack who are too scared to confront the monster leading them.

I'll fight.

And when Blair arrives at our pack, when my brothers try to steal her for themselves, I'll fight then too.

No matter the consequences, no matter the pain.

I'll fight until the air leaves my lungs and my heart beats for its last time.

Maybe now that I know about Blair, now that I've found my fated mate, I'll get lucky.

Fight.

Protect.

My wolf's fur bristles in preparation, his ancient, heavy gaze fixed on my father before traveling to my four grinning brothers.

Sarai's smile is cruel and sharp, a razorblade dripping in blood. "I accept your challenge."

16

BLAIR

DAY 12

It's been five days since that man's murder. Five days since I saw his skull explode and blood splatter the pretty garden he'd been tending to.

Vincent still hasn't told me what he did to deserve such a fate.

And honestly? I haven't bothered to ask.

I truly think a piece of me will cease to draw breath if I discover the man I watched die did nothing but exist. Because isn't that why the other wolves hunt me and my people? Because we simply exist?

As I stared into Vincent's ineffably calm gaze on the way back to the mansion, I couldn't help but wonder…am I living in the house of a monster? This isn't some *Beauty and the Beast* type of story. I'll never fall for someone who encompasses pure and unrelenting maliciousness. But at the same time, Vincent Davenport is a fire that burns so fucking hot, it's nearly impossible not to get burned. At the very least, his mere presence draws all of the oxygen from the room.

I can't quite tell if that's a good or bad thing.

I'm so fucking furious that I don't trust myself not to stab Vincent in the face if I were to see him. Maybe I won't kill him. After all, I'm nothing if not cautious when it comes to my people, but I *can* make him wish for death.

I spent those five days scouring online for any news about the man. I recognize the neighborhood as Springfield, some pompous middle-class section of town that believes they're richer and grander than what they truly are.

But when I type in every possible combination to learn more about the man—surely, news articles would've reported his death and the police have been investigating his murder—I come up with nothing. Not one article. Not one police report.

It's like…

It's like the man never existed. Like he was nothing more than a horrible nightmare that leaves you with crusty eyelids and ragged breaths. When you wake the next morning, the horrible dream slips through your fingers like icy water, leaving you feeling oddly bereft.

I mull this information—or lack thereof—over as I sit on the edge of my bed. Well, the Davenports' bed. I really need to stop thinking of anything in this mansion as belonging to me.

It's there Valentina finds me a few hours later, floating into my room without a care in the world. I quickly school my expression with a monumental amount of effort before she can take note of my distress.

"Get dressed," she instructs breezily, making a beeline towards my closet and sifting through the clothing options. "We're having dinner tonight."

Today, Valentina's hair is twisted into a stylish chignon near the top of her head, a few long strands cascading around her face. Her pouty lips are painted red again, though they're currently pursed in a frown. She wears a black dress that wraps around her neck, pushing up her cleavage, and then stops just above her knees. It sparkles in the dim lighting of my room, almost as if the dress is made up of thousands and thousands of black, glimmering stones.

She looks fucking gorgeous, and I have a feeling

that no matter what I wear, how I do my hair or makeup, I'll look like a Cabbage Patch Kid in comparison.

"This? No." She tosses a bright pink dress aside with a sneer distorting her pretty features. "Maybe this? Ugh no." She throws that one away too, not even bothering to watch it land on the floor. I immediately bend to start picking up the discarded clothes, ignoring the glare she tosses my way. Oh, right. They have *maids* to do this for them.

I said this before, and I'll say it one thousand times again.

Fucking. Rich. People.

Valentina squeals, turning towards me with a beatific smile on her face and holding up a silky dress.

"This. Is. Perfect," she gushes, all but tossing it to me. "Put it on. It'll fit, obviously. I had it custom made for you." She pulls her phone out from inside her bra—the sight actually makes me snort, because hellooo, this girl is the epitome of class and dignity—and moves to perch delicately on my desk chair.

I eye the dress like it'll suddenly grow fangs and bite me, sucking my blood. Huh. Death by vampiric dress. What a way to go.

The strapless, dark magenta dress is flirty and stylish while still maintaining the formality that all the Davenports exude. It has a sweetheart neckline and a crisscross pleated bodice that cinches at the waist. The dress is completed with an asymmetrical skirt, short in the front and longer in the back, and an open back design. To be frank, it's gorgeous, and a part of me wants to caress it like a total creeper.

But instead of doing any of that, I sigh, outwardly displaying a reluctance I don't truly feel.

A trickle of guilt settles in my gut. I shouldn't be enjoying all of these nice things, not when my people are in desolated and dilapidated trailers. They may have been gifted new clothes—something that Valentina claims to have no knowledge of, despite the twinkle in her eye—but they're still living in poverty while I'm hiding away in a mansion fit for a king. Or an ice prince and princess, as the case may be.

Bile rushes up my throat, but I work hard to keep my expression placid.

"And just who will be at this dinner?" I question as I strip out of my T-shirt and jeans and step into the dress. Valentina's right—it fits me perfectly, accentuating my naturally heavy breasts and smooth, pale legs. Once more, I wonder how the fuck she knew my exact measurements before I even arrived at the Davenport mansion.

I'm still convinced that she's, say, some creepy clothing wizard.

"Vincent, of course," she drawls, her words like a garrote, digging into my neck so deeply, I run out of oxygen and blood trickles down my throat. Our eyes meet, and a bolt of ice slashes through me, especially when she smiles. "And my mother. Annabelle Davenport will be attending dinner as well."

AN HOUR LATER, I STEP INTO THE DINING ROOM feeling like...a fucking Disney princess.

If Disney princesses had been forced into marriage and—

Oh wait.

Read the original Grimm fairy tales. Trust me. They're not as "Bibbidi-Bobbidi-Boo" as they appear on screen.

Sleeping Beauty? My home girl was raped and actually woke up to her children kicking inside her womb. True story. And don't even get me started on Cinderella...

Valentina insisted that I needed makeup to go with the dress, so she applied light purple eyeshadow, nude lipstick, and blush. And then, she spent another forty-five minutes curling all of my hair and expertly pinning the upper half away from my face. If there's one thing I learned about Valentina, it's that despite having the money and resources to hire people to do this for her, she prefers to do it herself. At least on other people. If she weren't rich as fuck, I imagine she would've gone to cosmetology school. Her golden eyes gleamed like liquid amber when she finished, a genuine smile erupting on her face before she schooled her expression.

For the first time that I can remember, I feel beautiful. It's an uncomfortable sort of beauty, like I'm wearing a skin that doesn't belong to me. I don't entirely feel like myself as I step into the elegantly decorated dining room.

Vincent is already seated, his profile to me as he stares absently out the window, watching the rain cascade down the panes. It's beautiful, that rain. The rhythmic pounding of it against the glass provides an almost melodic soundtrack to what is probably going to be an awkward as fuck dinner. Lightning slashes across the dark sky, followed by rumbling thunder, but Vincent doesn't peel his eyes away.

"Come, bestie." Valentina sashays forward, pausing only once to tousle Vincent's hair in a way that has his gaze sharpening on her. But then his ebony eyes slide past her, towards me, and pause. I can't be certain, but I swear they widen almost imperceptibly. Heat enters their black depths as he slowly, almost lazily, runs them down my body. I try to ignore the feeling of warmth that blazes through me as I hold my head high and rip my gaze away, effectively breaking the spell he put on me.

And though I can feel his gaze like a physical brand on my skin, I don't look his way as I stalk around the table, choosing the chair at the very end.

"That's Mother's seat—" Valentina begins, but her protest is cut off by a tinkling laugh, one that reminds me of the rain tapping against the window.

"Now, now, children. The guest can choose where she'd like to sit." A woman moves to stand in front of me, and it takes considerable effort to keep my expression placid and indifferent.

She's probably the most striking woman I've ever seen in my life, and that's saying something, considering Valentina resembles a runway model.

Annabelle Davenport has golden hair that hangs down to her shoulders in perfect ringlets, the blonde highlighted by strands of pure white. The effect is striking, and I half wonder if she dyed it at some point. But...nope. No dark roots. Just like with my brown hair and honey-blonde highlights, her locks are all natural.

The silver dress she wears is a surprising combination of modest and scandalizing. It flows around her like liquid starlight, the dress skin tight and stopping just above her ankles. It's the bodice, however, that would cause a person to stare. The neckline swoops downwards in a V-shape directly between her breasts before reconnecting just above her belly button. On anyone else, the style would look slutty, or at the very least, immodest.

But somehow, Annabelle Davenport manages to look like English royalty, her lean, athletic body displaying a grace and elegance I'll only ever dream of replicating.

"Mother." Vincent stands to give her a chaste kiss on the cheek while she beams at her only son. I search that smile for any hint of malice, of deceit, but it's as genuine as her gorgeous blonde hair.

"My boy," she purrs, cupping both of his cheeks between blood-red nails, the shade similar in color to Valentina's lips.

"Mom!" Valentina is a lot less graceful than her brother, practically sprinting around the table to wrap her arms around her. The woman chuckles good-naturedly, patting her daughter's upper back, before pulling away and placing her hands on Valentina's shoulders.

"There's a lot you need to catch me up on," she warns, but not in an unfriendly or threatening way.

More in a...teasing manner. Annabelle's eyes slide purposely towards me, and Valentina blushes.

"I will. Promise. But first, how was France?"

Oh yes. Annabelle Davenport has spent the last few months in Paris on a "business trip." I don't know for sure if that's true or not—my sources were inconclusive—but apparently, she's arrived home early. She wasn't due to return until next month.

"Busy," Annabelle exclaims with a breezy laugh. "But I won't regale you with my boring tales. I'm more curious about..." Her eyes slide to mine, even as she quirks a perfectly manicured blonde brow.

Feeling awkward—and realizing I'm the only one still sitting, in her seat, no less—I rise gracefully to my feet and stroll around the table to shake her hand.

"Blair Windsor." I beam. "Prisoner for the next eighteen days. Potentially Vincent's wife. If I live that long, I mean."

Vincent's eyes darken at my words, and I can't tell what part of that statement pisses him off the most—me calling myself his prisoner in front of his mother, me potentially being his wife, or the inevitably of me dying. Probably a mixture of the first two, if I'm being honest. He couldn't give a shit about what happens to me.

"Oh." Annabelle's perfect lips pop open in

surprise, and she slowly turns her head to stare at Valentina and Vincent. "Maybe you two should explain this to me?"

"It's simple," Valentina begins in a dismissive tone, her eyes begging Annabelle to drop this conversation. "I went to the summit and told them that our family will build an alliance and relationship with the bitten wolves...if Blair married Vincent." I notice that Valentina doesn't mention the incident in the warehouse. You know, the one where we shot at each other and I almost blew them both up.

Just an everyday, casual dinner conversation.

"I see." Annabelle's face clouds over, but she doesn't say anything more than that, waiting for Valentina to continue.

"Of course, I miscalculated how conniving and evil the other wolves are," Valentina states with a wicked sneer, her hands balling into fists. "Sarai and Grim both demanded their own shot of marrying Blair off to their sons. Apparently, if we want her, she must be something special." She rolls her golden eyes, and I can't decide if I should be offended or not.

As long as she doesn't mean a "dropped on your head" type of special...

"I see," Annabelle repeats, casting her eyes

towards Vincent, her expression inscrutable. "And do you agree with what your sister did?"

Vincent simply reaches for his glass of wine on the table, taking a tiny sip as he considers what to say.

"Sometimes you don't get much choice in the matter," he decides on at last.

"Yeah, sometimes Valentina gives you an offer that's literally impossible to refuse. At least on my part," I quip dryly, resisting the urge to steal an entire glass of wine and devour it in one sitting.

Oh god. Are the Davenports turning me into a raging alcoholic? Because I swear I want to get shit-faced ninety-nine percent of the time I'm with them.

Turning towards Vincent, I bare my teeth in a semblance of a grin. "But other people *do* have a choice, and instead of doing the right thing, they choose to take a stranger as a prisoner. Tell me, Vincent, why did you agree to this? What do you even get out of this arrangement?"

Vincent's expression doesn't change, not even a twitch, but his eyes heat. A fire blazes a pathway up my spine, even as my hands curl into fists. I don't know whether or not I want to claw his eyes out...or demand that he keep his gaze on me forever.

"I get you," Vincent answers simply, and the breath leaves me.

Is he joking?

I search his face, trying to find out if he's being sincere, but the fire in his eyes has cooled to warm embers instead of the inferno from before. His lips twitch cockily before he compresses them into a thin line, giving his attention back to his mother.

I swear, Annabelle's face is so pinched, I can't help but wonder if she swallowed a sour lemon when I wasn't looking. Her brilliant green eyes—so unlike her children's—are troubled.

"Regardless of how this came to be," Annabelle pointedly glares at both of her children before turning towards me, "we're happy you're here, Blair. I've been wanting to reach out for months now and work together to foster a better relationship between our two packs."

"Yeah, well…" I plop myself back down onto the chair, my legs unable to keep me upright anymore. I want to snap at her, tell her that it's too little, too late and we don't need her pity, but at the same time, that's not true. We *do* need her help. All of their help.

I just don't know what to do with the sincerity emitting from her eyes. The truth evident in the tentative twist of her lips. She wants to offer me an olive branch of friendship, but I don't know what will happen to me if I accept it. Will she light a match and use the branch as kindling to burn me?

Will she dismiss me and my wolves if I choose not to marry Vincent?

And then there's the issue of her husband, the twins' father.

The stronzo *is dead, and he's still causing problems for me.*

But instead of saying any of that, I simply smile at all three of them. I imagine it's wickedly sharp. Blade-like.

"Shall we eat?"

17

BLAIR

DAY 13

The next morning, I don't hesitate to head downstairs to the dining room for breakfast. If my time here has taught me anything, it's that rich people eat breakfast like champions. French toast, pancakes drowning in syrup, fluffy scrambled eggs, crispy bacon, sausage links, and an entire serving bowl of fresh fruit.

My mouth quite literally waters as I skip into the dining room, surveying the selection of entrees. I settle on French toast with strawberries and whipped cream—a girl can never have too many sweets in the morning—and a portion of scrambled eggs. Setting my plate down, I wait for a waiter—

because that's a thing, apparently—to arrive with a cup of coffee. Black, of course.

Groaning, I sip the nectar of the gods before digging into my feast, my mind replaying the strange dinner from the night before.

Annabelle had been...pleasant. At least, as pleasant as any Davenport could be. We didn't really talk much as staff brought out a five-course meal and we all dug in. The twins asked their mother questions about her trip to Paris, but I didn't learn anything that I didn't already know. Apparently, she was meeting with a contractor for her international shipping company. It's a legitimate business that hides a wickedly malicious underground corporation of money-laundering and drug trafficking. And skins, though my sources claim that they stopped when Mr. Davenport passed away.

I didn't throw in my own input as she regaled her children with tales from her travels, simply ducking my head and digging into my lamb.

And if Valentina was intensely focused on their mother, Vincent was focused on *me*. His obsidian gaze remained on me all throughout the night, even when they took away our plates and brought bowls of ice cream. Don't ask me the flavor. I wouldn't be able to pronounce the name of the chocolatey contraption even if I try. Hell, I'm not even able to *describe* it.

But god, I must've had three food-gasms throughout the meal.

This morning, I eat in relative peace, staring out the same window that captivated Vincent the night before. Only instead of rain, sunlight shines through, illuminating the dark mahogany of the dining room table in shades of gold and pastel.

No one joins me for breakfast.

Not Valentina, who I already know sleeps in until noon most days.

Not Vincent.

Not even Annabelle.

When I finish stuffing my face, a pretty lycan wolf hurries to remove my dishes, casting me furtive glances through her sheet of pale hair. I recognize her from the dinner last night, and I'm pretty sure— if her wide-eyed, reverent glances are any indication —she's in love with Vincent. She stares at him like he holds the sun in one palm and the moon in the other.

He can't even be bothered to remember her name.

Honestly, I don't understand how anyone could fall in love with Vincent Davenport. He's an ass, plain and simple. Sure, he's meticulously-groomed and handsome as hell in his dark suit and with his slicked back hair. And his bronze skin. And his ebony eyes…

Growling sharply at the direction of my thoughts, and causing the poor girl to jump five feet in the air, I stalk out of the dining room.

I don't know where I'm going until my feet land me in front of Vincent's office, the same one I visited him in after Valentina gave me a makeover. I haven't been here since.

I don't bother knocking. Instead, I push the door open, my eyes first dropping to the hearth. A fire burns hotly inside, the flames an incandescent red and a brilliant orange that eat away at the wood. With great effort, I wrench my gaze away and survey the rest of the office—the painting above his chair, the distressed, archaic wooden desk, the bookshelf, and then…

Vincent Davenport.

Like before, he's sitting in the same armchair, but instead of a book, he has a leather journal that he balances on one knee. He taps a pen against his mouth as that dark gaze of his fixes on me.

"Blair." His voice rumbles through me, causing delicious heat to flare between my legs.

But I reprimand my vagina for being a little,

needy bitch and carefully school my features into an expression of indifference.

"Vincent," I reply, matching his stiff, formal tone. Very, very slowly, he closes his journal and places it on a side table where a lamp sits. He doesn't remove his eyes from mine.

"Are we barging into each other's private quarters without knocking now?" He quirks a brow, even as his eyes dance with amusement.

Scowling, I cross my arms over my chest and tap my foot against the soft carpeting. "This isn't your bedroom. It's not like..." I trail off, and I swear his eyes glimmer in the scarce lighting from the flames. Besides that and the orange light from the lamp, the room is dark.

"It's not like what?" He leans forward, placing his elbows on his knees and clasping his hands together. His posh, elegant voice sends goosebumps rippling across my skin. "It's not like I'd be masturbating in the safety of my private office?"

Vincent. Masturbating.

I suddenly have a vivid image of him sitting in this exact chair, his suit coat draped over the arm and his dress shirt sleeves rolled up. His face slackens in pleasure as he strokes his throbbing cock from base to tip, running his finger over the precum beading at the tip. Is he thinking about me? Some other girl?

Fuck!

With great effort, I erase the fantasy like shaking an Etch A Sketch.

Not today, Satan. Not today.

"That would be kinda weird, considering your twin sister barged in on you just a few days earlier," I comment, trying to play off my flustered reaction.

His smile simply broadens, revealing blinding white teeth, and he settles back in the chair, crossing one leg over the other. His posture is relaxed, casual, but there's a sudden tension to his muscles that hadn't been there prior.

"What is this about, Blair Windsor?"

"I want to know about the man you killed," I say at last, infusing my voice with a confidence I don't necessarily feel. When he continues watching me, his hands steepled together, I continue. "The man you shot the brains out of. The man—"

"I know which man you're speaking of." Vincent's lips curve up halfway, even as his eyes turn guarded. "Despite contrary belief, I don't just kill every man I come into contact with."

"Well, I find that hard to believe," I snap. "But come on, Vincent. You need to give me *something*."

There's something so final in death. Something

so…absolute. Even when I was turned into a wolf, I knew it wasn't the end. I knew I would wake up the next morning, my heart still beating and my lungs still taking in air, and I would live to fight another battle. It would be rough, the road littered with explosives and deadly traps, but the rewards reaped would make it worth it. But death? There's no tomorrow. You can't just say, "I'll do it some other day." Everything just *stops*. Your goals. Your future. Your potential. It becomes trapped in a tiny coffin with only memories to keep you alive. But even those memories become obsolete, diminishing over time until you sink into peaceful oblivion.

Vincent… He thought he could play judge, jury, and executioner, and I want to know why.

"There are some people," Vincent begins slowly, finally lowering his gaze to his hands. He clears his throat. "There are some people so depraved and twisted that they don't deserve to live."

I don't respond, simply allowing him to gather his thoughts.

I'm not judging him, mainly because I've killed people too, but that doesn't negate the fact that I want—no, *need* to hear his justification.

"And this man was one of them?" I ask, hazarding a guess, watching his face carefully.

He swallows heavily, one of the first cracks I've

seen in his façade so far, and lifts his head up to spear me with an inscrutable look.

"The man's name was Harry Levi. He was human, as you might have suspected, but he had ties to the Bloody Skulls." Another swallow. Another dip of his head to stare at his clasped hands. Another shaky inhale. "We discovered that he was kidnapping young girls, most of them under the age of ten, and selling them on the black market on behalf of BS. As you probably know, the Bloody Skulls have been looking into taking over the skins market after the death of my...after the death of my father." His shoulders sag, almost as if there's a pressing weight resting on them. I can't help but notice the way he stuttered that last sentence, the way his face turned hard when he spoke of the man who raised him. "Harry Levi trafficked children, Blair. That crime... I couldn't allow him to live. Not after what he did. Not after I learned of the things he did to those poor little girls..."

Torment splays itself across his face when he finally lifts his head. His dark gaze is rife with agony, haunted with ghosts of stories he must've heard.

The man he shot...? He trafficked little girls?

Anger like I never felt before vibrates through me. Claws sprout from my hands before I can stop my instinctive reaction.

A bullet to the head was far too lenient.

I've never tortured a person before, but for him, I feel like I could learn.

But…

"How do I know you're telling the truth?" I hate that I have to ask it, I honestly do, but the bad blood between our two packs can't simply evaporate because of a few sincere words. For all I know, Vincent Davenport is a damn good actor. A skilled liar with a beautiful face and a tongue that drips honey.

He sighs, that wounded expression once more flickering across his features before he masks it with impassiveness. Without a word, he reaches towards a cabinet, thumbs through the files, and pulls out one labeled 'Harry Levi.' He hands it to me and then relaxes in his chair once more.

With heavy trepidation, I take the file and open it to the first page.

And instantly feel sick to my stomach.

Each document is more of the same—doctor and police reports, witness testimonies, photos of Harry and those girls…

I slam the folder shut and all but throw it onto the desk.

"I don't need to see anymore," I murmur. "I believe you."

"I'm not a liar, Blair." At some point while I was reading, Vincent rose and is now standing next to a tiny bar I didn't notice before. He hands me a glass of scotch before moving to reclaim his seat with one of his own.

"You're just a killer." It's not an accusation.

"Sometimes." He shrugs, putting the glass to his mouth and drowning it in one go. "Some may even call me a serial killer. Sometimes, I'm a thief. Other times, I'm a spy. But you would know all about that, wouldn't you?"

I perch on the seat opposite him, staring intently into my dark liquor. It appears almost black in the flickering lights.

After a moment of silence, I dare ask the question that's sitting on the tip of my tongue. Hell, I'm pretty sure it's been sitting there for thirteen days, since I first arrived at the mansion.

"Why haven't you killed me?"

Very tactful, Blair. Very tactful.

But once the words are out, I find that I can't take them back. I don't *want* to. They settle in the air between us like a fly buzzing but never settling.

Because he could. Kill me, that is. Shifter law dictates that my death is his to claim and his alone, especially since Tai passed up his chance to kill me for the death of his wolf. Yet I'm sitting here across from him, playing trophy wife to the handsome, aloof gangster. A part of me wonders if this is a form of psychological torture—luring me into a false sense of safety and security...and then stabbing a knife in my back when I'm not aware.

Vincent smiles, and it's like clouds moving away from the sun on a stormy day, when humidity replaces the rain and the air turns muggy. It's not an entirely uncomfortable sensation, but I still find myself fidgeting, sweat coating my skin in nervous anticipation.

"Haven't you realized it yet, Blair?" He cocks his head to the side, the firelight casting eerie shadows on his dark brown hair, making the strands appear almost black. "Maybe I'm not the monster you always accuse me of being. Maybe I'm not the bad guy. Maybe you've only read chapter one of a story, while I'm on chapter ten."

His eyes seize mine, heat building between us until it feels like an inferno. When I speak next, my voice comes out breathless and husky.

"Is that what you're doing?" I nod towards his journal and pen. "Writing our stories?" When he doesn't immediately respond, still staring at me with that unnerving intensity of his I find both endearing and terrifying, I ask, "And is it a happy ending or a sad one?"

"Now that..." He picks up his journal and pen, balancing the former on his knee and tapping the pen against his lips. It's the same position I found him in when I first arrived at his office. "*That* is an interesting question."

18

MASON

DAY 15

I don't consider it stalking.

On the contrary, actually.

I call it 'getting to know the woman I'll potentially be forced to marry.'

Though I don't like the word 'forced,' either.

Because Blair Windsor? She's the type of girl men would start wars over. Move mountains and all of that romantic, sappy shit. There's something so... hypnotic about her Caribbean stare, one that resembles the freshest of water sources, where the sunlight hits the surface in such a way that the color glistens with white specks.

And...

Fuck.

Once again, I'm waxing poetic.

Fuck. My. Life.

"You're pathetic," Grunt signs, a shit-eating grin on his scarred face. Instead of detracting from his looks, those scars give him an air of ruggedness.

"No," I huff, staring around the dilapidated club. Near the fight ring, a rapidly growing crowd cheers for the sweaty fighters exchanging blows, and across the room, a blonde bartender gives me blatant 'fuck me' eyes. "I'm...curious."

"About this girl?" Grunt quirks an eyebrow as he drops his hands back to his sides, still grinning at me.

"She's my girlfriend, apparently," I retort, moving through the crowd. I won't admit to anyone, let alone my best friend, how desperate I am to catch a glimpse of her. Of the tiny bitten wolf who's stormed into my life like a streak of brilliant, white-gold lightning, her presence louder than even thunder. The girl who even now occupies every spare second of my thoughts.

And I hate it. Fucking loathe it. People like me? We don't settle down. We fuck lots of woman and ride our bikes until they run out of gas. But I haven't been able to even touch one of the club whores since

I first set eyes on Blair Windsor. I don't even want to.

All I want is to wrap my thick arms around her petite, willowy frame. To devour her perfect breasts and slide my cock into her wet heat. To...fuck, I'm gonna regret saying this...hold her. Cuddle and snuggle her. Worship her, the way a goddess like her deserves.

Yes, I'm gagging just thinking about it.

Pussy-whipped already, and I barely even know the girl.

If my father knew the direction of my thoughts, he would beat me black and blue. And then, to prove a point, he would beat Blair the same way. He truly believes that a woman's place is in a man's bed. No strings, no attachments. He has an entire harem of women to please him, and he believes as the VP, I should have one as well.

But the thought of being with any woman other than—

Nope. Not going there.

Not now. Not ever.

Because it's almost as if...

It's almost as if Blair is my fated mate, which is utterly ridiculous. She would've said something if she felt the bond between us, wouldn't she? And mate bonds are most definitely *not* one-sided.

But like, why do my balls shrivel up into raisins when I even look at another female? And I fucking *hate* raisins. Those fuckers are the devil's work.

I clench and unclench my hands, my fingernails digging into the flesh of my palm, as I turn my attention towards the fighting ring and stare with love-struck eyes. I'm not gonna lie—I stare at the ring the same way I stare at a pretty female. The way I stare at tits and pussies.

Because I totally want to fuck the shit out of the ring right now.

Grunt snorts beside me, no doubt seeing my wistful stare, but he understands more than anyone the ever present bloodlust that sears my very soul. It's a constant presence, a wound on my arm that I'm desperate to itch but know I shouldn't. Grunt assures me that I'll never turn out like *him*, like my father, but I'm not so sure. The beast in me, the wolf that isn't quite a wolf, demands to be set loose. Set free. Destroy.

Which is odd, because most wolves don't have a cognizant presence in a person's mind. They're one and the same. Except for totemic wolves, of course, which are spirits of warrior wolves who enter the Native Americans during a special ceremony.

Fenrir are often feared by the other species of

wolves, mainly because we don't actually shift into a four-legged creature. Well, *most* don't.

I never said I was normal, did I?

The majority of our people turn into these... these mindless drones. Unlike Lycan wolves, fur doesn't cover our hands and legs, our arms and torsos. Snouts don't erupt from our decidedly human features. Our ears don't get larger, more pointed, like the Big Bad Wolf attacking poor Little Red Riding Hood...

We look human, but our minds are anything but.

Not-wolves.

What does Blair think about fenrir wolves? Does she fear us, the way I know the other wolves do?

Try as I might, as desperate as I am, images bombard me, completely unbidden. Visions...of the future. Hopes and dreams, to be precise, though I hate those two words with a bloody passion.

I see Blair smiling up at me, her dewy features magnificent in the splash of white moonlight. Her hand in mine as I kiss her passionately, the Bloody Skulls nothing but a distant and horrible memory. A nightmare. Would she be a doctor? A teacher? And what about me? What am I good for?

Maybe a mechanic?

Yes...

She would come to visit me in my shop, her bright blue eyes sparkling with mirth, almost as if she has a secret she doesn't want to share with me. Her brown hair, highlighted by the sun itself, would cascade around her waist in silky strands I yearn to run my hands through. And then she would—

Stop it, Mason! I scold myself. *You don't even know this girl. You can't start fantasizing about a future with a complete stranger, especially when she might not choose you.*

The thought makes me feel hollow and oddly bereft. Not blinded by rage or anything, but just... depleted. Weak. Destroyed. Fucking crushed, as if my insides have been completely demolished by a wrecking ball with the name of Blair Windsor.

But then I smile.

Because even if she falls in love with the other two men, even if she enjoys her time with them, enjoys their company...if my theory is correct, if she truly is my mate, she'll inevitably choose me. The bond will be impossible to ignore.

I'm not saying that a mate bond instantly causes love or even lust, but there's a reason the universe deemed those two souls to be together. We're quite literally the perfect match. Everything about us aligns like two beautifully broken pieces of the same puzzle.

Blair and me? We're endgame, fuck the others.

Mate.

Even I can't deny the sheer rightness of that word.

I'm pulled out of my thoughts by the sight of a familiar man sitting in a shadowy corner of the room. Mike's shaggy blond hair is pushed away from his cold, arrogant face, and he wears the BS cut over his jacket.

What the fuck is my father's sergeant at arms doing?

Don't get me wrong. It's not uncommon to see him, or any members of BS, here.

But why is he talking to Sarai's eldest son, Ash?

Why would my dad's right-hand man, someone he trusts above even me, his own son, be whispering to the Totemic Pack's evil prince?

As I watch, confused, the two men shake hands before Mike slips out of the booth, moving in one direction, while Ash heads the opposite way.

I didn't see anything—nothing that could constitute treason, at the very least—but I can't deny the bitter taste that takes up residence in my mouth, a heady combination of acid and bile.

But while I'm suspicious, especially since Mike is one of the biggest assholes I've ever met, I know better than to confront him or even contact my father about it.

Instead, my eyes follow after him as he exits the club, running a hand through his disheveled blond hair and casting furtive, suspicious as fuck glances in both directions.

"Did you see that?" I ask Grunt, but his attention is elsewhere.

Or more particularly, on the three people who have just now entered the club.

I recognize the Davenport twins immediately. Valentina is, as usual, texting on her phone, her red lips pursed as if she just ate something sour. Vincent has his arm linked with hers, guiding her through the throng of horny, raucous shifters. But his eyes aren't on his sister. No, instead, they're fixed firmly on the woman standing beside him, her eyes oceans of unfathomable depths. The smile currently on her face softens her features, gentling the severe angles of her high cheekbones and the brown slash of her eyebrows.

My heart stutters, skips a beat, and then races with renewed vigor. The connection between us...

I can practically taste it, something so painfully sweet that my teeth ache. The peace and tranquility I feel when I stare at her reminds me of the noise machine I used to play when I was a child in order to fall asleep—the gentle ripple of waves lapping at the craggy rocks of a cliff. Soothing. Beautiful. Enchanting.

Air saws in and out of my mouth with every gasp, each inhale like blistering flames.

Mate.

My fucking god.

I know it as surely as I know my dick is large—not trying to toot my horn, but it's definitely above normal size—and I have a birthmark on my left hip.

This girl, currently smiling at another guy, is my fated mate, gifted to me by the moon goddess herself.

Fuck. Fuck. Fuck.

Does this mean I'm gonna have to romance her? You know, buy chocolates and flowers and all that shit? I'm not really good at that type of stuff. The only time I tried to be romantic was...

Well...

Never. Unless you count the time I put a bow on my dick for one of my old girlfriends when she asked to suck it.

Fuck it. I am gonna woo the shit out of Blair. And then when she finally admits that she's mine, I'm going to fuck her senseless, dig my teeth in her neck, and complete the bond once and for all.

The intensity of my emotions startles even me,

but no one ever said the mate bond made a person rational. It's different for every shifter who experiences it. Some claim that it makes them lose complete control. Others describe it as a calmness that floods their systems.

Me? I'm a combination of the two. Possessive and serene. Desperate and calm.

I turn towards Grunt, ready to comment about her arrival and my plans—especially the ones that involve the two of us fucking—only to see that his face has drained of all color. My best friend looks horrified, his eyes wide in his rugged face as he stares at Blair with the same unnerving intensity I imagine I give her all the damn time.

What the hell?

I bite down on my lip to contain my growl as Grunt continues to stare at her. Just stare. He doesn't make a move to run towards her, but I can see a myriad of emotions flicker across his face. Confusion, hope, despair, anger... They're all there, etched onto his face.

Yeah, I don't like that. Nope. Nada. Not today. He can take his stare and shove it up his ass, thank you very much. That's *my* mate, dammit, and he can go to hell. I say that nicely, of course, because he's still my bestie. We have friendship bracelets and the whole shebang.

His entire body goes rigid, almost as if he's been struck by a lightning bolt, and I watch his hands clench into fists by his sides, something dark settling across his face. Before I can ask him what's wrong, he turns on his heel, growling beneath his breath, and all but runs out of the room.

What. The. Hell?

Grunt is a rather odd man—no surprise, considering his background—but that takes the cake on the whole oddness scale. Yes, it really is a scale. And he's at the top of it currently.

I'm just about to chase after my best friend when someone taps me on the shoulder.

No, not someone.

Her.

I can taste her presence, her scent so damn intoxicating, I practically drool. I want to bury my teeth into her porcelain throat while my cock slides in and out—

"Your staring is creeping me out," she says with a huff, folding her arms over her chest and drawing my attention towards her impressive cleavage. Today, she's wearing a bright pink tank top that molds to her impressive figure and blue skinny jeans. Her hair is loose, cascading around her in natural waves, and her lips have the slightest hint of pink lipstick.

I'm beginning to think my girl has a thing for pink.

Interesting.

I make a mental note of that for later—maybe I'll paint my dick pink?—before remembering she said something to me. Is she flirting?

"I would say I'll stop...but that would be a lie." I flash her a smile, even as she makes another irritated sound in the back of her throat. Fuck, I can't figure her out. I have no idea if she's aware of the bond that's growing more and more prominent the longer I'm in her presence. Does she know the truth? Because if she does then—

"Just...stop, Choir Boy," she retorts. "Or I might have to get a restraining order against you."

I laugh out loud at that, scratching the back of my neck with my fingernails. "That might be kinda hard since we're dating. And isn't it funny? Last time we had a conversation, you accused me of atrocious, despicable things. And now, we're flirting because you sooo want to ride my dick. Funny how the world works, am I right?"

I still feel a sliver of anger when I think about our previous conversation. Our *only* conversation. But I know I can't blame her, not when she doesn't know me. Not when the only experiences she's had with

BS members have been horrible. Not when my father…

Well, he's a sadistic piece of shit, and the things she accused me of doing are better suited to describe him.

She glares, those pretty eyes of hers narrowing slightly. "We're not dating." Her lips purse. "And I'm definitely *not* flirting."

"Aren't we?" I take a step closer to her, wishing almost desperately I could place my hand on her tiny waist. "If we're not, it'll make it kinda awkward when I take you out on dates. And, pretty girl? I don't do platonic relationships."

"T-Take me out on…?" she sputters, her face turning beet-red, and I bite down on my lip to hide my grin.

"I don't know what the Davenport devil has been doing with you, but I have every intention of wooing you. A new date every night for thirty days." I shrug my shoulders, causing her eyes to drop to my chest. "Maybe we'll do even more than date, if you know what I mean…"

She huffs out a laugh, tossing a strand of brown hair behind her shoulder, one of those golden high-lights catching in the dim club lighting. "You think I want to fuck you, Choir Boy?" She takes a step closer, canting her head back to stare up at me.

She's so fucking tiny and petite compared to me that all I want to do is protect her. What a strange thought. Yes, I want to fuck her, but more than that, I want to keep her safe.

God, I'm gonna punch myself in the face when I get home.

"You think I want your hands on my body?" As she speaks, she grabs my wrists and gently places my palms on her tiny waist. Her pink shirt rides up, revealing a sliver of porcelain skin, and my thumbs instinctively rub tiny, soothing circles into the smooth flesh. "You think I want your cock in my wet pussy?" she continues, lowering her gaze to my rapidly hardening erection. "Or your lips on my tits?" She slowly slides down the strap of her tank top, revealing that she's forgone a bra, and I wet my lips in eager anticipation.

Now that I'm paying attention, I can see the visible outline of her nipple through the thin material. The damn temptress wore this with every intention to tease and entice…though I suspect that her intended target of the night hadn't been me.

Jealousy unfurls in my gut like a wilting flower, one that has petals made of decay and green acid. I don't like the thought of her doing this same dance with Vincent fucking Davenport. I don't like that she came here to tease him.

As wolf shifters, we're not opposed to casual nudity. I've seen my fair share of cocks and tits and pussies throughout my life. Even my girlfriends would walk around naked in the clubhouse after a shift and I never gave a shit, even when other men stared hungrily at them. Hell, a few of my girlfriends even fucked other men in front of me and I didn't give a damn.

But when Blair slides her strap down even farther and one of her tits spring free, the dusky-red nipple already beaded, jealousy like I've never felt before pounds in my head, a marching band of drums and cymbals and trumpets.

No one is allowed to stare at her tits but me.

Fucking no one.

I'm such a possessive asshole.

I growl low in my throat, removing my hand from her waist to capture her wrist. My hand grazes the underside of her breast, and she smirks at me, cocking an eyebrow. Challenging me.

"Fix your damn shirt," I snap, sounding completely unlike myself. I fucking love it when girls get nasty in public, even if it's not with me. But Blair? Fuck no. I don't want people looking.

"You sound just like Tai," she murmurs, sounding both amused and curious. That jealousy? Yup, it's a fucking slithering snake pit in my stomach.

When the fuck has Tai told her to put her shirt back on? Why did she have her shirt off in the first place?

I'm gonna murder the asshole. And then spank that pert ass of hers until it's bright red.

But instead of letting her see how much she's affecting me, I school my features and adopt a cocky grin, still keeping my hand on her wrist.

"Are you gonna touch me, Choir Boy?" she taunts.

"I think your boyfriend might get a little mad," I say, matching her cocky tone with one of my own. 'Mad' is an understatement. Vincent, standing at the bar with Valentina, looks positively mindless with rage and jealousy. It's plain for anyone to see that the tiny bitten wolf has wormed her way past his unflappable exterior. There's a dark glint in his normally unruffled gaze, and he casts me a contemptuous, frigid glare.

And he can't even see what I'm doing. What *Blair's* doing, all in an attempt to rile me up.

He doesn't know that right now, the girl he's so obviously obsessed with has her tit hanging out just inches from my hand.

I think he'll quite literally murder me if he discovered the truth.

Call me a masochist or suicidal, but that makes me want to do it even more.

Come to papa.

Wait. Does that make me a daddy? Fuck that. Abort mission. Abort.

Blair grins at me, her bright pink lips that I yearn to suck between my teeth stretching, and I flash her a dark smile of my own, one painted on my lips with shadows and sin.

I crowd my body even closer to hers, ensuring no one in the immediate vicinity can see, and slowly bring my hands up to cup the ample flesh of her tit. Lazily, I run my thumb back and forth over her nipple, enjoying the way her breath hitches and her face flushes.

She hadn't expected me to actually do it.

The thought makes me grin even wider as I pinch her nipple between my thumb and forefinger, tugging enough to make her yelp before releasing it. Her breasts are fucking amazing. Supple and easily a handful. I could play with them all day.

And one day, I will. You mark my words. I'll memorize everything there is to know about her body, starting with her boobs.

"Don't challenge me, pretty girl," I whisper, leaning forward to press my lips against her ear. I continue to knead the tender flesh of her breast as she pants in front of me. "Because you already know I'm down to play."

She finally steps away, forcing me to drop my arm, and flashes me a smirk, her damn tit still hanging out. Most of the wolves don't pay it any mind—again, nudity is common with us—but a few males give her appreciatory once-overs. I all but growl at them, resisting the urge to throw her over my shoulder and spank her tight ass for showing others what belongs only to me.

Woah. Calm yourself, man. You're beginning to sound like a possessive asshole. Gross. Maybe you're the one who needs a spanking.

Ohhh. I could get behind that. Blair, in leather, holding a whip while I—

"You know, Choir Boy," Blair begins slowly, bringing her own finger up to run lazily circles around her already beaded nipple. "I think this little experiment just proved something."

My eyes are drawn to the way she flicks her nipple, the way her breast seems to jiggle when she breathes.

I'm so fucking hard that even the slightest friction against my clothes will cause my cock to explode. I'm, like, nearly one hundred percent sure I begin to dry hump the air. But don't quote me. So what if my hips thrust a little bit, trying to enter a pussy that hasn't been revealed yet?

That's human fucking nature.

Literally. Humans fuck by nature.

She grabs her breasts fully, still staring at me through a fringe of dark eyelashes.

"What?" I growl out as she pinches down, letting out a breathy noise that gets swallowed by the crowd around us. Thank fuck. I might just have to kill everyone in this club if they heard that sweet, decadent noise.

"I want your hands on me, Mason. Your mouth on my nipple. Your cock in my pussy. Fuck, I can see how big you are, how much you'll stretch me. I want your cock in me. Please, Mason. Please."

Holy hairy balls.

My hips begin to jerk even faster, my cock rubbing deliciously against my underwear.

She begins to play with her breast as her other hand travels to her jeans, rubbing herself through the denim. She's so fucking hot, so perfect, and the fact that we're doing this in public only amplifies my arousal. Because while one part of me is so fucking jealous that other men could be staring, another, larger part of me feels a surge of male satisfaction that she belongs to me. Even if she doesn't know it yet.

These men can look—*Vincent* can look—but no one but me can touch.

"Fuck, Mason," she mewls. "I need your big cock."

And I…

I fucking explode.

I come in my pants like I'm a preteen all over again. The orgasm's completely unexpected, and all I can do is ride the wave like a damn surfer, praying no one notices. Cum gets trapped in my tight boxer briefs as my breathing turns ragged, erratic, and my skin burns.

Blair's smile is fucking luminescent, her eyes crinkling.

All at once, she pulls up her strap, covering her tit once more, removes her hand from her crotch, and begins to walk backwards.

"You just came in your pants without me even touching you," Blair singsongs with a saucy wink. "I think we both know who has all the power in this relationship."

What the fuck?

"This was a fucking test?" I ask, borderline incredulous but mostly impressed. Cum sticks to my boxer briefs uncomfortably, but I'm still aroused. I swear my damn, horny dick is already getting hard again. Ugh. What an asshole.

"Maybe." She shrugs her shoulders, that cunning

smile still playing on her perfect lips. "Maybe it's nice to see how much power I'm going to have over you when I'm forced to play girlfriend. And if that stunt was any indication…I think I'm going to have it all. I'll see you in fifteen days, Choir Boy." She wiggles her fingers in a semblance of a wave and then sashays back to where Valentina and Vincent are standing. The former is completely oblivious, still typing away on her phone, while the latter…

He looks as if he wants to kill me.

Actually, if my death wouldn't start a war that he'd be unable to win, he probably would. It's obvious he figured out what was going on, and now he's livid. Jealousy emanates from his gaze, along with something fiercely possessive that has my wolf rising to the surface, a growl thundering from my throat.

He thinks of her as his.

Game on, Vincent Davenport.

Game fucking on.

But for now, I need to go home, take a long, cold shower, and plan thirty different dates capable of wooing a girl who doesn't want to be wooed. And think of ways to protect her from everyone in my MC who seeks to do her harm.

Blair Windsor, you may have won the first round, but this isn't over.

Not until you're on your knees, screaming my name.

Not until my cock is inside of you, my mark on your neck.

Not until you love me.

Not until you're mine.

19

BLAIR

DAY 15

The almost painful beating of my heart in my chest does little to temper the blood flowing straight to my core. I'm sure my face is on fire as I saunter away from Mason, putting an extra sway to my hips.

On the outside, I appear confident. Sultry, even.

But on the inside, I'm a tangled ball of nerves and anxiety.

Why did I just do that?

No answer immediately jumps to the forefront of my mind, and that only heightens my confusion. I'm not the type of female to blatantly...do *that.* Touch myself in public, I mean.

For a brief moment, I wasn't myself. I was sin and

lust personified, wanting this man to bleed for me. To worship me. I felt like some sort of goddess, an ethereal deity with a shrine created in her name. A connection I never experienced before reverberated between us like a live electrical wire.

I still remember the feel of his palm on my bare breast. His finger stroking my nipple. And then the scent of his arousal as my dirty words made him explode in his jeans.

A part of me wanted to see Mason lose control, to know that in some way, I affected him as much as he seems to affect me. At the same time, I barely know the man. I mean, what *do* I know besides the fact that he's a shameless flirt? That he has an angelic face and smooth, cutting features that belie a wicked man?

And in fifteen days, I'm going to be his prisoner.

The realization settles like a bowling ball of lead in my stomach. It balances precariously on my internal organs, the pressure applied just enough to make me nauseous.

Prisoner.

I fucking hate that word.

When I return to Valentina and Vincent, the former is grinning at me over the rim of her martini while the latter stares at his hands. The slashing, unforgiving tilt of his lips might be considered sensual, even inviting, if they weren't currently ravaged by a frown. The stark white dress shirt clings to his muscular arms and lean frame as he stares, just stares, at his hands.

"I'm proud of you," Valentina says with a smirk. "Standing up for yourself like that. Being...sexy."

Vincent's face grows tighter, even more strained, the harsh lines at odds with his dressy attire.

"Well," I slide onto the bar seat next to a still standing Vincent, "sometimes things happen beyond our control."

"And is that what happened?" His voice is a breathy hiss, though he still keeps his expression schooled and unreadable. "Something beyond your control?"

Is he...pissed? Jealous?

But why would he be?

We don't owe each other anything, and he hates me.

I hate him.

I'm screaming those three words into the abyss, but I'm not sure if the universe hears me. And if it does hear me, it sure as fuck doesn't believe me.

Without another word, Vincent pushes himself off the counter and stalks briskly down a hall that leads to the bathrooms and the back door. I don't know where he's going, and that lack of knowledge causes my heart to thump painfully.

What the fuck is wrong with me?

"Don't mind him." Valentina waves a manicured hand after her brother dismissively, her red lips stretching into a grin. "He's just pouting."

I force my gaze away from the hall Vincent disappeared down.

"He'd probably kill you if he heard you say that," I reason as the bartender arrives and asks for my drink order. I decline, swiveling on my stool to face Valentina fully.

"He can try." She glances down at her phone resting on the bar top. "But with one swipe of my finger, I'll have twenty assassins ready to take him out."

My god…

I gape at her, at a loss for words and honestly unsure if she's joking.

"You're terrifying. Has anyone ever told you that?" I ask, and her golden eyes turn hard, the color bleeding until they're almost the same shade as Vincent's.

"I'll do whatever it takes to protect my family," she states in a voice infused with steel. Goosebumps pebble on my arms. "Even if that means I need to protect them from their own idiotic decisions." The last is almost a grumble, and she glares pointedly in the direction Vincent disappeared down.

And then all at once, her expression changes. Where there were once dark, dreary storm clouds, now has a setting sun so brilliant, you need to shield your eyes to see clearly. But also like the sun, it doesn't immediately chase away the cold permeating your system. Instead, it simply blinds you, the harsh glare causing you to pause as you force your eyes to adjust.

What decision does Vincent need protecting from?

And why do I have the distinct feeling that Valentina is somehow alluding to me?

The thought of Valentina warning Vincent away from me for his own protection causes a bitter ball of acid to take up residence in my chest cavity. It suddenly hurts to breathe.

"Don't get mopey on me now," she says with a huff, casting me a side-eyed glare. As if coming to a decision, she throws back the rest of her drink and slides the empty glass down the bar. Standing grace-fully, she runs her hands down her tiny black dress and then takes my hand. "Come. We're going to watch hot men beat the shit out of each other."

"I don't really—"

My protest falls on deaf ears as she drags me towards the edge of the ring where two shifters are engaged in a fierce battle. One is a lycan wolf, his eyes burning hotly with rage, while the other is a totemic, his skin a shade of light brown similar to Tai's.

As I watch, transfixed, the lycan throws punch after punch into the totemic's meaty center, causing the latter wolf to release a roar of frustration. In a move that is so fast I nearly miss it, the totemic lowers his head, ramming it into the lycan's chest, and then tosses the other man over his shoulder.

The crowd goes wild.

"I wouldn't mind being tossed around by him," Valentina murmurs with a conspiratorial wink. I try to smile, but it's feeble at best.

Because I think there's something wrong with me, something I can't put into words.

The man fighting...

He's someone I normally wouldn't hesitate to take home with me. He's a fine example of rugged masculinity, his muscles flexing with each punch he delivers into the other man's face. A formidable opponent in both the ring and probably the bedroom. But...

I don't want him.

At all.

It doesn't make a lick of sense. How can I flirt shamelessly with Mason, lust after Tai, and ogle

Vincent, but not want to fuck anyone else? It's not as if I have feelings for the three men. Hell, I barely even know two of them, and the other is a serial killer I'm beginning to empathize with.

So what's wrong with me? Did something snap inside of my brain, a tenuous string that the slightest provocation is capable of destroying completely?

"I never actually engaged in a physical fight before," Valentina muses. I want to describe her tone as conversational, but it's not. Not really. There's something very pointed about what she's saying and how she's saying it, like she's trying to get a point across.

But what that point is, I can't tell you.

"Oh?" I honestly don't know how to respond to that.

"If this were a movie, I probably wouldn't be the leading character. But I also wouldn't be the comedic relief side character..." she muses, tapping a painted nail to her chin. "I would probably be the shallow viper who dies in the first fifteen minutes."

"That's...perceptive," I state, because honestly, what else can I say?

"You would be the creepy, badass girl who stands in the shadows caressing a knife while whispering in demonic tongues," she continues in a deadpan voice.

I slowly turn to stare at her.

"...the fuck movies are you watching?"

But she's already staring vacantly at a spot on the wall, her face drawn tight.

"When I was a child, I got diagnosed with a rare heart disease," she says, her voice faraway. "The doctors weren't sure if I was going to make it." Shaking her head, she gestures down her body with a wry twist to her lips. "Obviously, I did, but I think Vincent knew how close to death I got. Even when we were both children, he was always extremely protective of me."

Her dark red fingernails, the color of blood, tap against her thighs. "I remember once, when I was maybe ten or eleven, this other boy liked to pick on me. He was bigger than me and a totemic wolf." Her eyes grow despondent. "Mom told me that he had a crush on me, but I didn't believe it. One day, when we were on the playground, he cornered me by the slide. Pushed me. It hurt—I remember that part vividly. My hand caught on a loose nail and..." A sad shake of her head follows that statement. "But then Vincent was there, this avenging angel of darkness, and he beat this guy up. Vincent was only eleven, like me, and this guy was maybe, I don't know, fourteen? Fifteen?

"But Vincent pounded him into the ground and then stood up, glancing over at me with cold eyes...

eyes I wasn't used to seeing on my brother. I hadn't realized until then how twisted my twin had become. How dark. He always had this...this *monster* inside of him, but while my mother and I tried to keep it away, my dad fed it lies." I tense instinctively when Val mentions her dad, but if she notices, she doesn't say anything. "But I also knew that this monster that made up my brother would always protect me and the people he loves, and I vowed right then and there to find the beauty to his beast. Maybe then he'd finally be happy. And that's all I want for my brother, Blair. I just want him to be happy. I just want him to go to sleep without worrying about death and darkness and sin. My brother... He was baptized in blood. I always thought that was a bad thing, but now? I'm not so sure. Maybe he just needs someone in his life who's a perfect dichotomy of light and dark."

She tilts her head to the side curiously, still watching the ring instead of me, just as the totemic wolf is declared victorious. He beats at his bloody, sweaty chest, and Val gives him an appreciatory once-over, licking her lower lip salaciously.

"Why...? Why are you telling me this?" My pain and confusion sour each breath, until even the air tastes like poison.

But this pain and confusion rumbling inside of

me? I have no idea where it's from. No idea what it's for. All I know is that grief is crippling me, squeezing my lungs in an iron vise until breathing is immensely difficult, and that I have the desperate, nearly uncontrollable urge to find Vincent and...

Comfort him?

No, that can't be right.

Valentina finally pulls her gaze away from the ring and spears me with an inscrutable stare.

"I think you know, Blair. Now come. If you're not going to fight, we shall return home."

I FIND VINCENT IN HIS OFFICE.

The first thing I did when I returned to the Davenport mansion was change out of my pink tank top and jeans, replacing the stylish clothes with sweatpants and a T-shirt. Valentina will probably kill me if she sees what I'm wearing, but at the moment, I need comfort over beauty. Familiarity over style.

Vincent is still dressed in his dress shirt, though the sleeves have been rolled up, and black slacks. Like the other two times I saw him, he's sitting on the brown armchair, his journal resting on his knee as he scribbles his pen across the paper.

His body stiffens when I enter, his hand pausing,

but he doesn't demand that I leave. Actually, he doesn't say anything besides stare at me with those dark brown eyes of his. Pitch-black pools that a girl can lose herself in.

I don't know if I came here to apologize or what, so instead of saying anything, I move to his bookshelf, gently running my fingers over the worn spines of his books. It's apparent that these aren't simply here for decoration. Every single one has the telltale sign of wear and tear, the words having become faded over the years and the spines torn in some places.

I select a book at random and slowly move to sit in the armchair opposite him.

His tense posture doesn't relax, not immediately. Only his pitch-black gaze flickers across my face, watching as I open the book and begin to read silently to myself.

Almost incrementally, his body relaxes. First, his shoulders lower from where they were pressed to his ears. Then, he releases a huge gust of air. And finally, he begins to write in his journal again, the silence stretching between us, pulled taut like the string on a bow, surprisingly companionable.

Until he breaks it.

"He creates a blazing pathway up my body, pulling my shirt up with each stroke of his tongue on my abs. I help

him take it completely off, and he pulls himself onto his elbows to stare down at me," he reads as I gape at him like an idiot. At some point, he must've replaced his journal with a Kindle. His black eyes are bright with amusement as he pores over the screen.

"Vincent!" I squeal when I recognize the book. From *my* Kindle. The same Kindle I got from Johnson, Gray, and Martha last year for my birthday. "Where did you get that?"

He continues on as if I never interrupted. I recognize the book as *Charming Devils* by Katie May. A weird author, that one. She's a crazy cat lady through and through. *"'Fuck, you're more beautiful than I imagined,' he whispers as he kisses the top of my breasts, directly at the edge of my lacy white bra.*

"'You imagine this often?' I tease breathlessly." He raises his voice in a high-pitched impersonation of a female as a laugh escapes me, unbidden. Vincent is a lot of things, but he does *not* have a career in narration.

"Stop it," I warn, though my lips curl into a smile before I can stop them. "Once you go reverse harem, you'll never go back. You'll be wanting to join my harem by the end of the day."

He casually flicks his finger across the screen of the Kindle, flipping to the next page. "Make me."

"Make you join my harem? Or make you stop

reading?" I demand, but he simply lifts a brow in challenge.

Before I realize what I'm doing, I'm off my seat and jumping onto his lap, wrestling the Kindle from his grip. He laughs, the husky, genuine noise curling around me, and I freeze, utterly enraptured.

His eyes meet mine. Hold me hostage.

Every breath drags up and down my throat like a dozen razor blades. A sudden pounding begins in my head. My eyes drop to his lips, so plush and firm, and I wonder how they would feel against mine. Would they be as soft as they look?

His own eyes turn molten as the laughter drains from his face. Wordlessly, he hands me my Kindle as I struggle to get my heart rate under control.

"You read weird books," he states, his gaze still locked on my lips. Instinctively, I lick them, and I swear his eyes darken in carnal pleasure.

"Yeah, well…" Swallowing, I slide myself off his lap. Goosebumps pebble on my flesh when his *large*, hard cock brushes against my leg, and he groans, a low, pained noise. My heart races like it's running a marathon as I reclaim my seat opposite him, heat entering both of my cheeks before I can stop my instinctive reaction. "Book boyfriends are better than real ones. And multiple book boyfriends?" I fan myself dramatically, and he graces me with another genuine smile. "Fuck yeah."

"Should I be worried?" he asks in amusement, reclaiming his journal from the table.

I smirk. "If my fictional boyfriends climbed out of the pages and became real?" When he nods, my grin broadens. "I would dump your ass in this forced relationship so fast, you wouldn't know what hit you."

Though from what I felt when I was on your lap, you might just put book boyfriends to shame in at least one *department.*

He chuckles, shaking his head from side to side slowly, before turning his attention back to his journal.

I come to his office the next five nights as well.

20

BLAIR

DAY 20

The Davenports are actually…
Not horrible.

Valentina seems to consider me her own personal Barbie doll, constantly entering my room at all hours of the day to do my hair, makeup, and choose an outfit for me to wear. And while half of the time, she's on that damn phone of hers, ruling the world or whatever it is rich people do, the other half, she's instructing me on what *not* to wear.

Namely, everything she doesn't pick out for me herself.

"Take that sweater off now."

"Those jeans look atrocious."

"What color even is that? Vomit?"

"Those shoes are hideous with that shirt."

Once, after she brushed my hair stylishly back into a bun, I asked her what she always did on her phone. I mean, I understand technology, I honestly do, but this woman is borderline obsessed.

Her bright red lips twisted into a cunning smile, one befitting her nickname of the ice queen, and she replied, "Destroying my enemies."

And I didn't question her again after that.

I've also been teaching her how to fight. Self-defense, mostly, but a few offensive tactics too. Sometimes Vincent will watch us, his eyes on me like two heat-seeking missiles. He'll never comment, never speak out of turn, but his eyes will follow my every movement. Every punch, kick, and tackle. Every bead of sweat dripping down my chin and into my sports bra. Every word that leaves my lips as I instruct Valentina. I don't know if the look in his eyes is awe, respect, or judgment, and I don't have the nerve to ask.

The last few nights, I retreated to Vincent's study and sat in the armchair opposite him, both of us losing ourselves to his collection of books. The silence isn't as awkward as one might think. It's tense, sure, and almost electrified, but I consider it comfortable. And once the clock strikes ten, we'd both place our books back on the shelf and head towards our respective rooms, not one word having been spoken between us.

It's confusing as fuck.

Groaning, I throw a hand over my head and reach for my phone on my bedside table.

It's already ten PM, which is when I'm scheduled to have my daily phone call with Papa.

As always, he picks up on the first ring, his gruff voice having a soothing, calming effect on my tattered soul.

"Blair?"

"No, it's your mom," I quip like the mature adult I am.

Papa snorts, and I hear the sound of papers being shuffled. He must be in his office in the rec center. That man always keeps that place a cluttered mess.

"My momma's been dead for thirty years, child. Nice try," he retorts with a chuckle. That laughter dies off as he becomes serious. "How's the world treating you, kid?"

"The world...or the Davenports?" I inquire, staring up at the ceiling. Unlike the cracked ceiling in my trailer, this one has no water stains. No cracks. Nothing but pale white paint.

"Aren't they one in the same?" Papa asks, his voice laced with grim amusement.

"The Davenports are rich as sin, but I don't

believe they actually rule the world. Well..." I think of Valentina with her handy-dandy phone, the way all of her problems seem to disappear with a flick of her wrist and a few well-placed texts. The way Vincent takes death into his own hands like some sort of sexy, suit-wearing grim reaper. "On second thought, I might have to agree with you."

He chuckles again, and I squeeze my eyelids shut to stop the sudden onslaught of tears. Because fuck, I miss him. A lot. He's a crabby old bastard, but he's *my* crabby old bastard.

"How's everyone doing?" I whisper, my hands tightening around the phone, squeezing to the point of pain.

"Good. Martha misses you like crazy, kid. As do the youngins."

"And you?"

He sighs. "I'm worried sick about you, Blair. So is Johnson. We both feel..." A weary sound drifts down the line. "We both feel responsible for you getting into this shit. If you hadn't—"

"Don't," I interrupt fiercely. "Don't put the blame on yourself. I chose to do this. For you and Martha. For Johnson. For Jacob. For the entire community. I don't regret it for one moment. Have there been any more attacks?"

"None," Papa responds. "Not one new attack on

bitten wolves since you left with that Davenport chick. I don't know what you did...but it seems to be working. They're holding up their end of the bargain. All of the wolf packs. And remember those clothes that were delivered? Well, we received another shipment the other day, this one containing toiletries and blankets. Blair, I think we have a guardian angel."

Not a guardian angel.

Just a Davenport.

This time, tears cascade down my cheek unbidden as I'm bombarded by emotions. It rushes over me like an icy torrent threatening to drown me. I wonder if this is how a sailor feels just before a seductive siren drags him beneath the ocean's surface—wonderment and awe, quickly followed by bone-chilling terror.

"I'm glad. Listen, Papa, I—" A knock on my door has my head snapping up. "I have to go."

"Be careful, girl. You hear me?"

"I hear you. Love you, old man. *Ti amo.*" My voice is almost a whisper.

"Love you too."

I hang up the phone and scrub a hand over my face, ensuring I've collected all of the wayward tears, before exiting my bedroom and heading towards the parlor. Throwing open the door, I'm surprised to see Vincent, of all people, standing at the threshold.

His hands are clasped behind his back as he stares at me with unwavering focus, his eyes darker than a turbulent sea at night.

"Come with me," he instructs, and without waiting for me to respond, he turns on his heel and stalks down the stairs.

My mouth drops open, indignation roaring within me, before I release a muffled curse and hurry after him.

Fortunately, I'm still dressed for the day, having not bothered to change out of the clothing Valentina put me in first thing this morning. She dressed me in a stylish pink blouse and jeans, pulling my hair into a loose French braid. And now I wonder...

Did she know what Vincent had planned?

"Are we going to murder someone else tonight?" I quip, hurrying to keep pace with him. When he doesn't respond, I resist the urge to smack him. "Do I need to put shoes on? I'm kinda bare-feeting this party here."

"Bare-feeting isn't a word," he responds in that succinct manner he has, each word curt and to the point.

"How do you know?" I ask, quickening my pace. "Do you have a dictionary on hand?"

I swear he rolls his eyes, but of course, I could be imagining it. That seems too...normal for a man as distinguished as Vincent Davenport. "I think I would be aware of a word such as bare-feeting in the dictionary."

"Maybe it's a difference in cultures," I continue, enjoying the way his eyes twitch. There's nothing I find more amusing than pissing Vincent off. "Maybe it's like a British word that Americans don't understand or vice versa."

"We're both Americans, Blair," Vincent all but growls, causing my smirk to broaden.

"Like the Merriam-Webster dictionary has the first definition of 'transpire' as 'to occur.' But the Oxford dictionary doesn't have that definition. It's a difference in languages and cultures. Of course, you'd have to be ignorant to believe that your language is better than another's. Like color spelled with a U and also spelled without one. Or 'towards' versus 'toward.' Or bare-feeting, which is totally—"

"Are you done yet?" Vincent whips around to face me, one dark eyebrow raised, but I simply grin up at him.

"If you accept that bare-feeting is a word, then yes, yes I am."

His lips twitch, but he doesn't allow himself to smile. Not fully. Not yet. He's still too tense, his posture too rigid, to allow himself to let loose and drop his frigid walls.

Why do I suddenly, desperately, want to be the one who breaks them down?

Why do I want to be the reason warmth seeps into his eyes and melts the ice currently residing there? Why do I want to be the reason his lips quirk into a genuine smile, just like the one he gifted me in his office when I caught him reading on my Kindle?

"Come with me," Vincent says once more, leading me towards a door I know leads to the backyard.

"You know, I thought you were mad at me," I begin awkwardly as we enter the fenced-in area.

Vincent goes still, only his eyes moving to stare at me. "Because you allowed a BS member to touch you?" I swear his eyes flash yellow as his wolf makes an appearance, his lips pulling away from his teeth. Before I can defend myself, though I'm not sure why I want to, he continues, "It made me realize some things. The most important one being, if I want to win you, I need to step up my game."

"Win me?" I ask with a scoff, tossing my hair back. "I'm not something you can win, Vincent."

"Aren't you?" His voice is quiet, lacking the cutting bite he usually reserves for me. "Someone as sweet and as loyal as you? Someone as beautiful and kind? Someone who will go to the ends of the earth for the people she loves?" He shakes his head, a strand of dark brown hair falling over his brow, and begins to lead me down a pathway created by lit candles. "I realized I can't just rely on our bond. I need to date you like a proper gentleman. Court you."

Our bond?

Date me?

Court me?

Did hell just freeze over?

But I can't deny the way my heartbeat picks up speed or the way my hands shake. Or the nest of hummingbirds that have hatched inside of me and are now flying about, their wings battering against my stomach lining.

And maybe…

Maybe that's all I ever truly wanted. Someone to want me. Someone to fight for me.

Maybe, just maybe, that person is Vincent, with his cold gaze that feels searingly hot and the impassive expression that speaks volumes to my battered soul.

We follow a twisting trail through the forest, pausing when we reach a clearing where the moonlight can't quite reach completely.

The grass here somehow appears even greener, almost fluffy in appearance. A blanket rests directly in the center, covered in numerous pillows and a large picnic basket.

What the...?

Vincent fidgets with his cufflinks, and I can't help but wonder...

Is he nervous?

"I had the staff prepare this for me today," he states curtly, moving to sit on the blanket. His movements are almost robotic, and when he finally sits, his back remains ramrod straight. Does he ever let loose?

"Vincent..." I'm honestly at a loss for words.

"Does it...suffice?" he questions, once more fiddling with his cufflink. He buttons it, unbuttons it, buttons it, unbuttons it. Again and again and again. "I've never done something like this before."

Wordlessly, I drop to my ass across from him, running my fingers through the grass.

"I asked the chef to make us your favorites," Vincent forges on, removing the lid from the picnic basket and pulling out a simple turkey and cheese sandwich, a container of strawberries, baby carrots, and then a gorgeous chocolate cake.

My heart swells, even as indecipherable feelings course through me.

How does he know what my favorite foods are?

Has he been...? Has he been watching me?

Maybe while I thought he was ignoring me, he's been paying more attention than I could've believed.

"I brought a few different drinks for your selection," Vincent continues, almost babbling. His hand shakes slightly as he pulls out a bottle of red wine. "But if you choose to go the nonalcoholic route, I brought a canister of coffee and a bottle of orange juice. If you don't like any of these options, I can call for—"

"Vincent." I lean forward to place my hand over his mouth, and his eyes flicker down to the offending limb, narrowing slightly. "This is perfect." When I'm sure he's not going to ramble anymore, I slowly sit back, making myself comfortable against the pile of pillows. "This is..."

"Hopefully romantic," he says, handing me a plate with a little bit of everything on it.

"Different," I conclude. When hurt flickers across his face, there and gone in less than a second, I hurry to elaborate, "Not a bad different, Vincent. Just... different. I honestly didn't think you even liked me."

He doesn't speak right away. Instead, his gaze holds me captive, a willing prisoner laid bare and bleeding before a dark and angry god. He licks his upper lip, his pink tongue eliciting a fire in my bloodstream, as he considers what I just said with that painstaking patience he's known for. When he speaks, his voice is low and husky and curls around me like smoke. *"And when the sun crests the tree line, and the world turns dark and desolate, my soul cries for my light. My heart. You, my beloved, shine with all the brilliance and ethereality of a falling star, one that I'm desperate to catch. But my hands are slippery from the blood staining them, and you constantly fall through. My fallen star. The fallen angel from the heavens above."* His husky voice curls around me like smoke, rendering me immobile, though he barely spoke above a whisper. Warmth permeates my body, seeping through my skin and taking residence in my very bones.

"Is that...?" I clear my throat. "I mean, did you write that?"

I see him writing in that journal constantly. Every night, actually, when he's not reading a new novel, but I never asked what he was writing.

He doesn't blush, but his hands continue to shake slightly as he brings a strawberry to his perfect, lush lips.

"I find that some thoughts can't be spoken out loud," he declares at last, his tongue licking away the juices that drip down his chin.

"It's beautiful," I confess, my heart crawling its way up my throat until it becomes lodged there. "Is it...?"

How do I ask him whom the poem is about?

"Is it about you?" Vincent finishes, cocking an eyebrow. I squirm beneath his scrutiny. "Tell me, Blair Windsor...would you like it to be?"

Yes. The thought comes to my mind unbidden, but I can't deny the truthfulness of that one word.

More than anything, I want Vincent's romantic poems to be about me.

A sliver of hate embeds itself in my heart, but I ignore it.

He's my captor, right? My enemy?

Why doesn't it feel that way anymore?

I'm beginning to think I haven't felt that way about the Davenport twins in a while. Valentina has become my friend, and Vincent? I've never wanted anyone as much as I want him at that moment. But despite my shifting feelings for both siblings, I can't ignore the sliver of guilt that squeezes my heart in an iron vise. The hate that floods my senses when I think about who his father is and what he has done to my people. My family.

"To be quite honest," Vincent dabs at his lips with a napkin, carefully avoiding my eyes, "everything I write recently is about you."

My breath stutters, as does my heart, as I stare into his proud and arresting face. To some, he might come across as cruel or even cold. Heaven only knows that I used to think so.

But just now...

He appears vulnerable. The way he's carefully avoiding my gaze, his too-acute eyes, his trembling hands...

"You act as if you hate me," I whisper, and his head finally snaps up, his eyes leveling with my own.

"Maybe I do. But maybe it's because you make me hate myself." Those dark eyes of his cripple me. Ruin me. I'm helpless to look away.

And then he's leaning across the picnic basket, grabbing my chin in his strong, capable hand, and kissing me.

It's the kiss to end all kisses. A meeting of souls.

As his lips slash over mine, as fireworks explode behind my eyelids, I know, right then and there, that I'm screwed.

So, so screwed.

Because in twenty days, I've developed a crush on Vincent Davenport.

That's not to say I'm in love with him—I don't know if a woman as jaded and bitter as me is even capable of it—but I do know that a piece of me is irrevocably tied to him, no matter what the rest of this adventure entails.

His kiss is hungry, claiming, possessive. When his tongue tangles with mine, deepening the kiss, I give myself to him fully. I want even more of Vincent. I want…everything.

A contented sigh leaves my lips as I lean into him, tangling my hands in his hair as his own squeeze my arms tight enough to bruise.

To claim.

But all too soon, he pulls away from me, a smile on his face that I've never seen before. Smug, almost. Happy.

He looks fucking ecstatic right now. Even his eyes are glowing with an inner light.

He plants one more tender kiss to the corner of my lips before leaning back, settling against the mound of pillows. He appears almost…comfortable. No longer is he sitting like he has a giant stick lodged up his ass. He even takes his suit coat off and rolls up his sleeves.

Me? I'm struggling to get air back in my lungs, my entire body flooded with desire.

With a brilliant grin on his face, Vincent nods towards my uneaten sandwich.

"Shall we finish our dinner?"

Fuck me.

I'm screwed.

21

VINCENT

DAY 20

There's a perpetual smile that won't leave my face, no matter how much I will it to dissipate.

After finishing our sandwiches in comfortable, companionable silence, I lead Blair back to her room, ending our time together with a kiss on her soft lips.

I can't remember a time in my life when I felt such...giddiness. Is that what this foreign sensation is? It electrifies my veins, causing my heart to thump with renewed vigor. Or maybe...maybe it causes my heart to beat for someone who isn't myself. Maybe my heart has been lying dormant, a piece of black coal in my chest cavity, and it's only now coursing blood through me.

As I move to my own bedchambers, conveniently on the other side of the mezzanine from Blair's room, I run into my sister.

Her dark hair is loose, hanging around her face in perfect curls, but her face is devoid of makeup and she's dressed in a white silk nightgown and robe.

When she catches sight of me, she folds her arms over her chest and glowers.

"Have you told her yet?" she asks curtly, blocking my way into my bedroom. I could easily move her aside, but we both know I'll never lay a hand on her. Not like…

My eyes reluctantly move to the portrait of my father, as large and domineering in paint as he was in life. I've been meaning to get the painting removed, but I haven't had the time. I've been a bit… preoccupied with a beautiful bitten wolf.

"Not now, Val," I say, my tone shrouded in ice. Most men and women would flinch, but not my sister. Not my twin.

She simply raises her chin and narrows her golden eyes, so unlike my own.

"You need to tell her, brother. Soon."

"I didn't know you developed a soft spot for the little wolf." Though my voice is taunting, I can't deny the sliver of happiness that grows in my chest. My sister and the woman I care about...

Valentina's face is devoid of her usual humor and cunningness. "Of course I am. She's kind to me. And she doesn't look at me with fear or like an object that can be used." A hint of self-consciousness ravages her face before she schools her expression. "But you need to tell her. Soon. Before she sees it as a betrayal."

"I don't know what you mean," I all but growl, shouldering past her and placing a hand on my doorknob. All I want to do is crawl beneath my covers and think about the fantastic night I just had.

But of course, Valentina refuses to let the topic go.

"You need to tell her she's your mate," she says to my back, and I just know that if I were to look at her, there would be a fierce glint to her eyes. That her lips would be compressed in a grim line as her foot taps against the smooth marble flooring.

"Valentina..." It's a warning of caution. Because while I love my sister, she doesn't know what the fuck she's talking about.

"Brother." Refusing to be cowed, she storms towards me and grabs my arm, shaking it vigorously. "I'm not going to allow you to destroy the one thing that has ever made you happy."

"What do you know about anything?" I snarl, wrenching myself from her grasp and finally getting my bedroom door open.

My sister's voice is cold, colder than I ever remember hearing it. Icy and deadly and dripping with scorn.

"You forget, brother, that I know you. I know you even better than you know yourself sometimes. And I understand why you're in denial, why you're lying to yourself and your mate."

"Val—"

"Do not interrupt me, Vincent."

I whirl towards her, anger a hammer inside my stomach, pounding my organs. "What do you want to hear? That I'm afraid to tell her because I'm not good enough for her? That my hands, as stained in blood as they are, aren't worthy of touching her? That I've done awful, horrible things...some of them to her people?" My voice rises with each word I say until I'm practically shouting, my teeth bared. The only saving grace is that most of the walls are sound-proof with ancient magic. Blair, in her room, will be unable to hear this heated exchange.

"That was *not* you," Valentina says vehemently, tears causing her eyes to look almost yellow in the bright white lights. "That was our father—"

"It was my hands, Val. I have a mind of my own. I

could've said no. I could've—" The ringing of my phone in my dress pants pocket fortunately ends this wretched conversation. I glare at my sister. "If you'll excuse me…"

"This isn't over," she warns before turning on her heel and stalking down the hall to her own room.

Her words feel like a premonition, one that claws at my skin, flaying me open until I'm weeping blood.

Scrubbing a hand down my face, I take a deep, calming breath before putting the phone to my ear. "Davenport. What do you want?"

LESS THAN FIVE MINUTES LATER, I'M POUNDING ON Blair's door until she opens it.

My heart jumps up my throat when she appears in the doorway, a look of annoyance stamped across her features.

"What?" She's wearing a baggy T-shirt, one that displays some sort of band I've never heard of before, and a pair of men's boxer briefs. Jealousy briefly consumes me, imprisons me like iron chains, before I realize that the only scent on them is hers. That they don't belong to some ex-lover of hers. That knowledge calms my beast.

"Get dressed," I instruct curtly, loving the way her

eyes flare with irritation. I never want her to lose that fire.

"Why?" She glares at me, her pretty pink lips thinning. Lips that only a few minutes earlier, I was pulling between my teeth. Sucking on.

Lust stirs in my groin, but I keep my face an apathetic mask.

"I got word of a weapons shipment arriving in a little under one hour. And, Blair?" I smile, one that I'm sure is cruel and jaded. "This time, you're coming with me."

IT'S A DIFFERENT WAREHOUSE THAN THE ONE I FIRST met Blair in. Unlike the first, there are no shelves lining the walls. Nothing but cement flooring and corrugated, iron walls on either side of us.

Blair, dressed in a pair of tight black jeans and a pink corset, begins to pace. Her hair is pulled back in a sleek ponytail, not a hair out of place.

"What are we doing here, Vincent?" she demands, that same fire I've come to love so much sparking in her blue eyes.

"You'll see," I respond in a silky voice. As if the universe is agreeing with me, the garage to the ware-house opens with an audible screeching noise and a semi truck backs in. I wait with my hands crossed over my chest, Blair stone-still beside me, as the totemic wolf, Dexter, jumps down from the driver's seat. He spreads his arms wide on either side of him, a cocky smile pulling on his too-thin lips.

"Vincent! My man! How are you?"

My cold façade doesn't crack.

"Do you have what I asked for?" I demand, ignoring the growl that bubbles to the surface when Dexter sets his sights on Blair. He gives her a slow, salacious once-over, and she bares her teeth, a fierce growl rumbling up her throat.

"You have a pet," the idiotic wolf remarks. He can't be more than a few years older than me, but while my life experience has made me ruthless and cold, his has made him stupid.

"Careful." This time, I allow him to see a glimpse of my teeth. I can't quite call what my mouth is doing a smile. "A wolf she may be, but a pet she is not."

"Either way, I fucking bite," Blair growls out, too low for him to hear. My lips twitch.

Dexter's face loses its mirth, his eyes hardening. "Whatever. Where's my money?"

"Where's my product?" I counter immediately, and I swear his face turns even redder as anger radiates from his beady black eyes.

Without removing his gaze from mine, Dexter raises his fisted hand into the air. At once, the back of the truck opens, and I see five wolves standing around four crates.

"We had to up our security after what happened last time." Dexter's face twists in disgust as he spits on the ground. "Fucking BS. Can't believe they attacked. Killed Leopold."

"Yes," I say, ignoring the way Blair stiffens beside me. But like me, she's gifted at masking her features, hiding her thoughts behind glacial eyes. I know her brain will be spinning with thousands of questions, mainly why this man thinks BS killed Leopold and the rest of his lackies, but my girl is smart enough not to voice them out loud. "War brings out the worst in people, doesn't it?"

"Bring the crates down, boys," Dexter instructs his crew, and when he turns his back to me briefly, I lean in close to Blair.

"Do you trust me?"

It's the same question I asked what feels like years ago. The same way she couldn't answer. Not truthfully, at least.

But now, her bright blue eyes, oceans that a sailor could drown in, are wide and open. She licks her upper lip, her gaze searching my own, before she nods.

She trusts me.

I don't have time to focus on the emotions surging through me, turning my brain and heart into puddles of goo. No, I have something I need to do first.

Pulling my gun from my jacket pocket, the silencer on, I aim first at Dexter.

The shot is clean and simple. A bullet through the brain that causes him to fall on his face.

At first, silence reigns, but like all silences, it implodes at the slightest provocation. The tiniest bit of pressure that causes it to shatter.

The other men reach for their weapons, but they're too slow. Too clumsy. Too surprised.

They didn't actually believe that Vincent Davenport would bring about their downfall. They think I'm too scared, too weak, too afraid to upset the precarious balance all four packs have lived in for years.

One. Two. Three. Four. Five.

Five more shots, and the rest of the men are dead, their blood pooling on the floor.

Blair, beside me, has gone rigid, her face ashen and eyes wide.

"What...?"

"They were mercenaries. Members of different packs that come together and take on odd jobs," I say, placing my gun back in its holster. "This group in particular provides weapons for the packs."

"I know about that, but I—"

"Don't understand why I killed them?" I finish for her, and she swallows. A tiny bit of color returns to her cheeks, though she still doesn't meet my gaze. Her guileless eyes are fixed on the lifeless bodies littering the ground. I know my girl is intimately familiar with death. She may think she's a ghost, but rumors circulate. Rumors about the beautiful bitten wolf with eyes and ears in almost every major pack. The silent shadow who wields the night like armor, slashing throats with little remorse. The bitten wolf who trades in secrets.

"But the war between our packs and the bitten wolves isn't the only one occurring at this moment," I continue, watching her face carefully. "A few months ago, I received word that the fenrir and totemic wolves were in the early stages of an alliance." When she doesn't outwardly react, I press on. "They want to eliminate my pack and yours. Completely. When you saw us at the warehouse that day, we had gotten word that Leopold planned to betray us. The weapons he delivered were faulty. And he was a bad, bad man, Blair." Anger is a tangible fist in my gut, squeezing until I see stars. "He did awful things to bitten wolves like yourself.

Trafficked women. Even without the knowledge of his betrayal, I would've killed him. Same with Dexter today. They had no intention of letting me walk away with these weapons. They planned to double-cross me—steal my money, kill me, and then sell the guns to the fenrir wolves. Mercenaries always go where the money takes them. They have no loyalty."

Her lips part, a rush of air escaping, before she closes them once more.

"So what you're saying...?"

"I'm saying that there's a war coming, Blair." Tentatively, I lean forward and take both of her hands in mine. Something loosens in my chest when she doesn't automatically pull away. "The fenrir and totemic versus me and you. Us versus them. I'm saying that we need to be ready for anything they might throw at us." I implore her with my eyes to believe me, to see the sincerity in my gaze. "This alliance...it's not just about you and me. If you don't align with the Davenports—" I swallow the bile that wants to rise. "—it means you're against us. And you *don't* want us as your enemy."

22

BLAIR

DAY 25

Five locks.

There are five locks on the door, each one painstakingly installed by Vincent Davenport himself.

I sit on the bed in my room, my knees pressed to my chest with my arms wrapped around them, as outside, low, haunting growls reverberate through the night air.

The full moon sits high in the sky, painting the velvety sky in shades of molten gold and silver.

And for three nights, the people I have come to know in this household have been nothing but mindless, raving beasts. Wolves. Creatures confined to a barn behind their house, where even more padlocks and chains keep them from harming anyone.

Their wolves...

They're not like my people's. Not like the Totemic Tribe or even BS.

And while they have the distinct appearance of a wolf—coarse fur that sprouts across their skin, a huge snout that shows keen, canine teeth, large, powerful bodies with legs that are made for running, jaws that are intended to clamp down around preys' throats, eyes that burn amber in the full moon's glow —they're also different.

Mainly because most of them stand on two feet, their powerful chests on clear display, but somehow wider than an average wolf.

All of them, that is, except for Vincent Davenport.

Through the window, I watched when he underwent the change. The way his back arched as pain splayed itself across his handsome features. The way the fur erupted on his tan skin. The way he shredded the sweatpants and white shirt he wore as his body enlarged.

Before he could finish the shift, he moved towards the barn, where his sister and mother were already chained up, and checked each of the locks. I could've sworn he turned back towards the mansion, towards my window, his now golden eyes shining like he chiseled off two pieces of the moon and stuck them in his eye sockets.

And then he shifted into a pale gray wolf streaked with black and got onto all fours. Instead of looking otherworldly and monstrous, he resembled...well...a normal wolf. A normal shifter.

But how can that be? How can Vincent Davenport, a known lycan wolf, defy the laws of the world?

I heard a rumor once before that the more powerful the shifter is, the more control he has over his emotions and physical attributes. It's what makes certain men and women alphas. I'd laughed it off as hearsay, but now? Now, I'm not so sure.

That was hours ago, though, and I'm currently stuck in my room with nothing but my own mind to keep me company. Vincent and Valentina made sure to stock my fridge—yes, I have my own minifridge and kitchen with foods and drinks, enough to keep me satisfied—and prohibited me from sneaking out of my room.

Not that I would dare.

Lycan wolves are known for their brutality when they're in their shifted forms. They're unable to see reason, listen to pleas, do anything but kill because of their wolf mentality. Tear into flesh. Eat. Destroy. Devour.

And protect their pack and territory.

And me? I'm nothing but an intruder. I'm living in their house, for fuck's sake. And despite them forcing me to live here, their wolves won't see it like that. They'll consider me an enemy, a fiend, something that needs to be destroyed with the same swiftness and brutality Vincent used to kill the men in the warehouse five nights prior.

Goosebumps rise like angry ants on my skin when I think about that night, but not for the reason one would assume. I feel...horny. Fuck, I hate admitting that even to myself, but it's the truth. To see Vincent mercilessly destroy his enemies...

It does something to a girl and her libido.

My mind thinks back to what I learned.

BS and Totemic...

Working together...

I remember my desperation that night when I called Papa, demanding to know he was okay. He was, of course, but I just know we're on borrowed time. If I believe Vincent's story, which I do, then the other two packs are just waiting for a chance to strike. They're sitting in our territory like a grenade missing a pin, and any second now, the entire world is going to combust around me.

What are they waiting for? I think as anger courses

through me, white-hot and eerily resembling the flames from hell itself. *What do they want?*

Horror and trepidation tango inside of me, spinning and spinning and spinning, at the prospect of entering my enemy's territory in five days.

Dating my enemies.

Bile rushes up my throat.

Mason and Tai...

I'll make them pay.

But at least I have a warning, though small, that I could pass along to my family. I told Papa everything I knew, and as expected, he went very silent. Almost too silent.

When he spoke next, his voice was hoarse, rubbing against raw vocal cords. "We'll be ready."

That was it.

An ominous statement that even now causes my heart to frost over in my chest.

What did he mean? Does he know about the impending attacks? Did he suspect that an alliance was forming between the Totemic Tribe and the Bloody Skulls?

And what the fuck am I going to do about this arrangement?

Grim himself made it very clear to me that in five days, I'll be in his territory with Mason. He sent a messenger to both the bitten camp and the Davenport home.

Only the first one made it back alive.

Rubbing a hand down my arm, I sift through possibilities to get us out of this mess. All of us. Even me.

Even the Davenports.

A rapid knock on the door interrupts my musings.

I tense, every muscle in my body locking tight, as I reach for the blade I keep underneath my pillow. On silent feet, I move towards the door, my breath sawing in and out of me.

No one should be here right now.

The human staff has all gone home for the night, the Davenports are in the barn, awaiting morning, and all of the doors have been locked. Wh—

"Blair." Vincent's voice reaches me, as if in a dream. "It's me."

It sounds like him, but there's something...odd about it. Raspy, almost, as if he's speaking through gritted teeth. Growly.

Wolfish.

Cursing, I keep my knife at the ready but open the door partway, my breath whooshing out of me when I set my eyes upon Vincent.

A very naked Vincent.

His eyes flash like amber gemstones, and a low growl rumbles through his chest.

"Vincent? How is this possible? Why aren't you still shifted?" I demand, but he's already pushing through the door, the heat radiating from his body sending sparks of lightning through my body.

"Needed to see you," he growls out, the words nearly indistinguishable around his mouthful of wickedly sharp teeth.

"You're strong," I say softly, hesitating only briefly before shutting the door behind me. A part of me knows better to be alone with a lycan wolf in the midst of a full moon, but...but a larger part of me knows that he'll never hurt me. It's an innate type of knowledge, almost like knowing your name when you're a child. A sense of surety and rightness settle in my chest. "I've never met a lycan wolf who can resist the change."

"Needed to see you," he repeats. Suddenly, his hands are on my shoulders and he's pulling me against his chiseled, bare chest. My eyes are instinctively drawn to the tan, almost golden, planes of his chest, before inching lower. His tapered waist leads to an impressive V, which leads to a—

He runs his nose down the side of my neck and inhales deeply.

"Did you just…?" I blink as a low rumble builds in his chest. "Did you just sniff me?"

"*Mine*," he growls against my skin, hungry and possessive. Wanton and needy. Desperate.

Indignation flares to life inside of me like a ball of fire.

"I'm not yours," I say with a huff, even as my hands land on his broad shoulders, my fingers digging into his perfect, unblemished skin.

Another sharp growl follows my statement.

Someone did *not* like that.

"Why do you have to be so insufferable?" Vincent snaps, pulling away from me and flashing a mouthful full of sharp teeth. His eyes burn hotly, the yellow eating away the dark brown I've grown to love.

"Excuse me? Fuck you." I bare my teeth, my wolf bristling, and I know that my own eyes flash amber as well. A part inside of me, a part that I always considered to be my wolf, pokes her head up, her shrewd, too-acute gaze roving over Vincent hungrily. I can feel her emotions as if they were my own, a primal sort of thought process that takes my breath away.

Claim. Devour.

Mine.

Obviously, I know that my wolf isn't technically

speaking to me. While I have a wolf inside of me, it isn't coherent like a totemic wolf. It's more of a presence, one that sits inside of me like a mosquito on an arm drawing blood. We're one, my wolf and I. One soul. One body. One mind.

And we want Vincent.

"You are excruciatingly—"

I cut him off. "You are the biggest piece of—"

"—arrogant, cocky—"

"—shit that I ever had the displeasure of meeting—"

"—and you drive me absolutely fucking crazy—"

"—and I—" My speech is interrupted by Vincent's mouth on mine, eating my words up. What we're doing can't even be considered a kiss. A kiss was what we did on our date. *This* is an angry, predatory mash of lips, teeth, and tongue. A war where only one of us will emerge victorious, where the battle is long and drawn-out. Where blood runs in rivulets down the streets as people mourn their loved ones.

Liquid fire blows through my veins, and I swear it's burning me alive. I actually have to pull away to make sure I'm not on fire, that my skin hasn't peeled away in charred, flaky ash.

"You're mine!" Vincent growls—no, his *wolf* growls. He grabs my hair roughly and pulls my lips back towards his. But despite the roughness in his touch, there's a tenderness to his movements, and I know that if I want to pull away, he'll let me.

But I don't want to.

A nest of birds takes flight in my stomach as he devours me like he's starving.

I grab his shoulders once more and dig my nails into his flesh. I'm distantly aware that we're walking backwards, towards my bedroom and bed, but I can't focus on that. Not when his teeth are clashing with my own. Not when his tongue tangles with mine. Not when every brutal slash of his lips feels like fire and lightning combined.

A groan tears from his throat, low and predatory, as he spins us so my back is on the bed. He stands above me, naked and so utterly beautiful that I find it hard to look away. Every line of him is pure, masculine perfection. He's not as muscular as Tai or Mason, but the smooth muscles of his chest and arms show that he spends a lot of time in the gym.

"You trying to top me, Davenport?" I ask breathlessly, a wry smile pulling at my lips.

He growls in response, no longer the frigid, icy man I've come to know. No, this version of Vincent…it's pure fire.

Need claws at me as I lower my gaze to his throbbing member, and before I realize what I'm doing, I'm leaning forward to take him in my mouth.

I circle my tongue around the head of his dick, reveling in the way his hips jerk and another growl escapes him before hollowing my cheeks and taking him as far into my mouth as I can. He's big, bigger than any of the other men I've been with, but not impossible.

I bring my hands up to fondle his balls as he fucks my face. I allow him to take control, to dominate me for only a moment before I grab his thighs, stopping his erratic movements, and slide him in and out of my mouth. On the fifth rotation, his dick leaves my mouth completely, hitting my cheek, and I lower my face to lick every side of his cock like a lollipop. His salty, almost musky flavor bombards me, and I groan low in my throat.

All at once, his hands are in my hair, pulling my face away from his dick as he pierces me with a golden-eyed stare.

"Tell me you're mine," he growls out as heat unfurls in my gut, shooting sparks straight to my core.

Breathless, I force a smile on my lips. "Make me."

He lunges towards me, his nails now sharp claws, and tears through my night shirt, baring my breasts to his hungry eyes. His claws accidentally nick my skin, but Vincent immediately lowers himself to his hands and knees, running his tongue across the trail of blood on my belly.

"Vincent..." I groan as he brings his lips to first one nipple and then the other, running his tongue around the beaded nub before pulling it through his too-sharp teeth. I tangle my hands in his dark brown hair, tugging until he's forced to meet my gaze, and then breathe out, "Kiss me."

He does, his cock thrusting against my sleep shorts. My breasts rub against his hard chest as he lifts me up, shifting our bodies so he's now on his back and I'm on top of him.

The position is the ultimate show of trust and respect. It's very, very rare for an alpha like Vincent to give up control to someone.

My heart thaws a little bit at the gesture, a warm feeling I can't quite name blossoming inside of me.

Before I can catch my breath, Vincent grabs my hips with one hand and uses his claws to cut through the boxer briefs I wore to bed. I give him a mock-scowl, but the lust in his eyes quickly has me softening. I lean down to kiss him as his strong, capable hands knead my breasts.

"Condom?" I question, and some of the animalistic desire flees from his eyes.

"I'm clean," he growls out gruffly, more wolf than man.

"Me too." I slide down his chest until his cock is lined up with my throbbing entrance. "And I'm on the pill."

His hand tightens and then loosens around my waist as he stares at me.

"Fuck, Blair. I need you. I need you so badly."

I stare into his proud, arresting face, and something fizzles inside of me. Something I've never experienced before that sends warmth rushing through my bloodstream.

Slowly, I lower myself down onto his thick length, and we both groan.

"You feel so good. So tight, baby," he whispers, digging his sharp talons into my skin. For some reason, that endearment is almost my undoing. To hear a man as impassive and expressionless as Vincent Davenport call me baby causes every nerve ending in my body to light on fire.

So when I ride him, it's not just sex. It's not just carnal lovemaking between two enemies.

It's something softer, something *more*.

His hands move from my waist to my tits, tugging on them as they bounce. I lower myself slightly so he can take one into his mouth, wrapping a strong arm around my back to hold me in place as he nips and sucks and kisses the tender flesh.

"Oh god, Vincent!" I scream as he thrusts his hips

upwards, impaling me even more on his thick cock. He removes my breasts from his mouth, staring up at me with eyes shaded in gold.

"*Mate,*" he growls, the fingers of his free hand moving to my clit and rubbing it.

I don't have time to process the word leaving his lips before he's devouring my tit again, alternating his attention between the two of them. That combined with his cock sliding in and out of me, his fingers rubbing my clit...

And then his mouth leaves my breast, and he bites down on my neck, the slight sting of pain blending seamlessly with the pleasure.

It sends me over the edge.

I scream my release, my pussy clenching around his girth as his hips stutter, slowing down only to renew their speed with vigor. I find myself tumbling through a second orgasm as he ruthlessly claims my body as if it's his and only his. And when he bites down even harder, sparks fly, coloring my vision.

I swear I black out for a second.

And when I come to, my head is nestled on Vincent's bare, sweaty chest and his arms are wrapped tightly around me. His cock is still in my pussy, almost as if he doesn't have any inclination to remove it. Wait.

Why does it feel like his cock has just *expanded*?

Did he just…?

I've only ever heard of knotting happening between mates—when the male's cock enlarges inside of the female's pussy, prohibiting him from removing it for an unforeseen amount of time after an intense session of deep dicking. Intercourse. Sex. Horizontal tango. The bang, bang, choo-choo train. Whatever you want to call it.

Mates.

Bond.

It thrums between us, the heat it emits almost tangible. Real and alive and vibrant.

A mating bond.

Fuck.

23

BLAIR

DAY 25

I bolt upright in bed, placing a hand on Vincent's chest and glaring down at him. I can feel his cock inside of me, the smooth edges brushing against my inner pussy walls and causing a groan to slip from my lips.

But then I remember.

Using every ounce of willpower I possess, I force the lust away, ignoring how good his cock feels stuck inside of me.

Unlike the horror coursing through me, distorting my vision and no doubt twisting my features, he looks calm and content. A lazy half-smile dances on his luscious lips, lips that mere seconds ago, I kissed to within an inch of their life.

"You knew." It's an accusation, a warning, a threat, a prayer...

It's everything. Those two words are stamped inside of my mind, playing on repeat while the world around me dims.

I focus on the slashing tilt of his lips as they twist into an unforgiving slant. His expression closes over, once more resembling the apathetic Vincent I first met. His golden eyes harden, black eating away at the color, until they're nothing but obsidian chips.

His silence is answer enough.

"My god..." Anger and hurt fight for supremacy.

Vincent...

My fated mate.

No.

No.

No.

Horror embeds itself in my very soul like a wooden splinter, one you can't dig out no matter how many times you try. All you can do is wait until your body expels it naturally.

"No," I say out loud, and for a brief, brief moment, his mask falters. Pain slashes across his face before he can conceal it.

I did that. I caused that pain.

Mate.

Vincent's my mate.

"I've never done this before," he confesses, and I can tell he has completely wrangled control back from his wolf. His voice is silky smooth, just as I always remembered it being. Icy and detached, as if he's discussing the weather instead of something as life-altering as fated fucking mates.

It's actually kinda admirable, considering the fact his cock is still inside of my pussy.

How long will this knotting thing last?

Fuck! My body desperately wants to move my hips, to ride him, but I force myself to remain still and glare down at him, despite the pressure growing uncomfortable.

"Have a mate? Or have your dick grow inside of a female?" I'm semi-hysterical, but I honestly don't know how I'm supposed to feel. For so long, I saw Vincent Davenport as my enemy. And admittedly, a part of me was terrified of him and all he represented.

How can we go from being enemies to...this?

Mate.

The rightness of that one word churns the contents of my stomach.

"Romance," Vincent responds, still in that monotone, inexpressive voice. His face is pained as his hands move to my waist. Before he can touch my skin, he drops them back to his side, his hips jerking once in desperation. I bite my lip to contain my groan. "I've never wooed anyone. Never dated. Never wanted to." He frowns, the miniscule tick of his lips barely noticeable. "Until you came along."

"How long have you known?" I whisper, my heart thundering.

"Since the warehouse." His hand moves to cover my own on his chest, but I jerk away from him as if I've been electrocuted. Another glimmer of pain flashes in his eyes as he sighs, the sound heavy with self-deprecation. "It's one of the reasons why I didn't turn you in. The other being that we planned to destroy the weapons anyway."

Pieces begin to fall into place.

Somehow, Valentina learned the truth. Either Vincent told her or she used that wickedly smart brain of hers to put two and two together. She traveled to the summit to steal me for her brother, a man who she loves and cares for above all else. In her mind, I was the only thing that would make him happy.

So she took me.

She just didn't plan on the other monsters placing a claim on me as well.

"You hate me," Vincent says softly, his expression cold. But his eyes...

His eyes tell a different story.

A story of pain and loneliness and heartache. A yearning that steals the air from my lungs until I'm gasping like a dying fish.

"I don't hate you," I reply immediately. "But you lied to me."

"I didn't know that having sex would strengthen the mating bond," Vincent confesses, scrubbing a hand down his face. It almost seems as if he's trying to get his emotions under control, as if he's trying to force all of them back inside a steel prison with padlocks and chains and ropes. "And honestly, I thought you knew—"

"I didn't," I interrupt, the bite in my tone startling even me. "I had no idea about the mate bond."

A growl escapes him before he can contain it. "That explains why you flirted with Mason." The words are spoken more to himself than to me, but at the mention of the flirty VP, my heart shatters. Because if Vincent is my mate, then why do I still have such strong lust towards the other man?

What the fuck is wrong with me?

"I never had to try for anything in my life," Vincent admits. "Everything was always handed to me. If I wanted it, I got it. But now...with you...I've never wanted anything so much in my life." He pauses, a muscle in his jaw ticking, before continuing. "And I've never been so afraid that I'll lose the one thing I want."

Damn traitorous tears burn my corneas as I stare down at him.

I think both of our wolves know that this is *not* the time to be knotted together. I can feel his cock contracting inside of me, and when I move my body, it slips out of me, something that leaves me empty and despondent.

"Did I ever tell you how I turned into a wolf? About the night I was bitten?" I ask, my voice breaking. Phantom memories wrap around my throat like barbed wire as I brutalize my lower lip with my teeth. Vincent waits, his expression still cold and empty while his eyes turn wary. Cautious. Afraid. "I was a little kid. We'd just returned home from seeing a movie in the theater." At this, I smile, remembering the way Brett shoveled popcorn into his mouth while Percy tried to steal a handful. The way Mom and Dad snapped at both of them to be quiet and enjoy the movie. I don't even remember which one we watched. "When we got home, there were men waiting for us. Bad men."

Vincent's body has gone rigid, something dark and malevolent entering his gaze like black tar.

"Apparently, my dad made a bad business investment. Lost money he needed in order to pay back a loan." A single tear slides down my cheek. Just one. That single tear represents the grief wreaking havoc on my insides, the memory of my family that will never be forgotten. "These men slaughtered my entire family." My voice breaks as delicate tremors shake my entire body. "Saved my dad and me for last. They wanted to torture him. Taunt him. So... they turned me. Told him that I'd be their new plaything."

A low, threatening growls rises up Vincent's throat as his eyes turn yellow, his wolf peeking through. I can tell he wants to comfort me, demand to know who the men were that attacked me, but he physically restrains himself, digging his nails into his palms.

"My older brother, Brett, was still alive, but just barely. He distracted them long enough for me to get away, but by then, I was already bitten." I run a hand self-consciously across my neck. The wound has long since healed, but I swear I can almost feel the spot his canines ripped into my skin.

"I didn't know where to go, what to do. I didn't dare go to the police station because one of the men wore a uniform." I stare into the distance, haunted by my ghosts. My demons. Haunted by the scars that riddle my skin, not all of them visible. "I learned later that the police ruled my family's death as a home invasion. A fucking home invasion." I snort at the absurdity. A home invasion didn't usually look like a torture chamber, with blood dripping from the walls and staining the carpeting a dark burgundy.

My mom's naked, broken body.

My little brother's sightless eyes.

I squeeze my own shut, willing the memories to return to the box I usually keep them in. The mental one lathered in poison and riddled with explosions.

"Blair, I'm so fucking sorry." His voice is a croak, but I don't comment on it. Neither does he.

"And do you want to know who was leading the attack? Who leaned against the wall and laughed when they murdered my baby brother? Who spread my mother's legs and did unspeakable things?" I finally open my eyes and rest my gaze on him, watching as his face drains of all color. He looks like a ghost, and I wonder if he's haunted by his own past just as I am mine.

"No…" Horror engulfs that one word, wrapping it in a spindly, shadowy hug. I can see he already knows, and though his mind is fighting against the ramifications, horror has stamped itself across his face. "My father…?"

"Was a monster," I say hoarsely.

A fierce light enters his eyes as he grabs my wrist, pulling me back down onto his chest. He immediately wraps his arms around me, and I let him. Maybe I need the security and comfort he—and the mate bond—offer. Or maybe I'm just weak.

"I'll fix this, Blair. I'll fix everything," he vows against my hair, his entire body trembling.

"You can't bring back the dead, Vincent," I tell him. I'm suddenly tired. So very, very tired. Even my bones ache as I tilt my head back enough to stare at him, stare into his wide, glazed-over eyes. "I don't blame you for what your father did. I never did."

"My father was always a cruel, evil man," Vincent says venomously, his teeth clenched together. "But I felt stuck. Trapped. If I didn't help him, he hurt Val, and I couldn't—"

Pain is an icy torrent threatening to drown me. I blink the moisture out of my eyes as I place my hand on his chest, stopping him mid-rant.

"I understand. You'll do anything for your family, as would I. And the bitten wolves? They're my family."

"I'll protect them." Vincent's voice is a harsh growl. "We can come up with a plan—"

"I need to go to the other two packs," I interrupt. "I need to finish what I started. For my family."

The harsh, elegant lines of his face go still. His lips curl downwards, even as his eyes remain wide open, unblinking.

Each inhale feels like fire scratching at my throat. He directs a frigid, contemptuous stare my way.

"What?"

"In five days, I'm going with Mason," I whisper, my heart stuttering in my chest. "If I don't, they'll hurt my family, Vin."

"I'll protect them!" The words are a roar. With his wolf so close to the surface, I know we shouldn't be having this conversation. At least not right now. But I need to get the words out before I never can, before he consumes me so entirely that I forget about everything that matters. "Do you not trust me?"

"It's not you I don't trust." I shiver, though the coldness I feel has nothing to do with the temperature and everything to do with the icy male still beneath me.

"You're my mate," he hisses out, his voice catching. And then I realize...

It's not just anger riding him. It's fear too. So while I want to snap at him that I never asked to be his mate, to be anyone's mate, I bite my tongue. Instead, I whisper, "I need to do this. I don't have a *choice*. Who do you think will be the first people killed if I don't follow through on the agreement I made with all of the packs on behalf of the bitten wolves? Are you prepared to go to war right now? Right this damn second? We both know you're not, and I'm not putting my people at risk. I don't *care* that it's a trap. I don't *care* that the other packs will more than likely betray me. Until we have a plan to protect my people, I'll do what I need to do and *pray* that the other pack leaders keep their promises." A growl rips from his chest, but I continue on before he can interrupt, my eyes beseeching him to trust me. "And hell, maybe I can spy on them while I'm there. If they're truly planning on betraying us, if we're truly going to war, we could always use an inside man."

"No." He shakes his head vehemently. "No!"

"Vincent—"

He jumps from the bed, his teeth elongated and his claws extended.

"No!" he growls, spearing me with a look.

I sit up in bed, pulling the blankets up to my chin. I want to be livid with him at his sudden overprotectiveness, furious that he kept the mate bond a secret from me, upset that he's related to the man who killed my entire family.

But instead of any of those emotions, I just feel tired. So incredibly tired.

I've found my fated mate, the man I'm meant to spend the rest of my life with, and I can't even enjoy it. I refuse to allow the tiniest bit of ecstasy to slip through my defenses.

Because the road I'm on is immensely dangerous. One wrong step will lead to my death and the death of my pack.

So I harden myself, school my features, and remind myself that Vincent will be better off without me. That I can't love him the way he needs me to.

"I'm going," I respond with a defiant tilt to my chin. "And you can't stop me."

24

BLAIR

DAY 30

I haven't seen Vin since the explosive bombshell, when my entire life crumbled around me in thousands of pieces.

Vincent's my mate.

His father killed my family.

And I'm leaving to enter the wolf's den.

In only a few minutes, Mason will pick me up for his thirty days. During that time, I won't be able to visit Vincent, won't be able to talk to him except for fleeting moments when we see each other at the bar, won't be able to kiss him—

I shove those thoughts aside and lean against the new suitcase Valentina gifted me. The girl herself stands on the other side of me, her red lips pursed as she taps away on her phone.

"I'll fix this, Blair," she tells me without looking up. "I swear."

"There's nothing to fix, Val." I try to smile at her, try to reassure her that I'll be all right, but it wobbles, turning into a grimace. "I need to do this."

"I know." She finally puts her phone inside her clutch and stares at me, her golden eyes uncharacteristically solemn. "I contacted one of my men on the inside. He'll look after you while you're there."

My throat closes with emotion as I do something I've never done before in my life—willingly initiate a hug. She tenses in my arms, seemingly just as surprised as I am by the contact, before her arms come around my waist and hold on for dear life. When we finally part, she sniffles, attempting to keep her features blank as she gently wipes under her eyes and then smooths down her skirts.

"You'll be fine, Blair. Just fine."

I wonder if she's trying to convince me or herself.

I glance towards the towering, monstrous mansion behind me, pain spearing my chest when I don't catch sight of Vincent. I thought for sure he would at least say goodbye to me. I know he was angry from our fight, but—

No, Blair. You know that a relationship between the two of you can't happen. Not until you know for sure that your people are safe. Not until you have a plan to protect them.

But that doesn't stop the incandescent pain reverberating through me.

Valentina, following the direction of my eyes, purses her lips once more.

"He'll be here," she tells me, removing her phone from her clutch a second time. Probably to send a scathing message to her brother.

The guards surrounding us suddenly stiffen as the roar of a motorcycle reaches us.

My pulse hammers, lungs shriveling, as Mason parks the bike directly in front of me. He removes his dark helmet, shaking out his shaggy, shoulder-length blond hair as his verdant green eyes land on me. He flashes me a wicked smile, one that makes me think of long nights tangled between the sheets. Of sinful words leaving even more sinful lips.

"M'lady," he purrs, winking. "Your chariot awaits."

Valentina scoffs beside me, eyeing Mason with visible distaste.

But Mason doesn't pay the beauty any mind. His entire attention is fixed on me and only me.

"You can leave your suitcases here," Mason

instructs, holding out his helmet for me to take. "We have someone picking them up for us."

"Oh." Feeling hesitant, I take the helmet and stare into the pitch-black visor. Unbidden, my eyes drift back to the mansion, and hurt explodes in my chest.

He's not going to say goodbye to me.

Trying to shove my pain away, I move towards Mason and study him in the waning sunlight. His easygoing grin. His perfect, chiseled features that give him an angelic appearance. The sunlight glinting off his golden-blond hair. He's so beautiful that my heart literally hurts.

And then I feel guilty for finding him beautiful when I'm apparently mated to a man I once despised.

And *then* I feel conflicted about feeling guilty when I know that a relationship between me and Vincent can never happen. Not when my people's lives are so irrevocably tied to the other two packs.

"Have you ever ridden before?" Mason's smoky voice recaptures my attention, pulling me away from my morose thoughts. "Do you like riding, baby girl?" he teases. "Is that something you enjoy?"

His dirty words have a delicate flush spreading through my body, even as I keep my expression aloof.

Valentina, still standing beside us, growls in irritation.

"Wouldn't you like to know, Choir Boy?" I taunt, reforging the walls around myself and my heart.

Steel. Solid steel.

No one can penetrate them.

No one—

The walls instantly shatter, crumbling into nothing but fine particles of dust, when a loud voice screams, "Blair!"

I spin on my heel, heart hammering, just as Vincent catapults himself over the fence separating his house from his neighbor's. He's missing his suit jacket today, and the first three buttons of his dress shirt are undone, revealing gorgeous bronze skin. His hair is wild, sticking up in all directions, as his eyes dart my way, burning white-hot.

There's no mistaking the possessiveness emanating from his eyes, a banked fire burning hotly just beneath the surface.

Before I can catch my breath, not that I even wanted to, he has his arms wrapped around my waist and is kissing me passionately. Every brush of his lips against mine, every growl against my mouth, is another way for him to claim me. To devour me.

When he finally pulls away, we're both breathing hard, and I'm sure my lips are as swollen as his.

"I'll fix this, Blair," he promises, repeating what he said five days ago after our intense lovemaking session. "I'll fix everything. Everything my father did to you. Everything we've done to bitten wolves—" He cuts off with a self-deprecating scowl. "I'll fix this." He presses something in my hand, something I doubt anyone sees, and I carefully move my hand until the object is in my pocket, out of sight and out of my mind. It feels like...a phone. A way to stay in contact with him if the BS members steal my other one.

"I'm sorry," I whisper sincerely. And I am. I'm sorry I have to leave him after we just found each other. I'm sorry I have to do this on my own.

I'm sorry I fell in love with him.

He must see it all on my face because he releases a mournful whine, one I feel all the way down to my toes.

"If you're done..." Mason's voice is icier than I ever remember hearing it. When I turn back towards him, jealousy burns in his gaze, along with anger. And something else.

Something almost...smug?

I don't have time to untangle the cocktail of emotions on his face. Not now. Maybe not ever.

"I'll fix this, Blair!" Vincent calls to me, his voice shaking, as I move towards the bike and straddle it.

At Mason's urging, I slide the helmet over my head. "I promise."

"Hang on to me, sweetheart," Mason says, capturing my hands and placing them around his waist so they're touching his hard, impressive abs. "And don't let go."

Mason throws the kickstand up, and suddenly, we're tearing down the driveway, the trees rushing past us.

Traveling towards a world so unlike my own. A world where bitten wolves and humans are seen as lesser. Where we're kept as slaves and pets and workers.

Behind me, a mournful howl permeates the night air.

I don't know if I'll survive this, but one thing is certain...

I refuse to be torn to bits.

WANT TO KNOW WHAT HAPPENS NEXT?
Pre-order Ripped to Shreds here!

KINGDOM OF WOLVES: A WORLD WHERE ALPHAS RULE.

Enter the Kingdom of Wolves, a shared universe created by a set of fantastic authors that feature psychotic and possessive wolf alphas, intoxicating relationships, fated mates, and strong, badass heroines. Kingdom of Wolves will keep you up all night, addicted for more.

Make sure to leave your manners a the door. These wolves don't play nice when it comes to the women they want.

The series are all set in the same world and can be read in any order. Some books are standalones and some are the start of a series.

This shared world will bring you books by the following authors:

- **Wild Moon** by C.R. Jane & Mila Young

- **Lost** by M. Sinclair
- **Torn to Bits** by Katie May
- **Crossed Fates** by Lexi C. Foss & Elle Christensen
- **Shift of Morals** by K Webster
- **Rabid** by Ivy Asher & Raven Kennedy
- **Alpha's Claim** by Amelia Hutchins
- **A Lycan's Rage** by Theresa Hissong
- **Lunacy** by Lanie Olson

ACKNOWLEDGMENTS

First, I would like to say thank you to all of the authors in the Kingdom of Wolves shared world. I'm incredibly grateful and humbled to be able to work with all of you.

As always, I would like to thank my amazing alphas - Ash, Ellen, and Kelly. Thank you for reading my book and providing such incredible feedback. This book wouldn't be where it is today without your help and support.

A huge thank you to Ann! Honestly, I don't know where I would be without your support. Thank you for listening to my mental breakdowns when it came to this book. And thank you for taking the time to read it and offer me suggestions on how to improve it.

Finally, I would like to thank you, the reader, for sticking with me! I love you all.

ABOUT THE AUTHOR

Katie May is a reverse harem author, a KDP All-Star winner, and an USA Today Bestselling Author. She lives in West Michigan with her family and cat. When not writing, she could be found reading a good book, listening to broadway musicals, or playing games. Join Katie's Gang to stay updated on all her releases! And did you know she has a TikTok? Yeah, me either. Follow her here! But be warned... she's an awkward noodle.

ALSO BY KATIE MAY

Together We Fall (Apocalyptic Reverse Harem, COMPLETED)

1. The Darkness We Crave

2. The Light We Seek

3. The Storm We Face

4. The Monsters We Hunt

Beyond the Shadows (Horror Reverse Harem, COMPLETED)

1. Gangs and Ghosts

2. Guns and Graveyards

3. Gallows and Ghouls

The Damning (Fantasy Paranormal Reverse Harem)

1. Greed

2. Envy

3. Gluttony

Prodigium Academy (Horror Comedy Academy Reverse Harem)

1. Monsters

2. Roaring

Tory's School for the Trouble (Bully Horror Academy Reverse Harem)

1. Between

2. Beyond (Coming Soon)

Supernaturalette (Interactive Reverse Harem)

1. Introductions

2. First Dates

3. Group Outing

4. Game Night

5. Exes

Kingdom of Wolves (Shifter Reverse Harem Duet)

1. Torn to Bits

2. Ripped to Shreds

CO-WRITES

Afterworld Academy with Loxley Savage (Academy Fantasy Reverse Harem, COMPLETED)

1. Dearly Departed

2. Darkness Deceives

3. Defying Destiny

Darkest Flames with Ann Denton (Paranormal Reverse Harem, COMPLETED)

1. Demon Kissed

1.5. Demon Stalked

2. Demon Loved

3. Demon Sworn

STAND-ALONES

Toxicity (Contemporary Reverse Harem)

Blindly Indicted (Prison Reverse Harem)

Not All Heroes Wear Capes (Just Dresses) (Short Comedic Reverse Harem)

Charming Devils (Bully/Revenge Reverse Harem)

Goddess of Pain (Fantasy Reverse Harem)

Demon's Joy (Holiday Reverse Harem)

Printed in Great Britain
by Amazon